FORT
ROSS

FORT ROSS

DMITRI POLETAEV

authorHOUSE®

AuthorHouse™ LLC
1663 Liberty Drive
Bloomington, IN 47403
www.authorhouse.com
Phone: 1-800-839-8640

Translation Consultant
TATIANA LAMMERS

Graphic Design
ITECHNET

Published by AuthorHouse 09/25/2014

ISBN: 978-1-4969-1241-1 (sc)
ISBN: 978-1-4969-1242-8 (hc)
ISBN: 978-1-4969-1240-4 (e)

PROLOGUE

The people of long ago are not remembered, nor will there be any remembrance of people yet to come by those who come after them.

—Ecclesiastes 1:11

1792. St. Petersburg, Russia. The Winter Palace. Chambers of the Empress Catherine the Great.

Catherine had not been herself since morning. Not that she had a cold or influenza. No; she just felt under the weather. *This is probably what Londoners would call a spleen,* the empress thought with a bit of sadness. The "English" version of her distress only added anxiety to her already-dark mood. *Damn it! All I need is to have a stroke on their account! I'd better take an emetic.*

The tsarina pushed a dish of nearly untouched braised veal away. She scooped sauerkraut with cranberries from a gold-edged porcelain tureen and cut a piece of lightly cured pickle. That did not help either. Although a sip of sherry did spread a pleasant warmth through her body, it was clearly not enough to dispel her grim thoughts.

The empress raised her eyes. Count Alexander Bezborodko, who had the privilege of dining with her that afternoon, was a privy councilor, her secretary of petitions, and one of the most powerful people in Russia. He seemed to feel her mood and tried to be inconspicuous, which, due to his considerable physique, was not easily achievable. With eyes cast down, the count was silently and rather modestly shoveling in oysters, washing them down with white wine—the latest gastronomic novelty from France.

Look at him! The empress sneered inwardly. *I am a foreigner by birth but prefer a simple Russian peasant soup above any Parisian delicacies. Look at how this one devours those oysters as if he were not born in the backwoods but in Europe itself!*

"Alex," the empress musingly addressed her advisor, "remind me, dear, where you were born? For I somehow forgot."

"In the town of Glukhov, Your Majesty. In the province of Sumy," the vice chancellor quickly replied.

Although Russian was not her native language, Catherine knew him well enough to recognize that the name of the town derived from the word *glukhoi* or *glukhoman*, which means "backwoods" in Russian.

"Yes, that's what I thought, Glukhov," Catherine replied absentmindedly. "Look here, dear, you have advised me to respond to the note of the British envoy, but you'd better do it yourself. I'm just not in the mood today. I'd better go lie down."

In the last two decades, the Russian Empire had quickly expanded; along with his other innumerous duties, the vice chancellor was also overseeing the Ministry of Foreign Affairs after the death of Nikita Panin, the tsarina's main ally.

Count Bezborodko fidgeted in his chair, trying to stand up in an attempt to bow while hastily wiping his glazed lips with a napkin.

"Your Majesty, but . . . but, you know—" Bezborodko stuttered.

"What?" Catherine frowned, trying to suppress her irritation.

"Well, Derzhavin asked—"

"Oh, yes—about his secretary, Rezanov!" Catherine continued to frown. "Platon was also trying to tell me something about it. Remind me, what is it all about? But quick!"

She had mentioned the name of Prince Platon Zubov to take revenge on the count for his mentioning of Derzhavin. She knew Bezborodko disliked Zubov who, as her new favorite, was thirty-eight years her junior and to whom she increasingly entrusted the affairs of state governance. Bezborodko considered Zubov an upstart, the tsarina's "puppy," and not particularly smart.

Well, maybe so, the empress though, *but we appreciate him for his other accomplishments.*

Derzhavin was one of the most enlightened people of the empire. The famous Russian poet had recently been appointed as the head of the tsarina's private office but had already managed to damage his relationship with Catherine. The old man Derzhavin was too principled, too straightforward, and not flexible enough for a successful career as a courtier.

Furthermore, he was afraid of nobody and often criticized the actions of the empress. Although Catherine did not like the criticism, she tried hard to restrain her emotions, understanding that a critical look at her reforms and affairs was much more needed than an admiring chorus of court sycophants and hangers-on. Nevertheless, it was hard, and mentioning Derzhavin's name didn't help improve the tsarina's mood at that morning.

Meanwhile, Bezborodko continued. "The thing is, Your Majesty, that this Nikolai Rezanov is the secretary of your imperial cabinet, which Gavrila Derzhavin is the head—"

"I'm well aware that Derzhavin is the head of my imperial cabinet. Can you just stick to the point?" the annoyed empress said.

"Well, as I was saying," Bezborodko continued, unruffled by the empress's short temper, "this Nikolai Rezanov wants to propose a project to Your Majesty regarding our American lands."

"Our lands!" Catherine snorted. "I wish your friends, the English, could hear you now!"

"They are not my friends, Your Majesty," Bezborodko parried. "They are friends of Your Majesty's previous adviser, His Excellency Count Nikita Panin, may his soul find peace in heaven. Your Majesty knows it perfectly well. But if you ask me, I would have supported any project that takes care of our lands in America if only to knock the stuffing out of London. For God's sake, these English are everywhere nowadays! They are like stinging nettle weeds! Forgive my words, but one can't take a dump even at the world's end without banging into them!"

"You, my dear Count, had better drop this bathroom rhetoric of yours at least while we are at the table eating! As for the British, there's no reason to quarrel with them right now. Panin was right about this."

"No doubt, Your Majesty." Bezborodko did not give up. "He was *so* right that in his time, the British envoy presented him with the carriage decorated with gold. I wonder what merits that was for?"

"That we'll probably never know, God rest his soul." The empress neatly crossed herself in the Russian Orthodox manner.

"As a former minister of foreign affairs, he had more than enough merits to Europe, too many to list them all. But I wonder where all his merits to Russia were? Why wasn't he zealous for the interests of our motherland? First, he had a feather in the cap for Prussia, and then for the British Kingdom. By God, Your Majesty, nobody gets a golden carriage for nothing!"

"First, you're the head of the ministry of foreign affairs at the moment," Catherine retorted icily. "Second, he wasn't the only diplomat who received presents from foreign ambassadors. Take, for example, Prince Golitsyn—our ambassador to Prussia, or Count Vorontsov— our envoy to London. I don't think they're in need of anything. This is normal. We also give presents to those who could be of any use to us. What is *not* normal is your mood. What's wrong with it? I don't like it at all. So I repeat, I wouldn't look for trouble with the English right now!"

The empress got up slowly and walked to the window with a heavy gait. The short winter day, unable to declare itself properly, was plunging into dusk. The leaden skies over the Peter and Paul Fortress looked as if they were promising snow. The changing of the guards occurring outside the palace's grand entrance attracted her attention. Catherine sighed. Oddly enough, that emotional outburst had done her good. She felt better.

"All right, my lord!" Catherine continued in a more conciliatory vein. "Let's get back to that issue about Rezanov."

"Would Your Majesty mind letting him speak for himself?" Bezborodko asked softly, trying not to disturb the fragile truce.

"Do you mean he's here?"

"He's patiently waiting in the reception room," the minister meekly replied.

"Ask him in! Why are you making the man wait?"

Despite the absolute power given to her by fate, Catherine had never been vain about it. Since the days of her youth, when she—the poor princess of an insignificant German principality—appeared before the granddaughter of Peter the Great, then Russian empress Elizabeth, with just a nightgown as her dowry, Catherine had vowed she would never tempt fate with even the slightest bit of arrogance. She would not tolerate the slightest trace of vanity in other people as well. The swagger that shared national character trait in Russia was perhaps the only thing that annoyed her about the country, which she had otherwise wholeheartedly fallen in love with.

Take this Bezborodko, the empress mused. *It has not been that long since he was a mere valet serving Count Peter Rumyantsev. And look at him now, how ruffled his feathers are! Yet he is still all right, a talented rare bird. His unique ability to memorize everything is worth a fortune alone, not to mention his encyclopedic knowledge. But take others who lift their muzzles from the dirt as soon as they get a few kopeks in their pockets and start puffing their breasts just like turkeycocks, avoiding the eyes of their former friends. A little man is no match for them anymore! Pfft, such nasty peacocks.*

The empress's thoughts were interrupted by the opening of the chamber doors. A young man of about twenty-eight gallantly bowed to Catherine. He had a chiseled chin and a straight, thin nose on his very European face. Clever, bright-blue eyes under long eyelashes peered at the empress without servility but with due respect. The man was dressed in an impeccable, knee-length, blue coat embroidered with silver, a light-gray silk waistcoat, and a white tie. A moderately powdered wig with a black velvet ribbon around its pigtail perfectly agreed with the newcomer's appearance.

Catherine found herself involuntarily admiring the young man. She gave a quick, knowing look over the man's well-built figure. Catherine averted her eyes from Rezanov's slender legs clad in tight-fitting knee breeches and met the young man's eye. She motioned him to come closer with a plump hand adorned with diamond rings. Rezanov took a few steps forward and stopped again in a reverent bow, mainly addressed to the empress but somehow including Count Bezborodko.

The count leaned toward the tsarina's shoulder and announced with respect, "Nikolai Rezanov, the secretary of Your Majesty's imperial cabinet!"

"Oh yes, I've heard Derzhavin has spoken with respect about you, and Prince Zubov has also shared many appealing things."

"I'm very grateful, Your Majesty. I'm only trying to serve Your Majesty and our motherland to the best of my humble abilities."

"Don't be so shy. You're well known for your knightly upbringing and good education. Please, remind me where you've been sent to us from."

"I was transferred to Your Majesty's imperial cabinet to take the position of its secretary from the office of the vice president of the Admiralty Collegium, Count Chernyshov. Before that, I had the honor to serve in the imperial guards' Izmailovsky Regiment." Meaningfully and almost daringly, Rezanov looked the empress in the eyes. Catherine, however, pretended to be deep in her thoughts.

"So what business brought you here?" she asked.

"To tell you the truth, Your Majesty, it isn't my business I'm here about but that of Siberian merchant Grigory Shelikhov, with whom I believe you are very familiar."

It was well known that the Siberian governor-general had repeatedly reported to Catherine on the achievement of the Russian merchants, or *promyshlenniki*, on the western shores of the American continent. He had especially mentioned the name of the merchant Shelikhov and his success in this endeavor.

"Is this again about the acquisition of the newly discovered lands in America for our crown?" Catherine frowned.

"Not exactly, Your Majesty. This time it's about a very smart proposition. Shelikhov is seeking your permission to establish a commercial enterprise, and in the best interests of our empire, he would like to give that enterprise the right to discover and cultivate lands on the American western coast, which is unoccupied by the other nations. The idea is similar to the royal charter the English, for example, gave its East India Company. Thus, newly discovered lands would belong *not* to the Russian Empire but to the private Russian trade company, like everywhere in the world. Europe will have no reason to look at us askance."

Catherine frowned. *How much times I would hear the word "English" today, I wonder?* "Well, and what does your Russian Columbus want in return?" The tzarina half-turned toward Count Bezborodko, inviting him to join the conversation.

"He just wants a monopoly, Your Majesty," Rezanov said.

The parlor became quiet. The empress rose and walked to the window, maintaining a pause. Turning to Rezanov and Bezborodko, she asked in an icy and menacing tone, "Just a monopoly! Does your merchant understand what he's asking for?" Catherine recalled that one of her first moves after seizing power and ascending the throne was to abolish a monopoly privilege on salt. Back then, it had belonged to Count Andrei Shuvalov and a handful of other very powerful and noble Russian aristocrats. That decision was not an easy one, but the triumph asserted her power and showed the nobility who was in charge.

The prices for salt went down, along with people's discontent. After receiving the first approval of her subjects, she could finally sleep more or less peacefully at night without fear of another coup d'état, this one directed at her. Ever since, the word *monopoly* had been prohibited at Catherine's court. Bezborodko and Rezanov knew this well. "That's not all, Your Majesty," Rezanov continued in a quiet but firm tone. "The merchant Shelikhov also humbly asks you to grant him as the highest favor and honor a loan for the construction of a fleet that would help develop these lands for the benefits of the Russian state."

"Russian state!" Catherine exploded. "If he had the good of the Russian state at heart, he wouldn't have dared ask me for this monopoly. Yet here we are! Who is going to control this monopoly, I ask you, when it's thousands of miles away and can't be properly supervised or controlled from here?"

"Please, Your Majesty, don't be cross, but let me add some words too," said Count Bezborodko, who had remained quiet. "Approximately seventy gangs of promishlenniks procure sea otter pelts and conduct trade on our shores in America, and, Your Majesty, I really mean 'gangs'! These merchants hire their crews of workers among the Cossacks, as peasants are tied to the land, and there is nowhere else to get the workforce. Those Cossacks, instead of hunting sea otters, batter each other as it's easier and more profitable for them to steal already-procured pelts from one another than to freeze their behinds sitting in the canoes with the savages. Letting one company control all the fur pelt business would make it better organized, not to mention that it's much easier to control a single company than all these gangs."

"But how, I repeat, would it be possible to control it?" the empress exclaimed, standing her ground.

"By issuing shares, Your Majesty." Rezanov maintained his quiet, firm tone.

In the long years of her reign, Catherine had become used to having the reputation of a well-educated monarch. She took pride in corresponding with French philosophers such as Voltaire and Diderot. She disliked it when anybody became aware of her ignorance on any subject. Yes, she had heard the word *share* and could even properly use it, but she didn't know how issuing shares would really work.

She turned to Rezanov. "Thank you for your commendable zeal and concern about the interests of the motherland. I'm pleased with you. Tell your protector, Derzhavin, I'm also satisfied with his ability to discover young and talented people to serve our state." Catherine couldn't resist appraising the well-built figure of Rezanov again. "Your diligence is duly noted."

A slight tilt of Catherine's head signaled the audience was over. Rezanov bowed low to the empress and then to the vice chancellor. He left the parlor, silently closing the door behind him.

The empress stared out the window. "That's why the other day Prince Zubov kept drumming in my ears 'a share, a share.' I said to him, 'Your share, my dear, is between your legs. Take good care of it so that it stays strong, and let me look after you.' And you know what happened? He got offended at me." The empress could hear Bezborodko's unease as he shifted his body slightly. She was surprised that despite all his years of service, he had not gotten used to her occasional German ribald expressions.

Snow started falling outside, and the empress turned to her chancellor. "My dear, would you find a moment sometime to explain to this silly woman how these shares work? It's almost the nineteenth century in our domain, and I'm still in the dark about it."

The tsarina leaned heavily on the arm of her privy councilor and with a slight limp headed for the exit. The guards opened the heavy, gilded doors made in Rastrelli's baroque style; the doors' gold sparkled in the twilight. Servants holding candelabras met them with deep, reverent bows.

Majestically, empress and chancellor—a battleship accompanied by a cruiser—passed the guards and headed into the endless, palatial suite of rooms.

The imperial chancellery carriage was whisking Rezanov home on runners sliding across fresh snow. He was wrapped in a fur coat, and his legs stretched toward the warmth of the small, cast-iron heater in the corner of the carriage. Rezanov gazed out the window deep in thought. Although his fate was still hidden from him, Rezanov felt in the deeps of his heart that the audience with the empress would make an impact on his life. What he didn't know was that events sometimes unfold in a way quite the opposite of what we imagined.

Rezanov's life will be short but full of glorious achievements and unfulfilled expectations. Shelikhov's petition will be denied. At the sunset of her reign, Catherine will not care much about the fate of the Russian-American colonies especially in connection with the looming threat of a new war with Sweden and the resumption of the old war with Turkey.

More than that, very soon, by imperial order, Rezanov will be sent to the town of Irkutsk, deep in Siberia, to inspect the fur-trading enterprise of that merchant Shelikhov Rezanov had advocated so bravely for before the tsarina, and the business of the fur trade will become the purpose of his life.

In Irkutsk, Rezanov will fall in love with Shelikhov's fifteen-year-old daughter, Anna, who will become his wife, though not for long. She will die just three years into their marriage while giving birth to their second child. Her father, the honorable merchant Grigory Shelikhov, will pass away not long after, thus making Rezanov the heir of his enormous estate and immense enterprises.

Only after the death of Catherine the Great and under the reign of her son, the next Russian Emperor Paul I, the company Shelikhov had dreamed about all his life will be established. It will be endowed by imperial charter with monopoly rights to discover and develop North American lands unoccupied by other European nations. Rezanov will be the most active in the creation of the Russian-American Company.

Ten years will pass after that memorable audience with the empress, and the Russian-American company will organize the first Russian circumnavigation voyage. The ships *Neva* and *Nadezhda* will sail under the command of Captain-Lieutenant von Krusenstern and Captain-Lieutenant Lisyansky respectively. Rezanov, as the chamberlain of the imperial court, will be appointed commander in chief of that voyage.

Along with the first Russian circumnavigation, Rezanov will also carry out the first Russian diplomatic mission to Japan, but most of all, his dreams of reaching America will come true.

There, he will reenergize the Russian colonies, the history of which will be forever connected with his name. There, in California, he will meet his second and last love, the beautiful Maria de la Concepcion Marcela Arguello, or Conchita, a beautiful sixteen-year-old daughter of the commandant of the Presidio of San Francisco. They will fall in love madly. From California, Rezanov will rush back to St. Petersburg to ask permission to marry a Catholic, but exhausted by the gallop through the endless expanses of Siberia, he will sicken and die trying to reach his dream. Conchita, unaware of his fate, will be waiting for him many years until she will get word of his death. After that, she will become a nun.

Thus, there will be love the poets will write songs about in the centuries to come, and there will be loss—all of which we simply call life.

Still, at the moment, these events were only flickers of mysterious flashes on the horizon. Through a thawed hole on the icy window of his carriage, the young man meditatively stared out at the snowy streets of St. Petersburg and smiled.

PART ONE

The River of Time

You cannot step twice into the same river;
for other waters are ever flowing on to you.

—Heraclitus of Ephesus, IV CBC

CHAPTER 1

1820. The Lands of the Russian-American Company on the Northern California Coast. Early Morning.

The rocky shoreline cliffs covered with pristine forest met the ocean's heavy, cold waves. The morning sun, like a white saucer, was peeking through the predawn fog. A fortress with its newly built wooden fence stood on top of the high cliff along the coast. An Orthodox cross crowning the pointed roof of the chapel shone as a beacon in the rays of the rising sun. From a distance, the fort could be mistaken for a hermitage or monastery, but upon closer inspection, cannon muzzles poking through firing ports gave evidence it was a fortress.

A field with ripe rye spikes swinging in the wind stretched from the fortress to the woods. Away from the fortress, closer to the creek that flows into the ocean, a very Russian village's huts dotted the creek's edge. On the other side of the creek, Indian tipis rose in the early morning bluish haze. Sleepy dogs yelped in the distance.

A warrior, hidden by the primeval forest, stood motionless. He knew how to turn off his desires. The Great Spirit had taught him well. The most important thing during such moments was to think about nothing. It was difficult but doable. He had to ask the Spirit of these amazing redwoods to let him become a part of them, at least for a while. This was scary. The warrior had never seen such a forest. Everything was different in his and his tribe's land, far up north. The great fiery Canoe sailing across the sky was fond of his people and took good care of them. It did not hide behind the edge of the earth as often as it did here. These giant trees made him feel like an ant. Such trees did not grow in his land. In his land, trees were small and insignificant. Sure, the fiery canoe would leave the sky and for a long time, but it would always come back.

While it was gone, it gave the people great white silence. If a warrior was lucky enough during the hunting season and if the spirits were helping him, then he could even relax through the great white silence, surrounded by his wives and family. Like his big brother bear he could just wait for the great fiery canoe to return.

The timing for thoughts about home was bad, and for memories of his wives even more so. It was the third moon since the warriors had dug out their tomahawks at the great council of the tribes and accepted an invitation from the palefaces to assist them in their military campaign in the far south. It was the third moon since the warrior had started his quest. It was the third moon since the warrior had had no women.

It would all end that day. He could feel it. His bloodthirsty tomahawk would quench its thirst. His tired, weary body longing for a woman would be satisfied. Most important, great gifts would await him and his brothers after the battle. Truly, the spirits of his ancestors and the great mother must really favor them since they had received this honor to go on this quest.

The warrior's nostrils flared slightly. He felt the Great Spirit honoring him by entering his body. He did not have to turn his head to know that his brothers, just like him, were also experiencing the same sensation, not that he would have been able to see them. Just like him, hundreds of them blended with the forest, standing motionless, awaiting for the signal.

CHAPTER 2

1825, December 15. St. Petersburg.
The Day following the Decembrists' Uprising.
11:00 in the Morning.

$\mathbf{A}$ low winter sun hovered grimly over the frost-bound Neva River. A single ray of sunshine escaped the darkness. It sparkled for a fleeting moment against the needle-shaped spire of the Admiralty Building before disappearing behind the heavy cloud again.

Pressing his forehead against the window of his private study, the newly crowned emperor, Nicholas I, stared at the square gloomily. The cool glass felt pleasant against the hot skin of his forehead.

The second day of his reign had started almost sleeplessly. He had not had anything but a glass of Madeira wine and a couple of almond biscuits, but he had no appetite for food or anything else. His only desire was for this nightmare to end.

He thought he had been prepared to face all the events of the previous night, but they had affected him much more intensely than he had expected. In the moments of weakness that came with the nausea and dizziness, which he had tried unsuccessfully to get rid of, he felt lonely. Worse, he felt abandoned and betrayed. Only the previous day he had stood in the piercing December wind dressed only in his officer's coat, and just like Alexander the Great, he tried to protect the power that had been bestowed upon him by God. On the current day, a shameful apathy had conquered his will.

Why had it all turned out to be like that? Our older brother, Prince Constantine, was supposed to have succeeded to the crown after the death of our brother, Emperor Alexander I. Instead, showing his scorn for the buttress of the dynasty, Constantine had remained in Warsaw, thinking of himself and his interests only. Our younger brother Mikhail, along with Mother, are clearly conspiring something. Everybody is waiting for us to make the slightest misstep or wrong move. Keep waiting, gentlemen! It is not going to happen! I am well aware of all your close intents and of everyone who pulls the strings! I know too well who you are accepting handouts from and whose money you are planning to use to rule half the world from Warsaw! There is only one thing that you have not taken into account: I will not be a pawn in your hands!

Nicholas mentally rehearsed his accusatory speech he planned to spit in their faces. *Though this is rather overstated. First, such an occasion might never occur. Second, it is too early to talk about it. The situation is still unstable. Right now, I have to deal with those rebel officers to teach others a lesson. After that, I will deal with them.*

Nicholas did not finish his thoughts. Movement outside the window caught his attention and snapped him out of his musings. A black carriage sled with a barred window drawn by four black horses careened around the corner. The square in front of the Winter Palace was still in chaos. It was a city under siege, with crowds of people gathering around the palace despite the growing cold.

The shock from the events of the previous day seemed to unnerve everyone, even the animals. The never-ending neighing of horses and the gurgling croaks of ravens were unbearable. Every now and again, horses carrying officers, couriers, and aides-de-camp crossed the square. The sound of hooves on stone pavement echoed painfully in the aching head of the previous day's grand duke.

Having added yet another share of hoofbeats and the light crunch of the runners on the cobblestone, the sled carriage stopped at the palace entrance. The cavalry platoon escorting the carriage dismounted and lined up just as the carriage door opened. A young second lieutenant jumped out. Several bareheaded officers wearing fur coats over their uniforms followed him out of the carriage. Tsar Nicholas I stared at their faces. The officers, pale and unshaven, dropped their fur coats into the arms of one of their convoy and, hesitantly looking around, started for the palace entrance. After grabbing swords from the carriage, the second lieutenant hurriedly followed the other officers.

Nicholas involuntary closed his eyes and turned from the window. Again, his vision darkened, and he felt dizzy. *Oh God, no! I need to pull myself together! I cannot show any weakness.* This powerless thought pulsed in his head, yet the overwhelming mortification spasmodically drummed in his temples. He again had a vision of something he feared most—the familiar faces of officers, the sons of the most noble and prominent aristocratic families of the empire!

My God, but what about officers' honor? What about officers' duties to their emperor! Traitors! How dare they raise a hand against their tsar! Criminals! How low can a man fall? God, help me!

All these thoughts throbbed in the mind of the twenty-eight-year-old emperor. Nicholas got a grip of himself. General von Benckendorff, who stood behind him, had been an unwilling witness to the young tsar's struggle with his emotions since the general took it upon himself to organize the palace guards, not leaving Nicholas alone since. During this most recent struggle, von Benckendorff had kept quiet.

Nicholas turned to him. His impossibly bright blue eyes stared at the general. For a few long seconds, Nicholas kept his eyes on von Benckendorff as if not recognizing him. He regained his presence of mind, and his shoulders softened.

"Please continue, general. I hear everything you are saying," Nicholas said in French in a tense voice.

With a soft shift of his head, the general returned to the interrupted report he had been reading. "Therefore, the board of directors of the Russian-American Company humbly plead Your Grace to grant mercy to the general manager of the company's office in St. Petersburg, Kondraty Ryleyev—"

Benckendorff stopped short, glancing at Nicholas.

"What?" The newly crowned emperor was furious again. He immediately switched to German, which was more comfortable for him.

"They want me *to grant mercy*? To whom? To the company? Never! Do you hear me? Never! I'd rather pardon Trubetskoy than this . . . this . . ." Nicholas gasped for air in search of the right words.

"Your Grace," Benckendorff started quietly, wincing under the tsar's intense stare. "May I remind you that no one has seen Ryleyev at the Senate Square during the revolt. As for His Excellency Prince Trubetskoy, the rumors have it that he dared to call himself a dictator and even dreamed to take your place, sir."

"His excellency is a fool!" Nicholas yelled at the top of his lungs. "This company and Ryleyev along with it—they are my true enemies! Do you hear me? Remember this, General—this is where all the abomination is coming from, from the company. They were the ones who set those stupid officers against me. These merchants decided to rule Russia with money and without the anointed one! It will never happen! Do you hear me? Never!"

The young tsar's voice abruptly fell silent. He coughed. After a moment, Nicholas pulled himself together as he had many times in these agonizing past twenty-four hours.

"*Mon General*, I hope you understand that my anger has absolutely nothing to do with you, *monsieur.*" The emperor switched to French. "We shall never forget your loyalty to us and Mother Russia. However, these criminals will be judged without remorse. We will do it ourselves."

Nicholas's insane blue eyes met von Benckendorff's calm, steady gaze. The general silently bowed his head.

CHAPTER 3

Present Time. New York. Dmitry's Apartment. 11:00 in the Morning.

Dmitry woke up but did not hurry to open his eyes. He did not want to go back to the realities of everyday life. His strange dream lingered with him and stirred his imagination. He had been having these dreams for quite some time. Though some had deviations and different perspectives, they were definitely pieces of the same sequence.

Sure, human consciousness is an amazing thing, but dreams on demand? It's too much. I should probably see a shrink. Although what could I tell him? That I've been watching something like movie sequels in my dreams? That sounds like such nonsense.

He clearly heard the words from his dream: "They decided to rule Russia with money. I will not allow it. This will never happen!" Dmitry winced. The voice changed to a more trained tone of a TV newscaster: "As was stated by the Russian president at the press conference with the representatives of the media. We will continue to inform you on Mister Khodorkovsky's case proceedings in our next news broadcast."

Dmitry sat up on his bed. *Well, that explains it. You, man, better not forget to switch off the TV at night or you'll end up in a madhouse! Less alcohol will also help, and if you do drink, at least don't smoke.*

With a heavy sigh, Dmitry stood and walked into the living room. He picked up the remote from the floor and pressed the power button. The TV screen went blank, and the steady sound of the air conditioner mixed with the distant noise of street traffic filled the room. Dmitry drew the window curtains aside.

A pale New York sun blurred by the big city haze was reflected in the mirrored skyscraper across the street. For over a year, he had rented this apartment in the center of Manhattan, at the corner of 54th and Lexington, but he was still not used to the panoramic view from his thirtieth floor, more precisely, the *feeling* this view offered him. It was like soaring above the city, watching taxis that looked like yellow insects far below, as if he had supernatural abilities. Of course, this was an illusion, but it was so strong that it alone was able to fend off his seasonal bouts of mild depression that, like all creative people, Dmitry was inclined to suffer periodically. The fall's endless rains brought the melancholy without fail.

However, the work he did saved him, as was not the case for many less-fortunate people. In the truest sense of the word, it was inappropriate to call it *work*. How could one call *work* something he would do even if he did not receive pay for it? It's impossible. Despite the years he spent in his position, every time he got a check for his television reports, Dmitry looked at it with disbelief and inwardly thanked his fate that at least he did not have to look for the "meaning of life" or deal with another soul-searching crap.

According to his job description, Dmitry was a reporter for *Russia Today*, the Russian TV news channel accredited in the United States, but in his heart, he was more than just a reporter; he was a storyteller with a capital S.

Each century brings something different in the way of narrating a story. From the dawn of civilization, from the psaltery and harp, humankind reached the age of radio and television, but all these means serve the same, ancient goal—delivering information to audiences in the most informative and effective way.

Just as it had happened in every age and time, some people were meant to stay at the level of informers or reporters, while others, thanks to their talent, rose to the heights of storytellers.

Dmitry definitely had talent. More than that, he was popular. Even when he told stories based on his personal experiences, he always respected the point of view of his viewers, whom he considered his partners in conversation. He let his immense audience draw their own conclusions, thereby including them in the interactive process of collective story creation. That's why he was loved and appreciated by many.

When he was interviewed after receiving regular awards at various television events, he liked to say the recipe for his success consisted of only one ingredient: his passion for what he did. It was not surprising that his last documentary about the history of America had earned him fame in Russia and sparked his move to the United States.

Dmitry wasn't married, but he didn't suffer from loneliness. As a TV journalist, his life was filled with many meetings with different people, both planned and spontaneous, which taught him to appreciate moments of solitude.

Besides, such times were rather relative. He enjoyed good company, good food, the endless choices of the restaurants New York offered, and an even greater choice of women.

He always preferred the company of Russian girls, though. It was not out of a patriotic feeling, nor was such preference prompted by the popular belief that Russian women are the best looking in the world. Not at all. In New York, he occasionally met local beauties who left him slack-jawed, completely speechless, but he preferred Russian ladies simply because of their common heritage. Also, it was not a problem to get acquainted with Russian girls in New York, just like with anything else in this unique city.

He was thirty-five, he had an apartment in Midtown Manhattan, good manners, a fit and trim body, and long, wavy hair. Dmitry was the kind of specimen that women—especially single women—simply could not pass by easily, and he used his advantage rather successfully.

Of course, there was a slight hitch in such relationships. Because he was such an enviable mate, practically every partner soon started having very high expectations of bringing their relationship to the next level. This was precisely what Dmitry tried to avoid. It was not because he did not want to have a family but because he had already had a family once. The divorce with the woman he once loved had quickly turned into a "divorce" with his six-year-old son. Dmitry suffered so much over this that even after several years, this wound refused to heal.

He did not want to step on that rake again. Whenever he sensed the situation with his next girlfriend was leading to building a "cozy nest" together, whenever he come across a female's items in every corner of his apartment and had difficulty finding his razor among the innumerous bottles of lotions, creams, and makeup in the bathroom, Dmitry always managed to get out of the relationship while still remaining friends with his spurned lover.

His phone beeped with an incoming text message. Dmitry turned from the window and for several seconds tried to remember where he had plugged in his iPhone to recharge. *Look at that. Even in the automatic mode, "all systems work normally."* He chuckled as he found his iPhone in its usual place, on the kitchen counter next to the coffee maker.

Almost immediately after the text message, a new signal informed him of an incoming email. To make sure its owner got his act together, the cell phone started to play a jazzy composition signaling an incoming call.

The day was surely coming into its own. The text message was short and laconic: *You were amazing. Kisses.* Dmitry cast a quick glance at his rumpled bed and regretted sleeping through the moment when Lena had left. His latest interest worked at the flower shop and had to get up when Dmitry was usually only heading to bed. Lena was about twenty-five, sexy, and smart, and she was in her last year of college, a step away from becoming a legal assistant. Both were busy people, but if they happened to coincide in time and space, they had nothing against spending a couple of hours together with no obligation on either side. Dmitry was happy with such an arrangement.

The email was from his new boss in the Moscow office. As for the incoming phone call . . . Dmitry immediately pressed the answer button: "Hey, what's up, guys?"

Along with the wailing of a fire truck and buzzing of New York traffic, a young, almost boyish voice sounded in his ear. "We're just around the corner, boss! We've got stuck on Forty-Second and Broadway. The traffic here is crazy, but don't worry, we're almost out of it."

It'll take them another fifteen minutes to get here, Dmitry thought while making coffee.

"Is Margo with you?" he asked.

"Yep, she's here, catching a nap in the back seat," the voice replied with unmasked envy.

"What about the SD cards?" Dmitry asked.

"Got three, sixty-four gigs each. Should be enough to cover all our production," the laconic voice replied.

"Get them out of the luggage and put them in the carry-on. We'll take them with us. See you downstairs in five."

Dmitry pressed the button to end the call, finished his coffee in two gulps, and started packing.

CHAPTER 4

1820. Off the Northern California Coast. Early Morning.

Cloaked in the early morning fog, approximately a half mile from the coast, a two-masted schooner without any identification rocked in the ocean waves. The vessel's bell melodically responded to the monotonous tinkling of the anchor chain. No other sounds broke the peaceful silence of the morning. The fog was so dense that the vessel's masts disappeared somewhere above the first gaff sail, while the bowsprit seemed like it had been chopped off at the very nose of the schooner. Big bronze letters behind the ship's stern indicated the vessel's name: *Pearl of the Seas*. A slate with the word *Portsmouth* written in uneven letters hung on the rusty nails in the spot reserved for the port of registry indication. Overall, the *Pearl of the Seas* looked as if the ship had known better days and a more caring owner, but that must have been a long time ago.

A group gathered on deck, listening intently to the silence, trying to see something through the fog. No one would want to meet that gang in a dark alley. Their unshaven faces showed neither intelligence nor kindness. Some smoked pipes; others chewed tobacco and spit overboard from time to time. They looked a lot like a group of thugs.

The captain—easily recognizable by the number of pistols tucked in his belt, the cocked black hat worn over a red bandana, and the way the rest of the crew obsequiously cringed under his gaze—turned to the short, fat man who stood next to him. The latter sweated profusely and kept wiping his face with a rag. If the rest of the crew looked tense, the real fear showed on the face of the obese man, for which there could be several reasons. First, the captain's eye bloomed with a freshly inflicted purple bruise that clearly was negatively affecting his mood. Second, in the place of front teeth, the captain had a hole that seemed to be a novelty for him as he kept self-consciously covering his mouth with a handkerchief, making his words impossible to understand at times. This made the fat man sweat even more. His instinct told him it wouldn't be a good idea to ask the captain to repeat his words.

Without even giving a look to the short man, the captain scornfully lisped, "So what do you think, boatswain? Will your redskins not let us down?"

The fat guy readily and much more zealously than the situation required whispered, "They should not, sir."

"You'd better watch them! I sure hope they will not take the fur pelts for themselves, because if they do, I'll have to go to Canton to sell *your* skin."

The captain became silent. He stared into the fog. The fat man evidently did not like such a prospect at all. "Why the hell would they need the fur pelts for themselves, sir?" His eyes bulged for emphasis as he jabbered. "When we offer them rifles and gunpowder, they would slit the throats of not only Russians but the Spaniards as well. Fur pelts! What do they know about fur pelts?"

The captain turned abruptly to him. "Shut up you fool! Stop yelping. The sound carries far on the water. You ask why they would need the fur pelts for? I'll tell you why! Because, you idiot, they can always sell them to the Bostonians! That's why! I hear they started coming here more often."

The boatswain refused to give up. "Well, the local Indians could do that but not these savages we brought from the north. How would they get home? Have we suffered their stink for nothing? Because of them, the whole ship smells like she just got out of the stable." To sound more convincing, the fat man defiantly screwed up his face.

"Stop sniffling!" the captain hissed sharply. "You don't smell of French cologne either. The locals wouldn't go against those damn Russians. That's why we brought those savages from the North, but it seems to me they somehow learned the real value of the sea otter fur better than the locals have."

The captain stared thoughtfully in the direction where, according to the compass, the unknown shore with a mysterious Russian settlement was. Everybody was silent, not daring to interrupt the thoughts of their moody leader. The captain sighed, indicating he had come to a decision.

"I don't like this silence! How'd I know whether they are ready and in position or not?" After a moment of silence, he continued. "Okay. Anyway, there is no way we can check it out. They'd better be. Let's start moving!"

The boatswain, happy to have things worked out, swiftly turned to the crew and snapped, "Enough of your quips! Haven't you heard the captain's order?"

The thugs broke from their reverent stupor and carefully, trying not to make too much noise, rushed to load the crates of guns and ammunition into the rowboats tied to the schooner's side and frantically dancing on the water.

Accompanying the predawn fog, heavy ocean waves steadily rolled onto the rocky shore covered with pristine forest. The rising sun peeked through a rainbow halo of oppressive clouds of vapor. A raft, as it is called, of sea otters warmed their furry bellies in the sun, scratching lazily while dreamily floating on the waves. The head of the raft, its wet fur ruffled in a funny way, lifted its small head and looked around. The hairs around its whiskers glistened with a silver color that spoke of its rarity and gave its fur a special tint. Of course, the otter was oblivious to the desires of the human world. Otherwise, it would be very amused by the fact that its fur, which the otter valued greatly, was worth its weight in gold, and the common pun, "Hold dear to your skin," would have no abstract value for the animal. The otter was not aware of human passions of course, but it felt far from relaxed and interested in frolicking. For otters, it has become increasingly difficult to survive to an old age as the whole world seemed to gang up on them.

The otter scratched behind its ear, fluffed its wet fur, and took a stashed pebble out of the fold in its belly. The animal was going to use the pebble to open a big oyster shell and have a relaxed breakfast, yet something was keeping it alert. Tired of fighting the instinct that hinted something was wrong, the head of the otters' raft gave a discontented whistle and ducked underwater. Not daring to disobey his order, the whole pack followed its leader; having flashed their gorgeous, copper-colored fur in the sun, they quickly disappeared under the water as well. Their collective wisdom, life experience, and instinct had rewarded the pack and its leader.

At almost the same time the otters dove into the water, three dinghies packed with armed men came through the fog in silence, gliding swiftly toward the shore. Judging by their stiff faces and their intense concentration, the rowers were in a hurry, and not for a picnic.

The group made haste in a rather professional manner, without any bustle or unnecessary movements. The reason for their rush was becoming apparent; the morning fog that was so useful for hiding the group was quickly dissipating. The contours of the high cliff were becoming visible, and the outline of a fortress could be seen distinctly. If any of the fortress guards looked in the direction of the ocean at that moment, the fate of the seaborne assailants would be unenviable.

The fortress's newly built wooden fence protected the entrance into a small but sufficient bay. A polished copper cross brightly shone above the chapel's dome behind the fortress's wall. The sun was steadily rising above the mountain ridge.

Trying to use the last patches of the fog for cover, all three dinghies quietly approached the shore. In one of them, the huffing boatswain sprawled on his belly to steady himself, keeping his eye pressed to a spyglass. The sweat streaming down his face prevented him from seeing clearly. He tried wiping it with the cuff of his coat to no avail. The dawn was far from being hot; it was rather chilly, just like most northern California sunrises. It was obvious that the fat man suffered not from external temperature but from internal nerves.

The reason for his jitters was rather more serious than the prospect of being pummeled by his captain. Firing ports with shiny cannon muzzles were already evident in the fortress's wall. It would take just a couple of shots and . . . The boatswain did not even want to think about what could happen then. So far, everything was going according to plan. Nothing but the distinct sound of cicadas screeching on the shore disturbed the pristine silence of the morning.

The bell in the chapel tower lazily chimed. As if in response, a saggy banner on the flagpole revived and flew a Russian tricolor with a golden, double-headed eagle on the seemingly bigger white stripe on the top.

Below the eagle, cursive letters were stitched in gold: Russian-American Company.

CHAPTER 5

1820. Russian California. Fort Ross. The Same Morning.

Dogs started barking but just as quickly became quiet as if gasping from their efforts. A sleeping man opened his eyes as if he had not slept at all. For a while, he cautiously strained his ears. He abruptly tossed his blanket aside and sat up in bed.

Except for footwear and outerwear, he was fully dressed. He pulled on tall boots and stomped on the floor. He took two pistols from under his pillow, checked the hammers, stuck the pistols into his belt in a graceful, habitual movement, and stood. He threw a Russian naval officer's uniform coat over his shoulders, crossed himself widely in front of the candlelit icon in the corner, and left the room, trying to be quiet.

Ivan Kuskov was the founder and commandant of Fort Ross, as it was called in a foreign manner. He loved his creation more than life itself. Practically everything there had been created by his hands, through his efforts, or under his supervision.

He stepped onto the porch of a massive, two-story commandant's house made with well-fitting hewn wooden beams. It also served as an armory. Kuskov involuntarily came to a halt before the scene unfolding in front of his eyes.

The whole vast courtyard of the fortress was filled with people. Despite the large crowd, no voices could be heard. The cicadas were not shy at the presence of such a huge audience and continued their deafening predawn concert. Dogs that had been left down in the villages barked sporadically. Tall, three-legged broilers had been placed along the perimeter of the fortress; their dancing firelight lit the faces of the people gathered, making the whole scene look surreal.

The crowd moved under the gaze of their commandant. Men got up and moved forward. Women who held sleeping children stepped to the back. A small detachment of military personnel in the uniform of the Russian Marine Corps grabbed rifles in a businesslike manner and lined up. A young officer grabbed his sword to prevent the metal parts of the sling from clinking and rushed toward the commandant. Kuskov lightly ran down the stairs toward the officer and with long strides started walking toward the wall gun battery. The officer rushed behind him.

The fortress garrison was a rather strange sight. Indians with bows and arrows stood by the gun ports between the gun crews. They were the warriors of the local Kashaya tribe of the bigger Pomo nation that inhabited the territory stretching up to the big Salt Lake behind the Rocky Mountains to the east.

Kuskov remembered perfectly well when he and Alexander Baranov, the governor of Alaska, had acquired this land. They followed the advice of Nikolay Rezanov, the managing director of the Russian-American Company at that time, to negotiate with the local Indian tribe the price for the parcel of their territory, which was supposed to be used for future

Russian settlement. They had bought the land to the mutual satisfaction of both parties.

What a man! Kuskov often thought about Rezanov. *What a visionary! He managed to foresee everything!*

Back then, Kuskov had not known that the years of his administration at Fort Ross would later be called the golden age of Russian California. At this moment, he believed the times would always stay the same: peaceful, good, glorious, and joyful. The friendship between the Russians and the Kashaya people could not be simply defined as a "friendship" anymore; they were more like relatives. Lacking their own women, Russian settlers had taken Kashaya women as spouses, more firmly rooting the colony in the new land.

Unlike the Spaniards in the south, the Russians did not force the Indians to be baptized. It went without saying that all the wedding ceremonies were carried out in the Russian Orthodox manner; Deacon Cyril had invented a shortened version of the baptizing ritual for Indian women marrying Russian men.

Still, everybody knew that although they were diligent wives, *tanias*—that how the settlers called their narrow-eyed spouses among themselves in commemoration of typical female Russian name Tatiana, or Tania—freely celebrated their tribal rituals and holidays also.

The Indian warriors wore full warpaint. Their hair was decorated with eagle feathers and twisted with beads of river shells. Otherwise, they looked quite civilized. They were dressed in shirts made of thin deer leather and decorated with beads and fringe, with similar pants.

Some wore their traditional moccasins, but others wore bast shoes! Kuskov inwardly chuckled. Who would have thought the simple Russian peasant's bast shoes and foot cloth that the Indian women learned to weave would become so popular here in California? The Russians were already building a second workshop to manufacture bast shoes, which they were selling all the way to Monterey, the capital of Spanish California. This city, just a four-day ride to the south of San Francisco, was the second-most important port on the Pacific coast of the Spanish Americas, after Lima in Peru.

Kuskov stopped. He looked around. Gun crews with lighted wicks stood in place. Everything was ready for the battle. Apart from the Russians and Indians, there were also the Aleuts. They had been brought there two days earlier from northern parts of Russian America, Kodiak and Sitka, as a replacement crew for the sea otter hunting parties. So far, they had kept to themselves, huddling together and tightly clutching darts with bone tips. *Poor guys,* sighed Kuskov as he glanced at those strange people. The Aleuts had holes pierced in their cheeks, and animal tusks protruded from those holes. *I should encourage them somehow since they ended up in a full-blown war instead of hunting party.*

Kuskov turned. "Corporal Zaborschikov," he called in a loud whisper.

The officer took this as a call to report and whispered back while blushing, "Sir, everything is ready, sir."

"Listen, Prokhor—that is your name, isn't it? Here is your order." Kuskov got quiet for a second as if searching for words and continued in a laconic military tone. "Save the cannonballs. Use shrapnel instead. Do not leave any wounded or take prisoners. Ask our Kashaya brothers not to let any of the strangers escape. We need to make it look like nothing happened here. Is that clear?"

"Affirmative, sir Commandant, sir!"

"We do not need unnecessary scandals," Kuskov muttered thoughtfully to himself. "I will describe everything in detail in my report to the company." Kuskov gave a deep sigh. As if remembering something, he added, "By the way, has Zavalishin's detachment left for the Rumyantsev Bay yet to intercept the pirates?"

"Yes, sir. They left before sunrise, sir Commandant, sir!"

"At ease, Prokhor! We are not on a parade! You're saying they left at dawn? Good! God help them," Kuskov said with satisfaction. "How about our *guests*?"

The corporal leaned conspiratorially toward Kuskov. "The younger one and their tanya left for the Kashaya village as if they had forgotten something there. The other one," the young officer motioned to the side with his head, "is there, waiting for you by the wicket gate. He says he wants to say good-bye to you."

Kuskov turned in the direction his officer had pointed. By the opposite wall, a man leaned against the doorframe of the inconspicuous wicket gate. It was difficult to say anything about him. His body was almost completely hidden under a shapeless monk's habit and wide hood. The loose garment was crudely made from pile woolen fabric. It was practically impossible to tell its color whether because of its age or by the design of its makers. Kuskov had seen similar garments on the Franciscans monks from the nearby Spanish mission, but that was where the guest's similarities with the monks ended.

The guests, who spoke perfect Russian, had made a timely appearance and had practically saved the fortress. They had come out of nowhere with the warning of an impending attack on the fort, which enabled the colonists to prepare for the hostilities. Kuskov and all the settlers were very grateful to them even if nobody knew where they had come from.

"To say good-bye, you're saying," Kuskov mumbled. "Why not? Wait for me here." He hastily walked across the courtyard toward the man in the monk's habit.

CHAPTER 6

1820. Russian California.
Rumyantsev (Bodega) Bay. The Same Morning.

A gorgeous view of the bay and the Pacific Ocean stretching all the way to the horizon opened from the cliffs and through bushes and small trees. It was unclear what the roots of these shrubs clung to.

No wonder they called it "pacific," Lieutenant Zavalishin thought while lying on the rocks. *The smaller and shallower the water basin is, the more its movements tend to be chaotic and unpredictable. The opposite is also true. It is practically impossible to rock this vastness, but if that happened, it would not be an easy task to quiet it down,* philosophized the young lieutenant.

In spite his youth, Lieutenant Zavalishin had already shown himself as an extraordinary man. Having descended from a renowned family of military officers, the son of a general who was the hero of the Napoleonic war, Zavalishin was a prodigy. After his enrollment into the Imperial Marine Cadet Corps, Zavalishin soon showed such capabilities that at age sixteen, while still a cadet, he had been appointed to teach navigation for sophomores part time. It was no wonder. Not only did the young man know how to handle the most complex mathematical calculations in his mind, but he also possessed clear, expressive rhetoric. At age seventeen, by the direct order from the Admiralty Collegium office and skipping all the formalities, he was given the rank of lieutenant in the Russian Imperial Navy, an unprecedented promotion.

Zavalishin was a living legend among the Marine Corps cadets. When the school received an order to select the most talented young officers and "guard-a-marines" of senior classes to join the naval circumnavigation on the imperial frigate *Kreicer* under the command of Captain-Lieutenant Lazarev, no one had any doubts about the candidacy of Zavalishin.

Apart from the main expedition goal—to demonstrate the power and glory of the Russian Navy on every continent—it was to update existing nautical charts. Zavalishin, who by that time was twenty, was fluent in German, French, English, Spanish, Dutch, and Swedish, and he was methodically conquering Italian, Greek, and Arabic. Lieutenant Zavalishin, a very remarkable young man, was indispensable for such an expedition.

Due to the thick fog, it was utterly impossible to see how the pirates had lowered their boats, but the young man's ears easily heard the slightest nuances of the enemy's movements. He heard them load the last boxes on the boats and push away from the ship with their oars. He heard the first strokes of their oars. He spied the boats emerging from the fog, rushing to shore at double speed.

Lying on either side of Zavalishin, the cadets and guard-a-marines of his detachment came to life and began clicking their rifle bolts.

"Nakhimov!" Zavalishin called in a low voice. A young officer who, just like Zavalishin, wore a new midshipman's coat, crawled over in a crouch. "What do you think, midshipman? Which maneuver is better for meeting the enemy?" Zavalishin asked the officer in a calm tone as if reading a lecture question. He nodded toward the pirates' landing party.

Nakhimov surveyed the surroundings. "Well, it would not be too hard to capture them now, but it would be even better to do it quietly so that the main prize would not escape. Do I understand your intentions correctly, sir?" The midshipman motioned with his head in the direction of the schooner, which was still shrouded in fog.

"You read my mind," Zavalishin replied, half smiling. "Here is your first combat mission, midshipman. Take half the squad and hide over there, behind that ledge, a bit down the path. Let them pass you and head my way. Then do not delay! When we stick our bayonets in their bellies, you and your people come from behind and catch them off guard."

"Yes, sir."

Without unbending to his full height, Nakhimov got up and quietly gave a couple of orders. A group of marines tried not to disclose their presence as they followed Nakhimov in short dashes.

He will make an excellent officer one day, Zavalishin thought as he followed Nakhimov with his eyes. *He is so smart.*

CHAPTER 7

1820. Russian California. Fort Ross.
The Same Morning.

Smiling broadly and offering his hand, Kuskov approached the man in a hooded habit. "You chose such a bad hour to leave. I wish you would stay here with us."

The stranger put something into his knapsack, took a step toward Kuskov, and shook his outstretched hand. "Thank you, sir, but we should leave before everything starts. We have to. Good-bye, Mister Kuskov. God help you!"

The stranger's gray eyes looked at Kuskov in a forthright, respectful manner. His long, dark hair escaping from under the hood did not make him look any less manly. He was unshaven and rumpled, which was probably simply the consequences of the hardships of travel, and yet an air of freshness surrounded the man. Kuskov could not find the right word to describe his feelings, but he was sure the traveler had nothing to do with the Franciscans; Kuskov would bet his last ruble on that. Observing vows of poverty, Franciscan monks went years without washing themselves, meaning they stank like pigs and could be smelled from afar. This man didn't stink. He emanated an unusual but very pleasant odor.

"Well, if you need to go, I do not have the right to keep you here any longer, Father," Kuskov said, still smiling. "We already owe you our lives for warning us against these enemies. For that, I bow to you on behalf of the company, Mother Russia, and all us sinners."

"Do not mention it, sir, and please don't call me 'Father' because I am not a priest at all. We . . . how should I put it?" The stranger was silent for a moment, searching for the right words. "As I told you before, we are just travelers."

"Well, if you say so," Kuskov agreed with him in a friendly manner, "let it be 'travelers.' The only thing I do not understand is why you seem to speak our language so well and yet it sounds so strange."

"There's nothing strange about it, sir." The man frowned. "We have been traveling to many far and unknown places for a while now, and we meet different folks. Some would even forget their native languages, but we still remember ours."

Continuing to pretend he did not notice the guest's uneasiness, Kuskov continued. "People say you know what is to come in the future. Is it true? I do not know about America, but in Russia, 'travelers' with such abilities would be always called 'Fathers,' because they would almost certainly be monks or magi. Look, you did not even take any food with you. Do you live on thin air? If so, what are you if not saints?" Kuskov gave the man a friendly smile, pleased he had politely managed to needle his guest. The man shifted uncomfortably from foot to foot.

"Dear Mister Kuskov, let's not go there about the 'saints.' There is no man without sin. By some standards, we are even bigger sinners than you are, but I can give you advice concerning the future. This attack that the pirates waged today—I mean, will wage—is just the beginning. The situation is going to get worse. Not only will they try to steal furs, but soon they will start hunting animals in your—I mean, our—coastal waters. From here all the way up to Alaska."

The smile and friendliness faded from Kuskov's face. He understood this perfectly well. The only thing he could not understand was the stubborn silence of the company's management in reply to all his reports and messages in which he wrote about the number of provocations in Russian territorial waters. Only once did he get a small hint that the final decision on the problem depended on the decision of the head of state, or rather the absence of it, and that the company's management was doing its best to acquire that decision.

"By God, what is their interest in our lands? Bostonians have just founded their own state thousands of miles to the east. They call it the United States. The British have their own share of lands in America: Hudson Bay Company is our neighbor, but these are our lands, the lands of the Russian-American Company, which we lawfully bought from the locals! I could understand if we were talking about the Spaniards. They are our neighbors but are not particularly happy about that. Still, we trade with them in peace. Why are all these people coming here now?"

The traveler sighed heavily. "Sir, if everybody in the world thought like this—this is mine, that is his, and I am not getting into it—our world would be a different place." The stranger shrugged. "Do not think that everything happening here today is done just by crazy outlaws. Sometimes, even governments use the same tactics to pursue their interests. They strive for domination and economic privileges. If sea otters' fur is worth its weight in gold in China, then this is it—expect the newcomers whether you welcome them or not. The Spaniards will leave you alone soon, but others will want a piece of this pie. Look at Baranov up there in Alaska. To avoid confrontations, he simply hires the Boston's captains and shipmasters to do business together for their mutual benefit. Try to do the same here. You will not manage to keep this lands with our sluggishness. We are bold, we are strong, we are smart, but as a nation, we are very indecisive. We all look back on our father, the tsar, and wait for his order, his approval.

"Different times are coming, my dear sir, different times. Bostonians, as British, are offshoots of the same tree. They think all the lands on earth are their own and only they should cultivate them. So to add a little arrogance to your policies here will not hurt. Believe me." The stranger finished grimly.

Kuskov's mood changed for the worse. *He says he left Russia a long time ago, but he cares about the empire so much, and he makes sense as well. Russia is a hibernating bear in its lair. By the time Mother Russia stirs, puts two and two together, and I get the answers to my questions, everything will have been taken from under our noses.*

Kuskov lifted his head to looked at the stirring flag with the Russian two-headed golden eagle. *Two heads, and each is looking in different directions. What another symbol would better reflect our innate indecisiveness?* "Your words provoke thought, brother, that's for sure. Yes, I shall try to mull over your advice. This I can certainly promise you."

"There is one more thing." The traveler paused. "When you have time, ask your artisans to dig in the ground along the creeks and rivers here. You might find some interesting minerals."

Kuskov stifled a laugh. "What? Our Indians have already told you about the gold? We learned this from them a long time ago. Not only have they told us about it, they have also shown us where to mine it. Don't worry, we are not that indecisive as it may seem. We are already adding local gold to the company's coins we mint ourselves. Here, look!"

With these words, Kuskov pulled a newly minted five-ruble coin bearing the image of the Russian emblem and the letters RAC, the

Russian-American Company. He weighed the coin in his hand and tossed it in the air. The gold sparkled in the sun and obediently landed in Kuskov's palm. "Take it to remember me, brother. Also, thank you for the advice. We'll try not to miss the opportunities that have been given to us, so keep your chin up. As the saying goes, 'There's a time to throw stones away, and there's a time to gather them.' Skillful hands—that is what we need here—and many of them."

The traveler respectfully took the coin from the commandant's callused palm. "By the way," he said. "I've always wanted to ask you, sir . . ." the traveler said, but he never finished his question.

CHAPTER 8

1820. Russian California.
An Indian Village near Fort Ross.
The Same Morning.

Across the river, the Russian log houses were clearly visible through the tilted canopy of the tipi's entrance. The mouth of the nameless creek, humbly flowing into the great ocean, could also be seen to the left of the Indian settlement. Outside the Russian village, a ripe field of rye stretched up the hill almost to the very walls of the fort built on top. A well-trodden road ran parallel to the ocean, across the creek, and to the fort's entrance. To the north of the fort was the same forest that grew to the south of the Indian settlement, thereby encircling the small valley in a dense ring of trees. Nothing disturbed the sleepy morning.

Light smoke rose from the dying coals in the tipi's hearth. Coarsely processed pelts covered the cone-type structure. The gently twisting smoke exited through a hole at the top. A young Indian woman sat on the sack by the hearth, her long, slender legs twisted in the lotus pose. She was smoking a roll-your-own cigarette. From under languidly lowered eyelashes, she was looking at the young man who, unlike her, was extremely busy. He was hastily packing knapsacks with numerous packages and bags. Unlike the young woman, the man wore modern jeans, sneakers, and a T-shirt emblazoned with the name of the famous Russian soccer team Zenit.

Upon closer examination, the girl's Indian look was clearly fake. In spite of her weird hairdo, she looked quite modern, and way cooler than the man. Her short shorts and spaghetti-strap tank top failed to hide her young, slender figure; instead, it emphasized her beauty. Her body was covered with a tattoo that somehow did not look vulgar on her. A Japanese or Chinese motif prevailed in the tattoo; it depicted a serpent or a dragon striking something under her top. The skin not covered by the main tattoo hosted symbols and hieroglyphs that also had an oriental aspect. Her black hair was in a Mohawk hairstyle but dyed like a three-colored Russian flag. Its red, white, and blue matched her dark-blue eye shadow and black lipstick. To top it all, the girl went completely overboard with her piercings. In short, a twenty-first-century rock—or vampire-themed club would happily let her in without any entrance fee and would give her a free drink and then some.

To complete her mind-blowing image, two eagle feathers were stuck in the girl's Mohawk in perfect harmony with the interior appearance of the Indian tipi.

"You didn't forget my earphones, did you?" the girl asked the guy in a languished drawl while she kept her eyes on the smoke rings she skillfully produced.

The young man did not have the time to reply. A small light on the walkie-talkie lying next to the knapsack started blinking. The man rushed to the device, but the girl was faster.

"Hey boss! What's up?" she sneered into the receiver.

"Margo, are you two ready?" a worried voice asked.

"Sure! We're just like Boy Scouts—always ready." Margo giggled coquettishly.

Without succumbing to the girl's playful tone, the voice continued talking in a businesslike manner. "Has Jeff packed? You haven't forgotten anything, have you?"

"C'mon, boss. I had my eyes glued on him all the time," the girl replied. "He can't be trusted to do anything alone without supervision, you know."

The guy stopped in front of her and theatrically rolled his eyes. The voice coming from the walkie-talkie went silent for a while before saying, "Margo, I have a big favor to ask."

"For you, boss, I'm ready to do anything." The girl kept talking in a full-blown joking mode. "Do you want me to leave Jeff here among the cannibals?"

The man in the walkie-talkie ignored her comment. "Listen, we need to leave—immediately. That's why what I'm going to ask you is very important. Do you understand?"

"So what's the problem?" Margo became serious. "If we need to go, let's go."

"We can't leave until the commotion starts. It would attract too much attention. I'm also worried about this prolonged quiet," the voice said thoughtfully. "They might sense something's wrong. That's why I'm going to ask you to do something, uh, rather peculiar. Listen carefully. I think they're watching us, so you're going to step out of the tipi and pretend you've just woken up and don't sense any impending danger. Pretend to be a naïve Indian girl, sort of a Pocahontas who has nothing to worry about. Get it? Stretch, yawn, whatever. I trust your creativity. Just don't overact. Be careful, all right? Stop joking around for a while, okay?"

"Okay, but I already handed in my costume for storage."

"Do it without the costume." The voice on the other end started cracking with static.

Margo shifted, changing her pose. She sat on her feet and cast anxious glances at Jeff, who kept packing all this time, stuffing rags into their knapsacks.

"What? Don't say you want me to unpack it!" Jeff whispered nervously, turning to her. "We're running out of time!"

Without taking her ear from the walkie-talkie, Margo flipped her middle finger at him. "Okay boss. Got it. A Pocahontas you'll get," she asserted cheerfully.

"Both of you be careful there, and meet me at the agreed spot, okay?"

"Roger that," Margo said, rakishly showing off her knowledge of international call signals. She turned off the device and tossed it on the backpack. Sitting on his haunches by the backpack, the young man closely followed her movements. With catlike grace, the girl got up. Her signature smile spread on her lips.

"Hey, yo! Where's the camera?" the girl asked, mentally mulling something.

"Already packed. Why?" Jeff shot back.

"Damn it! The real cinematographer always packs his camera last. Loser!"

"You yourself told me we were leaving," the young man replied indignantly.

"Have you seen *Pocahontas?*" Margo asked.

"The cartoon? Sure. Why?" Jeff tried rather unsuccessfully to follow the abrupt changes of the woman's logic.

"Because I'm going to act a scene from that movie right now, *Pocahontas bathing in the waterfall.*" Margo giggled happily.

"What waterfall?" asked Jeff, clueless as to what she was talking about.

"You'll see. Too bad you've already packed your stuff, cameraboy," she added without any malice. "Such a scene, and you're going to miss it."

Margo stretched. In a blink of an eye, she dropped her shorts and took her tank top off. Jeff gaped dumbfounded. Before his astonished eyes, the tattoo-covered beauty stood in the sunlit opening of the tipi, dazzlingly naked.

"Pick up your jaw and wait for my signal," Margo chuckled, giving Jeff a quizzical glance. She stepped out of the hut.

An excellent view of the entire small valley opened up through the trees at the edge of the rye field. It revealed the field itself, the hill with the fortress on top, and the creek. A solitary, naked Indian girl stepped out of one of the tipis. She stretched and shuddered slightly from the early morning chill as she headed toward the creek.

Not a muscle flinched on the mask-like face of the motionless warrior hidden by the trees. Maybe his nostrils flared a bit. He could clearly see the naked female's body covered with tattoos as she bent toward the water in the river. The woman had well-built hips, long legs, and a round, perfectly shaped butt. That broke the warrior's resolve. Every feeling that had collected in him during his long period of abstinence resulted in a chilling, blood-stopping cry.

Almost instantly, the whole forest surrounding the small valley of the Russian dominion echoed with the similar wailing of hundreds of throats.

CHAPTER 9

1820. Russian California. Fort Ross.
The Same Morning.

The traveler's question was interrupted by blood-chilling cries from the forest. Nobody could understand where the attack was coming from, as the sound seemed to emerge from every direction; the wails filled the valley. When the deafening war cries joined the monotonous wailing, it became clear that the sounds were coming not from animals but from humans.

The fortress sprang to life. The bell in the chapel tower, which was also used as a watchtower, started to boom loudly. Gun crews began banging the lids of ammunition boxes. Crew commanders yelled orders. The courtyard filled with the noise of military actions. The defenders rushed to the fortress walls.

Already in motion, Kuskov turned to the stranger and yelled above the rising hubbub, "If you can't find a ship in Monterey, come back here! We'll be setting afloat a new packet boat from our shipyard in

September. We can give you a lift to Novo-Arkhangelsk, in Alaska, and from there you sure can get to Kodiak and then to Petropavlovsk on Kamchatka Peninsula. It is the shortest way to Russia."

"Sir," the stranger said while running after the commandant and trying to yell over the cacophony of sounds in the awakened fort, "I only wanted to ask you—"

Kuskov's attention had already been captured by the young corporal by his side who was wildly gesturing about something. His cheeks flushed with excitement; he was pointing toward the woods with a spyglass in hand. Having heard what officer had to say, the commandant started walking briskly in the direction of the gun battery. Yet, the question the stranger wanted to ask Kuskov seemed to be very important. Not afraid to seem intrusive, the traveler rushed after Kuskov, asking him something on the run. Kuskov stopped for a moment and shook his head negatively. The stranger froze on the spot. By then, it was completely impossible to hear whatever Kuskov was saying, but it was clear that the stranger was totally taken aback by his answer. Kuskov, in turn, seemed to be very surprised by the stranger's reaction. He hastened his step and yelled something to the traveler again.

At that moment, the sky suddenly lit up with a myriad of lights. Just like all the defenders of the fort, the stranger looked up. The hood slipped off his head to his shoulders. *It's so beautiful!* Forgetting about Kuskov for a moment, the stranger admired the celestial extravaganza. The lights in the air froze for a second. They changed directions and started falling down, gaining speed and turning into burning dots racing toward the ground.

Dmitry—with his hood fallen, it was obvious he was the stranger— did not even think about danger. He still could not get used to what had happened to him and looked at his new surroundings as if through someone else's eyes. *Arrows! Friggin' burning arrows!*

41

The defenders seemed not to share his admiration for the illumination. As if by someone's order, everyone rushed to the protections that had been prepared. Women and children raced to hide under the horse carts. *That's why the horse carts are piled with the sandbags!* Dmitry thought. *All the barrels with water around also make sense now!*

Someone running past Dmitry pushed him hard on his shoulder, and Dmitry flew under the protection of the terrace just as several arrows made a long hissing sound, piercing the place where he had just stood. Without slowing down or looking back, his unknown savior grabbed a bucket, scooped water from a barrel, and in a wide, sweeping arc, emptied the bucket on the burning bush.

Still dizzy from the action around him, Dmitry jumped to his feet. "I can't believe it!" Whom or what he was addressing was not clear. Mechanically, deep in his thoughts, he pulled the arrow from the ground and put it in his bag. He touched the wicket gate and indecisively froze. He turned in the direction of the gun battery, trying to spy Kuskov. Then he took his iPhone out of the bag, opened the gate and slipped out. None of the fortress defenders noticed his departure in the surrounding commotion.

CHAPTER 10

1820. The Russian California Coast. Rumyantsev (Bodega) Bay. The Same Morning.

A dozen heavily armed pirates swiftly scrambled up the trail that ascended the cliff from the small beach. With a rifle at the ready, the puffing boatswain led his assault squad. To his credit, he was walking ahead of the group.

A strategically bright thought flashed in his mind. *When we get to that shrub there, at the edge of the cliff, we can take a breath.* It was quite sensible indeed. Yet fate clearly had a different idea about the expression *to take a breath.* At that moment, fate has already been winding the last inches of the boatswain's life thread on its spindle and had already lost interest in him. The boatswain luckily was unaware of fate's cruel intentions for him.

He grabbed a long branch that stretched toward him at the top of the trail as if offering its aid, but he failed to catch his breath as he planned. With his sixth sense—or maybe a third eye that suddenly grew at the back of his head—the boatswain saw a rifle butt closing in on him, but the fat man did not have time to turn or duck. The horizon shattered into a thousand tiny, blinding shards.

When he regained his senses, he found himself lying in the middle of the path and tied up. His gallant crewmembers were all gagged and spread on the ground around him like silent logs taking a rest. Suddenly, somebody leaned over him. The boatswain could not see the person's face because the risen sun shone from behind the stranger's head and was blindingly bright. The fat man felt a painful prick on his neck. He recognized the cold sting of a blade. He heard excellent English spoken in a low voice. "Welcome to Fort Ross! One word and you're dead! Do you understand?"

Careful so as not to hurt himself on the blade, the boatswain blinked with all his might to show the stranger he understood perfectly.

"Good!" he heard. Someone grabbed him by the collar and in one strong pull made the boatswain sit up. He was able to take a good look at his conquerors.

To the boatswain's surprise, he saw a handsome young man dressed in a Russian navy uniform. The look in the officer's eyes radiated confidence. It was clear that, despite his youth, he knew perfectly well what he was doing. The boatswain's first impression of the young man was confirmed by the fact that the soldiers, who stood around the officer, listened to him with focused attention.

Fail me to hell! The phrase flashed in the boatswain's mind. He would come to regret this phrase later and not only once during that day, for it was not a good omen to express one's wishes in vain simply because you never know which of your desires the capricious fate will choose to grant. *These damned Russians have the whole army here—the bastards set us up!*

The fat man did not have the time to finish his thinking process and explain, at least to himself, who exactly had set them up when he heard a new order.

"Take off your clothes."

That's it. They're going to kill us, the boatswain thought, somehow completely unemotionally. *Well, they're doing the right thing. I'd do the same. There's no reason to ruin good clothes. They can still be of use.*

The thought that his clothes would soon be worn by someone else brought a single tear to the boatswain's eye. When Russians started stripping him out of his clothes, he sniffled as pitifully as he could. The next order confused him not because he did not understand the language but because of its logic, or better, its lack.

May it be mercy? The boatswain's heart skipped a beat. *Is it possible?*

Hope, that faithful companion of any vagabond, spread like a warm wave of Jamaican rum inside him.

CHAPTER 11

1820. Russian California. Fort Ross.
The Same Morning.

Dmitry hunched over as he ran down the path from the fortress toward the village. The ocean breeze was blowing the monk's garment like a sail. Realizing that it hindered his movements, he took it off and stuffed it into his knapsack in one swift motion. Moving around became much easier in his jeans and T-shirt.

The fortress wall separated Dmitry from the open space that stretched from the fortress to the village. The first salvo of the fortress's cannon boomed just as he ran into the field in front of the fortress. The Russians' first volley consisted of incendiary ammunition. It was a pity to burn unharvested grain, but as the French expression goes, *"Á la guerre, comme à la guerre."*

Dmitry paused to size up the situation. Like an avalanche, the savages were running from the woods and surrounding the fort. The rye field had already caught on fire in spots, and though it had not stopped the attackers, it had at least dissipated their ranks. They still had close to a quarter of a mile to cover until they would reach the walls. Pungent, black smoke filled the sky. Dmitry managed to notice the two small figures running from the other side of the field with all their might toward him. Just like the attacking savages, Jeff and Margo had to make it through the rye fields before they could come into the clearing where they had agreed to meet.

The attackers also noticed the two running figures. A small group of warriors separated from the main wave and headed to intercept the runners. Feeling cold with fear and stepping into the open, Dmitry dashed toward his companions.

Margo, who had somehow managed to get dressed while running, was galloping like a gazelle and was at least thirty feet ahead of Jeff. Ripe ears of rye kept whipping her tanned legs. Jeff, who was carrying all the bags like a gentleman, was running in long, camel-like strides.

When he was still a short distance from the clearing, one of the straps on a backpack broke. He stopped to readjust his load. The savages noticed this and doubled their speed. The situation was not in favor of the running duo. With all his effort, Dmitry lunged toward his companions. No more than twenty feet separated them from the clearing.

"This way! Faster! Margo, help him!" Dmitry tried to yell above the noise of the battle while gasping for air. "Jeff! Drop the backpack!"

Snatching his own knapsack from his shoulder, Dmitry took out his iPhone and hurriedly pushed buttons. He threw the device on the ground in the clearing. The iPhone obediently lit up with a blue, pulsating glow. The blinking flashes made a circle ten feet in diameter.

Dmitry was the first to jump into the circle. Seconds later, Margo threw herself into his arms. Gasping for air, Jeff literally stumbled into the glowing portal with his bags.

At that same moment, a hissing sound sliced the air; a tomahawk flew like a lightning bolt through the smoke, followed closely by the figures of the savages. With a dull thud, the tomahawk embedded itself in the backpack hanging by one strap across Jeff's back. The long-suffering backpack, as if it could not withstand such abuse any longer, fell at the feet of Dmitry and Margo with the tomahawk stuck in it. The force of the impact threw Jeff out of the glowing circle, and he sprawled on the ground about ten feet away.

As if in a sign of farewell, a faint bluish lightning bolt outlined the border of the portal, the blue circle shrunk to an intolerably bright point, and it disappeared along with Dmitry, Margo, the backpack, and the iPhone itself.

Jeff, spitting dust, picked up his head to meet the approaching Indians and squeezed his eyes shut.

CHAPTER 12

Present Time. Northern California. At the Entrance to the Museum of the Fort Ross State Historic Park. Morning.

The parking lot at the Fort Ross State Historic Park was packed as it usually was on weekends. A few years earlier, rumors had leaked to the press about the possibility of the museum's closing to save money for the bankrupt state. However, that only attracted more crowds. People had different opinions about the governor of California those days, but that decision had been criticized practically by everyone. The common verdict was, "What else would you expect from the Terminator?'" Since that time, the flow of people had not decreased.

The public hastened to pay tribute to their soon-to-be-trampled freedoms. People liked this museum albeit in different ways. Russian communities, especially in San Francisco, treated it as holy ground. National holidays and various events were celebrated here with the participation of the Russian Orthodox Church abroad. These events, like any other Orthodox celebrations, were replete with icons and the rise of the cross. To an outsider, such celebrations might look like funeral processions, and in a sense, they were funerals of unrealized dreams. Russian history was rich of such hopes.

The Americans liked anything that had at least something to do with the history of their multinational and relatively young country. Whatever the reason, these celebrations constantly attracted many people. Some gawked at the exotic props while others shed tears for missed opportunities.

The next group of tourists was leisurely getting off the red, double-decker bus with the word *Ohio* across its side. The group included many overweight people, so everybody was preoccupied with helping each other down the several steps at the tight exit of the bus. Therefore, no one could confirm or deny the words of an extremely fat man assuring everyone that the odd-looking couple of "hippie scumbags" had appeared next to the bus out of nowhere. He even offered a logical explanation to the phenomenon, stating that they were aliens from outer space. The man claimed he had witnessed with his own eyes how they had appeared out of thin air. The tourists who had already gotten off the bus stared in amazement at the strange couple. Some reached for their cameras.

Dmitry was the first to come to his senses. He brushed off his jeans and picked up his iPhone. Without meeting anyone's gaze, he took Margo by her arm and almost dragged her toward a nearby Toyota minivan.

With her eyes full of unshed tears, Margo, silently biting her lips to keep from crying, followed him while clenching the ill-fated backpack with the tomahawk sticking out of it. The minivan's doors slammed simultaneously. Seconds later, the van's tires screeched as it dashed from the parking lot toward the highway.

The fat alien hunter from Ohio kept on snapping pictures of them as the bewildered tourists watched in disbelief the scene from pulp fiction movie unfolding before their eyes. The big man was very excited. His trip had already paid for itself. If he could manage to get photos of genuine transvestites on the streets of San Francisco, he would have enough stories to tell his neighbors for years to come.

PART TWO

Anomaly

The wind blows to the south and goes round to the north;
round and round goes the wind, and on its circuits the wind returns.

—Ecclesiastes 1:6

CHAPTER 13

Present Time. New York. On the Highway to JFK Airport. Two Days before the Events Described in the Previous Chapter.

A silver Toyota Sienna with the words *Russian TV* on its side was slowly crawling along Manhattan's congested FDR Highway. The driver skillfully used any gap in the endless stream of cars to inch his way forward. The Toyota followed the road signs that directed the traffic toward the airport. Having escaped the never-ending queue of vehicles trying to get to Brooklyn and then to JFK via the toll-free Brooklyn Bridge, the Toyota sped up and dove into the Battery Tunnel.

"Geez! How do you guys drive here? I don't get it! There's nothing but traffic here!" grumbled Jeff, the driver. Dmitry, sitting next to him, held an open computer notebook. Margo had the back seat to herself. Taking full advantage of the situation, she lay down with her feet comfortably up on the windowsill.

"Well, we don't drive here much. We mostly walk or use the subway," Dmitry replied absentmindedly while retrieving his cell phone from his pocket.

"Besides, it's so hot here, people can't breathe! Even the asphalt is melting! It's so much better in Brooklyn! There's always a breeze from the ocean."

"And the stink of borscht from Brighton Beach!" Margo added waspishly. She has deliberately cut herself off from Jeff's constant mumbling with music piped through earphones, but it was clear she hadn't missed a thing.

"What do you have against borscht?" Jeff frowned and looked in the rearview mirror. "I was little when our family emigrated from the Soviet Union, so I don't remember much, but my mom used to tell me that in Odessa, people took borscht even to the beach! They would just put it in a jar. Why not? One cannot live without liquids."

"How many times do I have to tell you, Jeff, that it's not appropriate to call soup a liquid!" Margo rolled her eyes. "It's called *the first course!*"

"Well, call it whatever you want, but in Odessa, we call our first course simply a liquid!" A red-faced Jeff was standing his ground.

"Here we go again!" The girl cut him short with fake annoyance. "Boss, please make a note that I tolerate this individual only because of you!" Margo did not want to let Jeff win their verbal duel.

Completely immersed in his thoughts about the upcoming trip, Dmitry didn't participate in their argument. He recognized Jeff as a great cinematographer. Even though Jeff was ten years younger, Dmitry valued his efficiency and reliability, the main virtues of the cameraman in Dmitry's thinking. During the years they worked together, they had become friends in spite of the differences in their characters, upbringing, education, and age.

Margo had just recently joined the team. She had worked for them as an intern after graduating from NYU. She had expressed an interest in continuing to work with Dmitry, and he had agreed. His numerous requests to Moscow for an assistant had been ignored. Margo turned out to be a great sound engineer. She compensated for her lack of TV reporting experience with her willingness to learn the profession. She wasn't what Dmitry had been asking for, but he decided she was okay. He knew that experience would come in time; he decided he would turn her into his field production manager along the road.

As far as Dmitry could judge from their short period of working together, she was trustworthy and very responsible, and that was of paramount importance. The crazy life of TV journalists, which mixed constant traveling and hectic schedules with sleepless nights and ever-changing deadlines, was much easier with a cohesive team.

One other of Margo's important attributes was that she was an American, and on top of that, one who spoke perfect Russian. To his surprise, her Russian was in many ways even better then Jeff's, who had been born in Russia. It was easily explainable.

Jeff, who had grown up in Brooklyn in a family of Soviet Jewish immigrants, spoke a wild mix of Russian, English, and vulgar Yiddish. Jewish émigrés from the former Soviet Union has not nurtured a special reverence for Russian culture. On the contrary, during the years of repression, they had developed a strict rejection of all things Russian, and besides, they were in a big hurry to become Americans. That is why their children grew up kind of lost. They didn't become Jews in its true religious sense, their Russian cultural roots had also been severed, and they never became *real* Americans. Most of them continued to live in Brooklyn as a lost generation in a marginal subculture where they became an inexhaustible source of ridicule and anecdotes for the American and Russian mass media.

Margo was raised in a family in which her Russian genes from her maternal grandmother were valued. She had grown up in California, in Orange County. When her parents divorced, she moved in with her grandmother, who lived in a prewar building on Central Park West and 79th, right across the Museum of Natural History.

Her grandma had recently passed away, so Margo wasn't very fond of dwelling on the subject, but from her fragmentary stories, Dmitry realized that her *babushka*, who had been brought to America after the Russian revolution when she was little, had belonged to a noble, aristocratic Russian family.

Despite the warnings from his colleagues, Dmitry chose her for his team and had never regretted it. Despite her relatively young age Margo, at her twenty-four, had a very professional attitude toward her job. Jeff would occasionally exhibit fecklessness by oversleeping or forgetting something, but Margo was as precise as a Swiss watch.

The only problem was her extravagant appearance, and *extravagant* is putting it mildly. Margo usually shocked people, especially those who saw her for the first time. Her hairstyles changed several times a day depending on her mood, and her tattoos and various accessories of the current youth fashion made her a traffic stopper.

Right from the start of their professional relationship, Dmitry understood that Margo's shell hid a kind, pure heart, and her ever-changing hairstyles concealed a fine, sharp mind. Margo's eccentricities struck him as amusing, and they had been at times a big help. She made young people feel closer to her, which was important, as the youth were often subjects of Dmitry's journalism. Her appearance was also a good distraction at times when Dmitry and Jeff had to conceal their shooting or make videos in a candid-camera style.

Margo's long, beautiful legs were crowned by a nice, tight butt. She was fully aware of her assets and never missed a chance to emphasize them. She usually wore miniskirts or tight shorts. As a last resort, she would wear jeans, but they were always form-fitting stretch jeans. Overall, Margo's becoming a member of their team had spiced up Dmitry's and Jeff's stale brotherhood. Jeff had perked up, his sluggishness had disappeared, and whenever Margo was around, he did his best to suck in his flabby paunch, much to Dmitry's amusement, especially when it became evident none of Jeff's efforts worked on Margo. It was not that she did not notice him; she never missed a chance to make him the target of her sneers and biting remarks. It was obvious to everybody with the exception of Jeff that he had no chance with her.

Jeff stoically endured it all, pretending complete indifference to Margo's remarks as well as to the girl herself, but he was fooling only himself. Dmitry had often enough caught a telltale look in Jeff's eyes when he watched Margo. No objective witness would have the slightest doubt about his feelings for her.

After a time, the bickering between the two young people started to resemble a well-staged comedy show put on mainly for Dmitry, their main and only audience. Dmitry sometimes roared with laughter at Margo's most successful remarks about Jeff. Since such bickering did not affect the working relationship of the trio, at least in a negative way, Dmitry followed the development of their relationship with great interest.

Although Dmitry was attracted to Margo, Jeff's vivid romantic feelings for her had prevented Dmitry from taking his own steps toward her. Deep inside, he appreciated that. Not that he was concerned about having a relationship with a coworker, no. It's just that he didn't think they could last together. He did not think their ten years' difference was a big deal, for his current girlfriend, Lena, was the same age as Margo; he just felt they belonged to different generations.

Maybe he felt that way because in his eyes, Margo wasn't really Russian. Of course, she spoke Russian well, but having been born in the

United States, she was already more American and had other interests and a different mind-set.

Whatever the reason, Dmitry decided not to "touch" the girl; he was just following, not without interest, the development of her relationship with Jeff.

CHAPTER 14

1825, December 13. St. Petersburg.
The Day before the Decembrists' Uprising.
11:00 in the Morning.

Right in the middle of Voznesensky Avenue, four magnificent horses thundering at top speed carried an expensive, black-lacquered carriage. The team and carriage were raising shimmering clouds of snow and scaring off oncoming coaches, which slid to the roadsides.

In front of the carriage, leading the way through the morning traffic, a *troika* of horses harnessed to a sled carried six bearded, armed Cossacks. A similar sled followed in the first sled's tracks.

Red-faced from the frosty morning wind in their faces, the Cossacks were excitedly whooping and hollering. The sounds of their whips cracking above the horses' heads and sometimes over the heads of careless passersby echoed in the wintry air.

Having passed at full speed the construction scaffolds of the future St. Isaac's Cathedral, the horses drew the sledded carriage over the cast-iron Blue Bridge, their clad hooves clanking loudly. Without slowing down, the horses turned to the right on the Moyka River embankment and stopped in front of the colonnade of a stunning, four-story mansion built in the classical architectural style.

The Cossacks jumped off their sleds and surrounded the carriage in a tight ring. A curtain fluttered on the frost-covered window of the carriage. The Cossack captain lowered the footrest and opened the carriage door. A plump gentleman in a long beaver coat glanced at the captain, who stood at attention. His gold-rimmed glasses glistened in the pale sun. The gentleman deftly climbed out of the carriage and disappeared through the main entrance.

Noticeably relaxed, the Cossacks and the carriage driver threw blankets over the horses, which were hot from the run, and moved the carriage with the sleds to the side of the embankment, opening the space in front of the main entrance.

The colonnade supported a large, Grecian portico with a sign that read, "Russian-American Company." The golden letters gleamed in the sun.

A wide marble staircase led upstairs from the entrance hall. Despite his size and his heavy fur coat, the owner of the fancy carriage deftly ran up the stairs and disappeared into the inner chambers.

In the center of his spacious study, Kondraty Ryleyev, the manager of the St. Petersburg's office of the Russian-American Company, sat behind a huge inlaid table of Karelian birch with a marble-like pattern to its grain. He was in the company of a six quite imposing men, the cream of St. Petersburg's society as well as the best people in Russian business and finance.

One chair was unoccupied. It was evident everybody was expecting someone. The very private meeting had been urgently convened by

Ryleyev; all the servants had been given the day off. Ryleyev and his assistant, Somov, acted as hosts, an easy task considering everything had been prepared in advance. Plates laden with biscuits and appetizers sat on wheeled carts positioned along the wall. Decanters of various vodkas, liquors, and wines sparkled. A cozy fire burned in the fireplace in the corner.

Such privacy measures had apparently not surprised the guests. Almost everyone in St. Petersburg's high society was crazy about various secret lodges and societies; such was a fashion of the time. So even if someone accidentally stumbled upon their meeting, it wouldn't be much of a surprise. However, those who gathered that day in the meeting room of the Russian-American Company had more grounds for secrecy than anyone else in St. Petersburg.

Count Nikolai Mordvinov, a member of the Cabinet of Ministers' finance committee, president of the Free Economic Society, and admiral of His Majesty's Imperial Navy sat at the head of the table directly opposite Ryleyev. The diamonds adorning his numerous medals and the gold of his epaulettes sparkled in the candlelight. Along with his many governmental posts and duties, he was also the owner of one of the largest number of shares of the Russian-American Company.

Next to him sat Mikhail Speransky, the former state secretary of the untimely deceased Emperor Alexander I and a former governor-general of Siberia as well as the famous Russian reformer. Speransky was leaning forward and saying something in a subdued voice. The fact that Speransky was also the owner of a large stake in the company, so large that the company management could not have refused to invite him to this extraordinary meeting of shareholders, evidently came as a surprise to Mordvinov.

The admiral listened to Speransky with half an ear and kept sullenly nodding his head at the words audible to him alone. To the side of them sat Peter Severin, chair of the board of the Russian Copper Bank who also served on the Russian-American Company's board of directors. He was scratching quick notes on a piece of paper.

The mayor of St. Petersburg, merchant of the top guild Nikolai Kosov, used the pause to munch on smoked sturgeon smothered in French mustard and to warm himself with brandy.

Prince Sergey Uvarov, chair of the board of the Commercial Bank, stood by the window, smoking a cigar and staring over the frozen Moyka River. As was the case with the other gentlemen in the room, he was a board member and belonged to the highest level of power in the Russian-American Company. Puffing on his cigar with visible pleasure, Uvarov watched through the frozen window as a guard who stood on duty in a sconce at the entrance of the Blue Bridge kept slapping himself and stomping his feet to warm up.

It was apparent everybody had been expecting someone else. As if in confirmation to that, the door opened, and Somov, who served under the patronage of Ryleyev as the company's head clerk, ushered in the last participant of the meeting.

"Gentlemen!" Somov announced formally, "His Excellency Prince Kurakin!"

It was absolutely unnecessary to introduce Prince Aleksey Kurakin to anyone present. As chairman of the St. Petersburg Assignation Bank and the son of the famous diplomat of Catherine's the Great epoch, he was well known to everyone; the clerk's announcement was simply protocol.

The owner of the black-lacquered carriage, his glasses misted up in a warm room dropped his fancy beaver coat into Somov's hands. With a guilty smile, as if apologizing for his late arrival, he readily joined the group.

Ryleyev rose after everybody had finally taken seats. "Gentlemen, first let me thank all of you for such a prompt response to our short notice of this meeting. I think we can begin." Ryleyev paused, taking in the elite group with his smart blue eyes. "Second, I would like to say that Mister Buldakov sends his greetings to all of you."

All faces immediately showed instant interest, respect, and surprise. Mikhail Buldakov was the last living founder of the Russian-American Company; he had survived Shelikhov, Baranov, and Rezanov. Due to poor health, he was spending almost all his time at his estate near Velikiy Ustyug and rarely participated in the company's business at the time.

"Third," Ryleyev paused again. "As you all know, the situation has become rather critical thanks to the military branch of our organization. Tonight, a meeting of the Northern Society lodge will gather in this room and Prince Trubetskoy will be present. I asked all of you to come this morning so we can make our final decision before the other meeting takes place. Because the army has to take the oath to the new emperor, Nicholas I, tomorrow, I have every reason to believe that tonight, our military staff will decide to start a revolt before the oath."

Through practically his whole speech, Ryleyev had spoken with a disdainful, sarcastic smile that left no doubt as to how he felt about the decision of the "military branch" of the organization.

"*Mon cher.*" Mordvinov turned to Ryleyev in a completely silent room. "I've heard that Prince Trubetskoy is very busy creating a manifesto or a constitution. Is it so?"

"This is true, Your Grace," Ryleyev answered with a slight bow. "As you know, our military commanders," Ryleyev pulled a face again, "are represented by Misters Volkonsky, Pestel, and of course Trubetskoy. They dream of forming a dictatorship upon elimination of the imperial family. His Excellency Prince Trubetskoy even dreams of becoming the future dictator, Your Grace."

"What do you think would happen when the prince learns about the real motives and the results of your, eh . . . efforts?" Speransky asked Ryleyev with a slight burr.

"*Our* efforts, Your Excellency, if I may." Ryleyev corrected Speransky, stressing the word *our*.

A little embarrassed, Speransky wiped his balding head glistening with sweat and corrected himself. "*Our* efforts, of course."

"You, Your Excellency," Ryleyev noted calmly, "apparently underestimate the ambitions of Colonel Pestel. They're very busy with dividing the positions and responsibilities for their future government. However, that is good for us! While the officers are busy, we will fulfill our duty."

Ryleyev became quiet. Expectant eyes turned to Mordvinov. The handsome admiral shook his gray mane and coughed into his white linen handkerchief. He slowly pulled out his golden Breguet and opened the watch's lid. The second hand was getting close to the number twelve at the top of the dial, very close to meeting the other hands. It was almost noon. When all three hands aligned, the watch played a pleasant mechanical melody. As if by command, everyone turned to the window. When the melody stopped, light smoke arose from the bastion of the Peter and Paul Fortress. Several seconds later, the expected sound of an artillery shot muffled by the distance reached the ears of those in the room. As if having proven something to himself, the admiral slammed the lid of his watch and with a theatrical gesture returned it to a special pocket in his uniform jacket.

"I had a talk with the empress dowager," the admiral began in the well-modulated, deep voice of a theatrical tragedian. "She is certainly one of the largest shareholders of our company, and therefore we can completely count on her support, but—" The admiral again paused. He looked around as if to make sure everybody was paying attention. The others were indeed clinging to his every word. Satisfied, the admiral started whispering as is required by the genre of high tragedy. "—but she is also a mother! She's already suffered too much when Constantine waived his right to the throne. Now she is concerned about Nicholas, knowing how unpopular he is with both the court and the guard regiments."

His listeners understood the matter quite well. The special "relationship" the empress dowager had with the admiral was no secret to anyone either.

Prince Kurakin, who had warmed himself up enough, joined the conversation. "I've heard that Trubetskoy insists on eliminating the whole imperial family?"

All those sitting around the table froze. The prince shifted his searching gaze to Ryleyev.

"You've heard it right, Your Excellency," the chair of the meeting answered while looking straight into Kurakin's eyes.

"He does insist on it, but I took measures. Kakhovsky will be sent to the Nicholas's quarters in the palace. He received all the necessary instructions. Nicholas will live."

Mordvinov rose slowly. He silently paced the room before turning to face Ryleyev. "You do understand, *mon cher*, that this plan cannot fail, don't you? I gave my word to the empress dowager!"

"I do understand it, Your Excellency. Kakhovsky will carry out this order as instructed. I will personally see to it."

"I had never any doubts in you," the agitated Mordvinov uttered while getting back to his seat.

"Gentlemen, we all understand the great importance of the upcoming events." Ryleyev had taken the floor again. "We understand that the fate of Russia itself will be decided tomorrow. We also understand how high the risk is, but we believe it would be very unwise not to use this situation to our advantage! The company has invested heavily in the process of destabilization of the government. Not to mention the fact that under the existing circumstances, there would be no future for the company or for our North American assets!

"We need to expand to the east, gentlemen! Every one of you around this table knows this well. You have devoted your life's efforts to this idea! For the economic future of Russia is there, in the east, not in overcrowded Europe! Isn't it so, Your Excellency?"

Every man followed Ryleyev's eyes to Speransky.

"The future of the Russian Navy is there too! Not on the closed, 'inland' Baltic and Black Seas but on the vast expanses of the Pacific! Isn't it so, Your Grace?"

This time, Ryleyev and all the rest turned to Admiral Mordvinov.

"Without the peasants' emancipation reform, which would free working hands needed for our colonies in America, our company will not survive! As it turns out, gentlemen, there's no other way! We must take advantage of the chaos among the guard regiments and military officers and intercept the initiative!

"Upon Nicholas's abdication, an interim government will be formed with the empress dowager as its head. Even Count Nesselrode, who for the last forty years guided Russian policy in Europe and who is the most conservative statesman of the whole Holy Alliance along with his English friends, will appreciate the change. After all, Russia was always more lucky with empresses than with emperors."

Ryleyev took his seat. A heavy silence hung over the table. The grim-faced men were deep in thought, seemingly contemplating their own positions. A sudden chime of the bell on the entrance door brought the statesmen back to reality.

"Are we expecting someone?" Uvarov expressed everyone's perplexity.

Ryleyev gave an eloquent look at Somov, who stood and left the room, tightly closing the door behind him.

CHAPTER 15

Present Time. New York.
On the Highway to JFK Airport.

"**I**f it weren't for you, boss, I would've been gone long ago," continued Jeff, happy to have found a reason to change the subject. "Cinematographers are in demand everywhere. It's just because of you and all our travels that I'm still here. That's what I love the most! By the way, what are we filming this time?"

Margo instantly shot a smart response. "Haven't you learned in all those years that we'll have a briefing when we get settled at the hotel? Don't you see the boss is busy at the moment? Dude, every time you act like you were born yesterday. Am I right, boss?"

Convinced she had given quite an earful to Jeff, Margo got back to her music. Dmitry, deep in thought, did not respond. However, over the years they had spent together, Jeff knew his boss better. The question he had asked had hit the point. It was exactly the upcoming shooting Dmitry was thinking about. His well-designed plan had been disrupted three days earlier when his new chief editor called from Moscow with an urgent order. According to changes that had emanated from the deeps of editorial politics, Dmitry had to fly to San Francisco at once to make a video reportage and a short documentary about the historical Russian settlement called Fort Ross. Of course it had to be done yesterday; he was to forget all he had planned.

Dmitry had already bought tickets to Fort Lauderdale to cover the opening ceremony at the International Boat Show and had already obtained press passes and hotel reservations for his crew. He also had arranged to film onboard of the newest mega-yacht that would have carried him and some other lucky invitees to Key West. Of course, the beautiful yacht was to be the focus of his story, but for the sake of a dream journey, he had gallantly decided to accept that little compromise.

Editors usually didn't like stories that had a commercial flavor. Dmitry perfectly understood the objections that might arise to such a report. Who knows, maybe the reporter got paid by the yacht manufacturer to get such a review, bypassing the hefty fees that would otherwise be paid to a TV channel's commercial department? Even though the story could have been interesting and informative, Dmitry understood the ambiguity of the deal. He just badly wanted to go there and thought that he would smooth the awkwardness of the situation by shooting a story about the Hemingway Museum. *For good measure and for the same money*, as the expression goes, Dmitry thought. His bags with swimsuit, mask, and flippers had already been packed when he received that call from his new boss that had changed his plans.

Moscow didn't even want to hear what he had planned. "Why're you upset? You wanted to go to a fort, so you're going to a fort. Fort Lauderdale, Fort Ross—what's the difference?" The new editor-in-chief happily snorted in the phone, extremely pleased with his play on words, and hung up.

Dmitry tried to pacify himself. *Well, I could probably understand him. Sitting in his office in gray, rainy Moscow, thinking that someone going to Florida was unbearable.* However, no persuasion, nor reasoning had done Dmitry any good. Knowing he did not have much time left to prepare, he gave up and started poring through various materials connected with his new assignment—Fort Ross and its history.

The closer he studied the materials, the farther away Florida sailed in his mind. The new project was awesome. As required by any journalistic sensation, it had a hint of a mystery.

At first, the material was a puzzle in bits and pieces with plenty of discrepancies and inconsistencies. Although all his documents repeated the same facts, he could find no logic in the historical events. Why had the Russian-American Company, the most powerful and rich organization in those days, which owned Fort Ross and the rest of America's Pacific coast from Alaska to northern California, suddenly abandoned its colony? What had been the rush to sell the colony? They seemed to have been in such a hurry; it was as if they had something to hide. It seemed that the company hadn't even bothered to collect the money from an American settler, John Sutter, to whom the company offered its Northern California lands.

Dmitry thought this commercial arrangement had been a "deed of conveyance"; he had no heart to call it a "sale." The cost of the transfer was nominal, and it was rather clear the Russians were not interested in money but in something else. What could that have been? Everything had been done in such a strange, puzzling way. Dmitry was convinced that they had tried to hide something. The questions were *what* and who were *they*. Dmitry first came across the word *conveyance* in the documents of the first historian of the company, Peter Tikhmenev, who studied and published the *History of the Russian-American Company* in the middle of the nineteenth century. That word stuck in Dmitry's head. Without a doubt, Dmitry's new subject for TV reporting had become much more promising if not downright thrilling! The more Dmitry immersed himself in the material, the more the events of those long-past years seemed improbable. He had a mystery on his hands.

It was then weird things started to happen. Dmitry suddenly began having detailed dreams that felt very real. It quickly reached the point that Dmitry could hardly wait to go to sleep to see the sequel to his previous night's dream. His subconscious did not let him down. All his dreams were surprisingly clear, constant, and frequent. He dreamed about Fort Ross and the Russian-American Company. Stories of a completely forgotten chapter in Russian history stirred his imagination.

The jazz melody of the ring tone of his iPhone made Dmitry snap out of his reverie.

"Dmitry?" He heard a female voice. "I am calling on behalf of the Russian-American Company."

"What?" Dmitry jumped in his seat.

"This is Vika . . . from Russian-American *Consulting* Company." The girl's voice in the phone sounded somewhat offended.

"Oh, Vika!" Dmitry exhaled. "I'm so sorry. I simply . . . I thought . . . I heard . . . Well, never mind! Please forgive me! I'm all ears!"

"Andrey will speak with you in a moment," the voice said in a tone that made it sound as though president himself was about to pick up.

Dmitry has imagined Andrey's secretary continuing to pout. *For some, Andrey is the big boss, but for others he's just old buddy Andy.* He chuckled inwardly.

Dmitry was always happy for his friends who had done well in the States. He had known Andrey since their college years; both had applied to the Moscow State Institute of International Affairs. Andrey had been accepted, while Dmitry's path was awaiting him elsewhere. He attended Moscow University to study journalism, which became his passion. They nevertheless remained friends. Back when, it would have been hard to imagine that one day, his old buddy Andy, who used to be a witness of and a willing participant in all Dmitry's parties, would become the owner of one of the largest travel companies in New York.

Dmitry often used the services of his friend's company. Of course, the majority of travel arrangements could be made on the Internet, but at times, trips could easily become so complex and traveling plans could be changed so often that only the help of travel specialists such as Andrey and his people could save the day. That's exactly what happened when he had to reroute his trip from Florida to California.

"Hey man, what's up?" Dmitry heard a familiar voice. "Everything's done. The car will be waiting for you at the airport, you'll get your return tickets at the check-in desk, and rooms are booked at the hotel near Fort Ross, as you requested. We even called the museum administration and got the permits for you to shoot in the proximity of the fort."

"Whoa! Andy, that wasn't necessary, but thanks! I have no words, brother. Thank you—" Dmitry started to say, but Andrey dismissed the gratitude.

"C'mon, Dim, forget it! Just remember, the woman's name is Marianne. When you arrive at the airport, call her. You can discuss the time for your shootings next day with her directly. Got it?"

"Sure! What's her number?"

"Vika will text it to you in a moment. I've got to run, man. I have a delegation waiting. Good luck! If there's anything you need, give me a call!"

Dmitry pressed disconnect.

"Well, seems everything's settled. We've got confirmation of the hotel booking. They even got permission for us to shoot in the museum!" Dmitry addressed to his friends with satisfaction as they were finally passing the sign, "Welcome to JFK Airport."

CHAPTER 16

Present Time. San Francisco.

"**D**ear passengers! In a few minutes, our plane will be landing at San Francisco International Airport."

Dmitry opened his eyes. He could feel the plane descending. Margo slept in the adjacent seat, her head on his shoulder. Jeff, gloomy as a thundercloud, was playing a game on his phone, trying not to look at them. Dmitry stared with surprise at his sleepy companion.

"Hm, that's what I call a . . . landing."

But Jeff just mumbled something unintelligible in reply. Carefully, Dmitry freed his shoulder from under Margo's head.

As promised, they had no problem getting their return tickets at the check-in desk. They retrieved their luggage and all their equipment and headed directly to the rental car terminal.

An hour later, another silver Toyota Sienna, only without any words on its side, drove over the Golden Gate Bridge and headed north on Route 1. Of course, they could have taken Highway 101, which would have significantly shortened their drive, but they would have missed the most picturesque road on the West Coast. Dmitry did not want that to happen to his friends; he had been to San Francisco many times and knew that Highway 1 was a true national landmark.

Winding between mighty cliffs covered with ancient redwoods on one side and the vast expanse of the Pacific on the other, the trio crossed bridges that spanned countless bays and rivers. Route 1 stretched from San Francisco to Oregon and Washington. It also led to their destination, Fort Ross.

The rented van was exactly like their television van back in New York inside and out; it almost felt as if they had not left home. Jeff was driving while Margo reclined in the back, stretching her legs and displaying her perfect pedicure. Dmitry sat next to the driver with his nose in his notebook.

As usual, Jeff was telling a never-ending story that neither Margo or Dmitry interrupted because they were not listening. Margo had cut herself off from the rest of the world with her music player and a magazine. Judging by her giggles, she was reading something amusing. Dmitry was engrossed in typing on his computer. He took his eyes off the screen for a moment. The van was driving along a very picturesque bay a sign said was Bodega Bay.

"All right, guys! Congratulations, we've arrived at Russian America!" Dmitry exclaimed in excitement.

"You're rushing things, boss!" Margo had wised up first, as usual. "We're at least thirty miles from Fort Ross. I'm following the route." Despite listening to her music player, Margo had not missed a thing.

"I'm not rushing anything at all," Dmitry shot back. "Bodega Bay was once called Rumyantsev Bay. It was named in honor of Count Rumyantsev, the minister of commerce during the reign of Tsar Alexander I. Officially, this was the most southern outpost of

Russian America. This place had a port, a wharf, warehouses, and workshops."

As if on command, everyone stared at the scenery.

"So why did the Spanish allow it?" Jeff sounded genuinely surprised. "If I remember correctly, California belonged to the Spanish then, right?"

"Yep, you're right, Jeff," Dmitry replied. "Believe me, they were greatly disappointed about that. Only the truth remains; what was then called Spanish California ended right here."

"What was from here?" Jeff did not give up.

"What do you mean, 'from here'?" Dmitry was confused.

"I mean, whose lands started from here?" asked Jeff.

"I told you already—Russia's lands! Also, my friends, from here starts the subject of our future documentary."

Dmitry was obviously enjoying Jeff's incomprehension and was not in a rush to lay all his cards on the table. Margo had taken her earphones off and had put away her magazine. She was sitting up straight.

"As I said, Russian America stretched from here along the coast all the way to Alaska," Dmitry said.

Jeff turned the radio off. The silence in the van was interrupted only by the slight whooshing of the air conditioner and the humming sound of tires on road.

"What do you mean Russian America? What about the Spanish?" Jeff still couldn't conceive that.

"What about the Spanish? Their progress to the north along the Pacific coast ended somewhere north of San Francisco. The overstretched, declining Spanish Empire did not have the means to effectively control its vast American territories. In the east, on the Atlantic, were the British and the French, and from here to the north were the Russians. What could they do? The Spanish weren't in the position to demand any rights. Also, when Russians arrived here, they developed a rather romantic relationship with them!" Dmitry smiled, enjoying the complete attention of his audience.

"Did you see or listen to *Juno and Avos*, that Russian rock opera? Guys, you got to see it! The music is awesome. Just go to YouTube. The plot is even better! The opera is named after the two ships, *Juno* and *Avos*, that brought Nikolai Rezanov, a Russian explorer and the founder of the Russian-American Company, to here. The plot's based on the love story of him and Conchita Arguello, a sixteen-year-old daughter of Jose Arguello, the commandant of the Presidio of San Francisco."

"At dawn you'll wake me up, and barefooted you'll come to see me off." Margo suddenly sang a piece in a beautiful, deep voice.

"You will never forget me, and I will see you nevermore!" Jeff continued eagerly though off-key. "C'mon, boss. Everybody knows that song!"

"Exactly!" Dmitry smiled. "You guys are well equipped for our trip, I can see."

"So what happened next, boss?"

"Well, Chamberlain Rezanov left a rather memorable footprint here. After he charmed Conchita, he managed to charm her father and befriend her brother, Don Luis Arguello, who by the way succeeded his father as the presidio's commandant. It's safe to assume that right from the very beginning, Russians established pretty good connections here!"

"Why did you say she fell in love with him?" Margo frowned. "Maybe it was *he* who fell in love with her, not charmed *her*!"

"I wouldn't argue with that." Dmitry grinned. "For a forty-year-old man to fall in love with a sixteen-year-old girl isn't that hard. Let's just say that after the first exploratory visit of Rezanov's ships, the Russians came here several years later and stayed for the next forty years. Aleksander Baranov, the governor of Russian America then, followed Rezanov's recommendation and gave orders to build a colony here.

That was done under the supervision and direct participation of Ivan Kuskov, Baranov's lieutenant-governor. Later, Kuskov came here as the first commandant of the fort and the Russian colony here. What a great time it was. What a great people they were!" Dmitry said dreamily.

"Then why hadn't we put roots down here?" Jeff asked anxiously, suddenly feeling a national affiliation with these remote, historical events. "It's way better here than in Alaska!"

"Oh that's because they forgot to ask your advice, Jeff!" Margo never missed a chance to needle the guy.

"Okay, I meant *they*. Why didn't they put roots down here?" Jeff corrected himself, rolling his eyes.

Dmitry suddenly became serious. "First, you're wrong about Alaska, Jeff. Back then, Alaska was the main source of sea otter pelts, which were worth a fortune then. Their value was comparable to the value of oil in our days. California's waters were less abundant in marine animals but had tons of other advantages. The main advantage was of course good soil for growing cereal crops. This was the main reason for Rezanov's decision to start a settlement here. Food was a serious matter for the Russian settlers in Alaska. By the way, what do you mean by asking, 'Why hadn't they put roots down here?' Who are *they*?"

"Why the Russians of course." Jeff was pushing on excitedly.

Dmitry did not reply. He stared out the window. The road ran down toward the coast again. *These ninety miles have flown by unnoticed,* he thought. He felt satisfied with his mastery of the subject. The days he had spent on reading various materials he had dug up in libraries and archives were paying off. Judging by the interest of his team, he was on the right track with the subject he had presented. Without even knowing it, Margo and Jeff were his own focus group. Dmitry always tested his ideas for future reports on them first. Although this time, not everything was going as smoothly as usual. Something was missing.

"Ah, the Russians!" Dmitry returned to the conversation. "This remained a mystery to me. There's something about it I still can't grasp."

Dmitry fell silent. The road had become more winding and was snaking unpredictably through mountainous terrain overgrown with trees. Jeff stopped talking. He was so concentrated on his driving that he even clenched his teeth, which prevented him from talking. Margo was quiet; she watched Dmitry from her backseat in the rearview mirror.

"They did put roots down here. The only thing is that it was not Russia that had done that. It was the Russian-American Company! Have you ever heard of that name?"

Margo and Jeff shook their heads.

"The historians came to the conclusion it was one of the first public companies formed in Russian history. It owned everything from Alaska to northern California. It's also interesting that many of the Russian nobility, including members of the tsar's family, owned shares in the company. At the beginning, everything was fine, but then—" Dmitry made a theatrical pause, "—I guess something happened."

At that point, their van was barely making any progress; they were driving at twenty miles per hour. Even the polite California drivers who trailed the van in a long queue started showing signs of irritation as they tried to pass the van.

"For some reason, no one paid much attention to the list of the company's shareholders. However, I found a rather intriguing fact. Many of the Decembrists—young Russian army officers who revolted in a protest against Nicholas I's assumption of the throne, which took place on December 14 of 1825 in Imperial Russia, held a significant number of shares in the Russian-American company or were otherwise connected to it. As for the well-known Kondraty Ryleyev—" Dmitry took another theatrical pause, "—he was not only the famous poet, 'the singer of the Decembrists' Uprising,' but he was also the manager of the company. So he probably wrote his 'calling for freedom' poems in its office in St. Petersburg in his spare time. However, what about the Decembrists' revolt? Was he planning it in his spare time as well, or it was the main goal of the company?"

I should use this phrase to finish the first episode of the documentary, Dmitry thought with satisfaction, rather enjoying the complete silence in the van. His companions' jaws had dropped in surprise about what they had just heard.

"Hey Jeff, park the car right here, would you? Let's take a short walk."

The van obediently turned into a gravel lot in front of a gorgeous bridge. Far below, a river flowed out of a gorge and spread out over the land. Its unrealistically blue waters smoothly flowed into the ocean.

The sign in front of the bridge gave it a name: Russian River.

CHAPTER 17

Present Time. Northern California.
A Hotel near the Fort Ross State Historic Park.

Two men and a young woman talked animatedly while they followed a trail that ran from the hotel down to the rocky ocean. The girl, jumping from stone to stone with the grace of a mountain doe, was empty handed. The men carried a basket with food and bottles of wine; a French baguette stuck out of the basket. They were occasionally passed by tourists who greeted them with understanding nods. Everybody strolling the scenic spot was in a great mood.

The sky, covered with high, spindrift clouds, promised a gorgeous sunset. The main character of the approaching celestial performance, the sun, slid slowly toward the horizon. A tall wooden pole, a totem for an Indian god, stood majestically in the center of the vista. A few hours remained until sunset.

The two men and the young woman settled down on the edge of the cliff right above the rumbling surf. They spread a blanket on the ground and started getting bread, tomatoes, cheese, and the wine out of the basket.

"Whoa! This is what I call service!" Jeff exclaimed excitedly while fishing a corkscrew out of the basket. "Check it out, guys. They even packed a corkscrew!"

"Thanks for the corkscrew, but look, those weirdos from the hotel's restaurant packed plastic cups instead of glasses!" Margo noted with a chuckle.

"C'mon, guys." Dmitry smiled. "Not every restaurant will serve you with the picnic basket to enjoy the sunset! Be grateful for what they did!"

"Hey, but they forgot to pack a knife!" Jeff played along with Margo, happy he had also found a fault with the restaurant's service. "It's been a while since I brought my own pocket knife with me since airport security would've taken it."

Just as he was speaking, a small blade sliced into the cutting board Jeff was putting tomatoes on. The knife quivered like a tight spring. Startled, Jeff yanked his hand away. "What the heck, Margo! You could've chopped my finger off! Are you nuts?" Jeff made a circling motion with his index finger at his temple.

"What do you need your fingers for, Jeff?" the girl sarcastically asked with a giggle. "What are you going to do with them?"

"Seriously, Margo, how did you manage to bring a knife with you?" Dmitry asked with a smile, trying to distract his crew from any battle.

With an innocent air, Margo clicked the knife into her belt buckle, of which it was an integral but occult part. "How else can a girl who wants to keep her chastity survive in this world without a weapon?" Margo theatrically rolled her eyes. "No way! Especially when she's traveling with two men!"

"Look at her! Some touch-me-not!" Jeff mumbled, still angry.

As ill luck would have it, his phrase hung in complete silence. The knife again stuck into the cutting board, dangerously close to Jeff's hand as he reached for a piece of cheese. Astonished, Dmitry and Jeff stared at the girl. It has become obvious now that her knife-throwing skills were not a fluke. Margo's face was red, and her eyes shot daggers.

"You'd better watch your mouth, you punk!" the girl said in a very quiet but threatening tone. "I, myself, will decide who will touch me and who will not! And without advice from any snotty assistant, okay?"

"Hey! You kids are getting out of control!" Dmitry clapped his hands to ease the tension. "Break it up! Get to your corners! Don't you have anything better to do? I can easily find tasks for each of you if you don't! Instead of fighting, you'd better check this beauty out!"

Dmitry raised his wine in a plastic cup and looked through it. Pink wine obediently sparkled in the setting sun's rays.

"Should we drink to 'the beauty which would save the world'?" Jeff raised his glass, avoiding looking at Margo.

The phrase sounded ambiguous, so Margo decided not to pay attention to it this time. Instead she quietly corrected. "The *love* will save the world!"

"You're both right, but let's drink to Russian America for now," Dmitry suggested. He gallantly clanged his plastic cup with Margo's first and then Jeff's. The girl's expression softened a bit, but she did not turn her head in Jeff's direction. They enjoyed the wine in silence.

"You know," Dmitry began philosophically, addressing no one in particular, "a long time ago, I came to the conclusion that wherever you are, drink local wine! There's simply nothing better than that. To be in California and drink French wine or to be in France and drink Italian wine is such pretentious nonsense! Wine is any land's bloodstream, so to speak, saturated with all its minerals. If you really want to know the land, drink its wine!" Dmitry happily spread himself on the picnic blanket with a smack of his lips.

"How amazingly generously Mother Nature shared her wealth with us, but we either don't understand it or don't appreciate it."

Margo looked thoughtfully into her glass and put it aside. She reached into her backpack for a baggie of grass and professionally rolled a joint.

"Good wine," Jeff said after he emptied his glass and licked his lips. He still felt out of sorts. "I'll go set up the camera," he said as he got up. "I can't watch such beauty being wasted."

"What's the rush, Jeff? We'll have plenty of time to use your camera," Dmitry said as he took the joint from Margo and drew on it while squinting from the irritating smoke. "We came here for longer than a day. You'd better get in the spirit of this place first. Listen to it, try to comprehend—"

"Here, take a puff," Margo said, offering a truce. "This will help."

"What would it help me with?" Jeff asked. He nonetheless took a hit.

"To pretend . . . shit, I meant to comprehend!" Margo giggled while slowly blowing rings of smoke.

Her slip of tongue seemed so funny to her that she burst out laughing. Jeff choked on inhaled smoke and joined her laugh. Dmitry could not help but join them, and very soon, all three were rolling on the blanket in fits of silly laughter.

"Mighty stuff," Dmitry said, squinting his eyes and scrunching his nose. "You start levitating just after half a puff!"

"Yep! Local weed!" Margo said with pride. "I bought it at a drugstore with a prescription."

For some reason, the phrase *with a prescription* seemed even funnier to them. They laughed for another five minutes till tears ran down their cheeks. Exhausted, Jeff fell to the ground.

Margo, wiping her tears, suddenly asked, "Hey, boss, is this the usual thing for around here, or am I too high?"

The guys were so stoned that at first they didn't understand her question. Dmitry turned on his elbow and looked toward the ocean in the direction Margo was gazing. Jeff hiccupped loudly.

"Ah that! Yeah, this place is well known for that kind of stuff. I mean, fog—" Dmitry started answering, but without finishing his phrase, he abruptly stood. On the horizon, stretching as far as the eye could see, fog was billowing toward the coast. San Francisco's fogs were famous even outside the state, but this fog was very unusual. It rapidly crawled up to the shore as if it had been created by a smoke machine at a rock concert.

"Whoa! It spreads like a blanket," Margo said.

"Even the birds got silent!" Jeff said as if in a trance. "What is this, Dim?"

Dmitry had not even noticed that Margo and Jeff had joined him, one on either side. It took Dmitry a while to spot what had seemed so unusual to Jeff. A myriad of bluish lightning bolts were flashing inside the fog!

"Holy moly," he gasped. "I've never seen anything like this before. Not here, not anywhere. If this is fog, why are there lightning bolts inside of it?"

The fog, or whatever it was, started climbing the cliff. The trio instinctively backed up.

"I think we'd better go," Dmitry said with deliberate calm, trying not to show his concern.

The fog reached the edge of the cliff right where Margo and Jeff stood in a trance. The huge mass of the fog and its lightning bolts swayed left and right like a living organism, and then, as if it had just made up its mind, headed for the trio.

Margo yelped softly. Dmitry and Jeff came to their senses and grabbed their belongings. A powerful thunderclap shook the ground. Bottles and cups toppled. Margo screamed at the top of her voice.

Dmitry stopped hiding his worry. As he grabbed the blanket, his iPhone fell out of his pocket. It was as if everything had been waiting for this split second. A lightning bolt hit the iPhone as Dmitry was reaching for it. Someone had turned off the sound, or so it seemed to Dmitry. He saw Margo silently screaming, her eyes filled with terror. He saw Jeff frantically gesturing and yelling something to him, but he was in a silent movie. On top of it all, his iPhone started shimmering with an intense blue glow that grew brighter every second. Mesmerized, Dmitry stared at the glowing device. The phone were pulsing invitingly.

This is so weird, Dmitry thought without taking his eyes off his phone. Out of the corner of his eye, he saw Jeff and Margo in slow motion, as if they were underwater, moving toward him and yelling silently.

Where are they going? What for? Don't they understand that the only important thing right now is the iPhone? It is so . . . beautiful! It so . . . weird! The fog is so thick! It swaddles me . . . I'm floating in the fog!

The iPhone, like a magical crystal, was shimmering in every shade of blue. The screen was lit, and a strange application, which Dmitry didn't remember ever downloading, seemed to be working on its own. It was some sort of calendar with a wheel indicating years, and it was rotating frantically.

Dmitry raised his hand with the iPhone as if it were a beacon. The last thing he saw was Margo and Jeff still screaming something to him and trying to reach him. They looked unreal in the ghostly, sparkling light. Dmitry cast a glance at the still rotating wheel of years on the app's calendar. He instinctively touched the screen to stop the rotation. A painfully bright flash blinded him for a second. With a cry, he squeezed his eyes shut. When he opened them, everything had disappeared.

Maybe "disappeared" is the wrong word, he thought, *but everything looks different!* What he had first taken as a flash from his phone turned out to be the bright sunlight of a gorgeous day! He was still standing on the same cliff, but Margo and Jeff weren't there. *No way! How could this cliff be the same?* Dmitry was irritated. *It looks like somebody just changed a movie set!* The air was saturated with a cacophony of unusual sounds and smells. The most prominent were those of sheep baaing, cows mooing, and horses neighing that mixed with cattle drivers' cries.

Dmitry realized the cliff was the same, but it was now part of a fairly broad, trodden, dirt road running along the coast. It was busy; heavy drays were traveling it in both directions. Oxen were pulling carts loaded with bags and baskets of fruits and vegetables. The cattle drivers, perched on bales, confidently managed the animals with slight whips on their ears. Indian boys chased a flock of sheep along the road. Shaggy dogs of various sizes and colors were helping the boys by running around the flock and barking loudly. Horseback Indians tried to control a herd of cows scattered along the road.

No hotel was in sight. As far as the eye could see, in between the rocky coast and the spurs of wooded mountains only a mile or so away from the ocean, rye fields spread out on both sides of the road and were interspersed with small orchards and vineyards.

In the distance, where a shallow creek flowed into the ocean, was a log fort on the tip of the cliff. A small village spread along the creek. A smaller road that turned toward the fortress led from the main highway where a startled Dmitry stood. His mouth was as wide open as the fort's gate.

A group of horseback riders in old-fashioned military uniforms lazily trotted along the smaller road toward the fort.

I'll be damned! Dmitry looked around completely stunned. *If that's the weed, I'll buy it all!*

He realized that the stir in the ranks of sheep and cows had been caused by his sudden appearance in the middle of the road out of literally nowhere. Dmitry jumped toward a branchy peach tree by the roadside. At the last moment, though, he noticed movement on the other side of tree trunk. He steadied himself by grabbing a branch and froze.

Almost in front of him, comfortably spreading in the shade, was a burly, bearded man lying on his back in flattened grass. A young Indian woman had lifted her skirt and was diligently riding him, moaning, with her eyes closed. She was obviously enjoying herself.

Dmitry's cheeks flushed. Feeling a new presence, the Indian woman opened her eyes and with a cry, rolled away, tugging at her dress.

The man raised himself on an elbow and tried to hide the scared girl behind him. He turned to Dmitry and opened his mouth to say something unpleasant to this insolent violator of privacy when Dmitry, completely embarrassed, touched his iPhone's screen again.

The man stared intensely at the spot where the stranger had been standing just a blink of an eye ago. He had apparently forgotten to close his mouth. The Indian woman gave a suppressed sob.

This time there were no flashes. Dmitry was back at the same spot. The cliff again changed to the one he remembered, the one with the right set decorations. His friends stood in front of him. Their dropped jaws left no doubt that what had happened to him had not been due to the weed he had smoked.

The fog dissipated as if it had never been there. A dark, stormy sky was over their heads instead. His throat dry, Dmitry tried to swallow. He looked at the iPhone lying peacefully in his palm. It looked normal.

Even innocent. When the first big raindrops fell on its screen, Dmitry turned sharply from his friends and briskly walked toward the hotel.

As if awakening from a dream, Margo and Jeff picked up the basket, the blanket, and the unfinished bottles of wine and ran after him.

CHAPTER 18

Present Time. Northern California.
A Hotel near the Fort Ross State Historic Park.

The rain began in earnest. Raindrops clattered on the roof of the hotel. The trio sat at the bar in the lobby. A vaulted ceiling of wooden beams in a Swiss chalet style hid in the shadows above. Quiet music drifted through the room. A huge fireplace at the end of the hall created a cozy atmosphere and granted the three a much-needed sense of comfort. Although the bar and the restaurant were almost completely occupied, it was not noisy at all. The three friends were silent, deep in thought, their glasses of red wine almost untouched.

"Listen, guys." Jeff fidgeted. "Maybe we just smoked too much, eh?"

Margo and Dmitry turned their eyes from the iPhone in the middle of the table and looked at Jeff. Their looks were expressive. No words were needed. Embarrassed, Jeff fell silent.

"Theoretically, this could be explained." Dmitry rubbed his chin thoughtfully. *"Time flow* is like a river. While you're going with the flow, you coincide with the events and therefore you are *present* in your reality. Let's suppose you have something that allows you to step out of the current."

"Of course! If there's a river, there should be banks one could step on," Jeff added excitedly.

"You cannot step twice into the same river," Margo recited thoughtfully while watching streams of rain running down the window.

"Yeah, Heraclitus was right, although that was not quite a precise interpretation of his words," Dmitry said. "The exact translation says, 'You cannot step twice into the same river, for other waters are ever flowing on to you.' No wonder that Greek magus was called a dark philosopher. By the way, physicists of our days believe that just by this phrase alone he proved in principle the possibility of time travel. So if we take as a basis that time is a flow of events, all we need to do for travel in time is to step out of that flow. Like stepping onto the banks of the river and reentering upriver or downriver!" Dmitry stopped. He took his wineglass, slowly brought it to his mouth, and took a sip. Margo and Jeff followed his example.

"Okay, but what does that friggin' iPhone have to do with it?" Jeff suddenly uttered as he put his glass on the table. His exclamation sounded unexpectedly loud. People sitting nearby gave them disapproving looks.

"Jeff, you'd better stick to Russian with your expressions." Dmitry made a sour face.

"Sorry," Jeff said. "I meant, what does the iPhone have to do with it?"

"We probably wouldn't be able to answer this question." Dmitry sighed. "I believe the iPhone in itself has nothing to do with it. The device simply has a calendar app that looks like a time wheel, which an . . . eh, *anomaly* . . . decided to use."

"Hey, you anomaly." Margo shook her finger at the window. "Why are you using someone else's iPhone?"

All three laughed, which lightened their mood.

"Let's step out for a smoke." Dmitry rose from the table. "The rain seems to have stopped."

The hotel, which they had gotten thanks to Dmitry's New York friend, was itself a local landmark. Built in the style of a Swiss chalet, it perched on the edge of the cliff like an eagle's nest. Its site included a considerable part of the coast, a beach, walking paths, vista points, and areas for barbecues and picnics. Stunning views of the bay and the ocean were everywhere. What was especially priceless for Dmitry and his friends was that on the other side of the bay, on a cliff, proudly stood Fort Ross.

It was dark. The lanterns cast uneven light on the wet parking lot full of cars. At the end of the week, on Friday, the hotel was packed with tourists who came for the hotel's great restaurant and local wine. The trio stepped on the porch and paused, soaking up the charm of the place.

"Okay, let's analyze the situation." Dmitry lit Margo's cigarette and his own. "So how did it all start?"

"Well, we . . . eh . . . we all took a puff," Jeff said hesitatingly.

"C'mon, man! Give us a break!" Margo cut him short with evident irritation. "Puff puff? That's all you can remember? You obviously shouldn't have to, that's for sure!" She turned to Dmitry. "The air smelled of electricity. That's how it all started!"

"Electricity doesn't smell," Jeff said gloomily.

"It's not electricity that smells," Dmitry said. "It's the ozone. Before the storm, oxygen molecules turn into ozone in the electrically charged atmosphere. Then what?"

"Then everything, eh . . ." Margo started snapping her fingers, trying to find the right word.

"Fucked out?" Jeff supplied hopefully.

"Yeah, you can say that!" This time, Margo relented. "And you, boss, started to shimmer!"

"Yeah, with hellish blue light!" said Jeff, who had perked up due to Margo's approval.

Dmitry unexpectedly laughed. "I just remember your faces when I came back!" He tried to imitate Jeff's and Margo's looks and laughed some more. They joined him, but their laughter was more of the nervous type and soon died out.

"What do you mean by 'came back,' Dim?" Margo asked. "Came back from where?"

Perhaps because of the excitement, she had addressed him informally as "Dim" instead of "boss" for the first time. Not understanding why, Dmitry took note and looked at Margo. Margo returned his stare while waiting for an answer.

"As I already told you," Dmitry began with a sigh as if talking to indolent students, "the time travel was clearly provoked by the iPhone, which for some reason got agitated. It suddenly reacted to the date on the calendar. I said I 'came back' because it was as if I had gone into the past! I saw Fort Ross!"

"So what? I can see it now" a puzzled Jeff said, looking from Dmitry to Margo. "It's across the bay."

"No, Jeff! I saw an *old* Fort Ross," Dmitry said passionately. He thought for a second and corrected himself. "Actually, I saw it when it was still relatively new. It was built in 1812, and I was in 1820."

Jeff and Margo watched Dmitry. Jeff opened his mouth to say something, but Margo was first.

"Where did such precise timing come from?" she asked, incredulous. "Why do you think it was exactly that year?"

"Because I remember the date I saw on the calendar—June 14, 1820," Dmitry answered.

The porch again grew quiet. Jeff shook his head and turned to Margo.

"Marg, can I have a cigarette?"

Margo silently got a cigarette out of the pack and handed it to Jeff without taking her eyes off Dmitry. Jeff asked something hanging in the air. "Do you think you can do it again?"

Dmitry didn't answer. He was looking at the night sky, deep in thought.

"If you could," Jeff continued, "then we—" He suddenly jumped off the porch railing he had sat on. "I've got an idea, guys! Boss, you came back fully dressed, not like a Terminator, naked, right?"

"Yeah . . . why?" Dmitry gave him a baffled look.

"Geez, don't you see? It means that if you can take your clothing into the time portal, you could probably take other stuff there too."

"So what are you proposing?" Margo looked at Jeff with genuine interest.

"Ha!" Jeff was triumphant in the limelight. "What I'm proposing is simple. We can take the video camera to the past!"

Margo turned to Dmitry with a wide smile. "That's great! What do you say, boss? Take us with you, and we'll shoot such footage that you'll get not only the Taffy but the Nobel Prize too!"

Margo and Jeff paused and enthusiastically stared at Dmitry. It seemed that the idea had not particularly impressed him. He continued leaning on the railing and thoughtfully fiddled with the phone. "Yeah, maybe so, but . . . the battery runs out of juice very fast," Dmitry said. "We can take something better than just a camera. I mean—"

He did not finish his sentence. The main door opened, and a group of very happy, loud guests filed onto the porch. Warm from the wine and the fireplace, they momentarily filled the space around the trio. A young man with a buzz cut gave Margo a blatant look and asked for a cigarette.

That dude's definitely in the military or something, Dmitry thought while giving him a light. *He looks like he hasn't seen a woman for quite a while. That's why he's staring at her legs like a madman.*

"Okay, good night!" Dmitry suddenly dropped their conversation and headed for the entrance. "I need to check something."

"C'mon, boss!" two voices protested. "We haven't finished our talk!"

"We can finish it tomorrow." Dmitry brushed them off as he walked through the door. Suddenly, as if remembering something, he turned. "Marg, have you brought that solar battery charger with you?"

"Yeah." Margo shrugged. "It's in the camera bag. Why?"

"Smart girl! I'll tell you later, but first let's check the weight." Dmitry said, already ascending the stairs. He turned and added, "Night! See you tomorrow!" Dmitry ran up the stairs to the second floor and disappeared into his room.

"Can I have another cigarette?" Jeff sighed while giving Margo a poke in the ribs. Instead of a cigarette, he received a sharp jab somewhere near his solar plexus. Margo's kick was short, professional, precise.

"What the hell—" Jeff gasped for air.

"First learn some manners. Treat women correctly." Margo cut him without even looking at him. "Second, learn to carry your own cigarettes." Margo turned and headed upstairs to her room.

"That's what I'd call legs!" The guy with the buzz cut followed her, his eyes almost licking her legs. Clicking his tongue, he gave Jeff a sly wink. Jeff was not in the mood to carry on a conversation with the insolent stranger. He gave him a frown and followed his friends.

The hotel room was lit only by the computer screen Dmitry sat in front of. His queen-sized bed remained untouched. On the bedside table, the iPhone lay plugged into the charger. The hotel clock's bright-red digits read 3:37 a.m. Dmitry leaned back in his chair and rubbed his eyes. The web page with the history of Fort Ross was open on his screen. *Actually, why not? Let's try it right now!*

Dmitry walked to the bedside table, grabbed his iPhone, and pressed the power button. The screen lit up in welcome. The green indicator showed the battery was fully charged.

CHAPTER 19

1820. Russian California. Fort Ross.

Lieutenant Zavalishin sat at the table in the officers' barracks, his navy uniform coat over his shoulders. The barracks was otherwise empty. He was sitting in front of a huge samovar, the traditional Russian metal pot that was heated with coal or charcoal to boil water. It was diligently puffing and whistling; all indications were that the water would be boiling any moment. A round loaf of bread lay on the table in front of the young man. Potatoes, corn, tomatoes, and onions were dished out on clay plates.

A huge corked gallon bottle filled with a cloudy liquid stood on the table between the plates. The young man had nothing better to do than to stare at his reflection in the shiny samovar. He was not in a good mood, to put it mildly, and there was no one to blame but himself.

All his adult life, Zavalishin had dreamed of visiting Russian America, especially California. Thus, when a rumor that the thirty-six-gun frigate *Kreicer* under the command of Captain-Lieutenant Mikhail

Lazarev was preparing to circumnavigate the globe and visit Russian America, Zavalishin had rejoiced. This expedition, as had been all the Russian naval voyages of the last years, was fitted out with the money of the Russian-American Company, and one of the main objectives of these expeditions was to protect the territorial waters of Russian America from frequent attacks by pirates and smugglers.

Zavalishin had every reason to believe his application would be accepted even without the help of his father, a major-general who was personally acquainted with Count Mordvinov. The count was not only the member of the Admiralty Board but also—as was widely known— had unlimited connections inside the company.

So it turned out exactly as Zavalishin had hoped. Moreover, since Mordvinov had heard so much about the exceptional abilities of the young officer, he appointed Zavalishin to be an assistant navigator and a commander for a detachment of guard-de-marines, senior-year cadets of the Imperial Marine Corps who were going to sail on the *Kreicer* for training.

If someone's lifetime dream comes true before he turns twenty, it's hard not to believe that such a person does have a special relationship with Fortune herself.

Upon arrival in Novo-Arkhangelsk, Alaska, Baranov—the unchallenged ruler of Russian America—begged Lazarev to make the trip to Fort Ross to deliver the Aleuts who worked for the company for the procurement of sea otter pelts. Of course, Zavalishin went with the frigate.

California captivated his heart so much that the young officer volunteered to stay there and wait for the return of the ship. The *Kreicer* was to deliver cured pelts to Alaska and head home to St. Petersburg.

As a senior officer, he knew about plans to go back to the *Kronstadt* around South America's Cape Horn. Therefore, traveling along the coasts of North and South America and visiting Fort Ross again was unavoidable.

The reason for the young man's discomfort was easily explained. Kuskov and almost all the military personnel at Fort Ross were preparing to depart for San Francisco at the invitation of the commandant of the presidio, Don Luis de Arguello. Kuskov had decided to leave the fortress under Zavalishin's command. The problem was not of course that Zavalishin dreaded his new duties but that he wanted to visit San Francisco. Indeed, when would such an opportunity present itself again if at all to the young officer?

The Presidio of San Francisco guarded the northern border of Spain's possessions in North America and was closed to foreigners. Only special neighborly relations between the commandants of the two fortresses based on the common objective of protecting their lands allowed exceptions to the rule.

After three months of his voluntary stay at the fort and waiting for the return of the *Kreicer,* the young man was bored. The prospect of not making such a fascinating journey was not a happy one. There was nothing special in the routine, everyday life of the Russian colony that required Zavalishin's intelligence or native resourcefulness. The Indians knew their agricultural duties very well, and the Aleutian hunters spent most their days at sea, procuring otter pelts. Knowing all this and simmering more than the samovar was from resentment, Zavalishin prepared himself for a week of infinite boredom.

Holy Mother of God! That cunning Kuskov used my kindness to his advantage, could not recover Zavalishin from the offensive decision of the fort commander.

Young man was sullenly staring out the window at the courtyard of the fortress. All the activities of the colony during the day happened beyond its walls—in the port, at the workshops and warehouses, or at the farms and plantations.

That morning, Kuskov as usual had inspected his domain. Zavalishin let his guard-de-marines visit the nearby Indian village while he stayed in the empty fort and tried to prepare himself, at least mentally, for even greater solitude.

Action outside attracted his attention. Indian boys were trying to drive away an annoying mutt from a huge sow and its piglets. The mutt, barking its head off, was trying to prove its superiority. The sow was screeching and getting ready to fight. The kids, divided into two groups, were trying to resolve the situation peacefully. Some were quieting the dog while others tried to move the swine away. The sow made up its mind and fled. The dog and the children chased it, and the whole company, raising clouds of dust, disappeared behind the wide open fortress gate.

The peace that pervaded the courtyard again was occasionally broken by the screech of saws coming from the shipyard being built. The sun seemed to have stopped at its apex. The vast ocean sparkling in the distance was visible through the open gates. Sighing, Zavalishin lifted a bottle with an unsteady hand to fill his glass with moonshine. *I'll show you how to leave a man alone!* Zavalishin mentally complained to his reflection in the samovar. *Look at them, going to visit the Spanish commandant, and I'm supposed to stay here and play housekeeper!* In a bad temper, the lieutenant cracked an egg on the samovar and peeled it. *"I can't leave the fortress without an officer in charge!"* Zavalishin's thoughts were mimicking Kuskov's words. *Well, but how about leaving a living person alone? Is that okay?* was Zavalishin's mental riposte. No answer. He lifted the glass of murky liquid to his mouth.

"What if something would happen?" Zavalishin continued, imitating Kuskov's voice. *Yeah, right, but what can possibly happen where nothing's going on?* His mental adversary was silent. Zavalishin took a big gulp

of moonshine, a daunting task for the young man who was not an experienced drinker.

He grunted, put his glass on the table, and stuffed the egg into his mouth. When his breathing became normal and his tears stopped, Zavalishin hiccupped, rose from his stool, and leaned out the window, sternly inspecting the empty courtyard.

"Hey you! Watch out there!" he shouted to no one. The victorious sow and piglets triumphantly entered the fortress but immediately decided otherwise. They quickly disappeared behind the fence again, having decided rightly that that day was definitely not their day.

Zavalishin hiccupped again, flopped on his stool with satisfaction, and stared at his unfinished glass with a sigh.

CHAPTER 20

Present Time. Northern California.
A Hotel near the Fort Ross State Historic Park.
Dmitry's Room.

Dmitry slowly selected the date on his iPhone—June 14, 1820. He stepped into the middle of the room and held his breath as if he were about to jump into a pool. He closed his eyes and pressed his iPhone's button with the short word *Go*.

1820. California. Fort Ross.

Zavalishin was looming over his glass, getting ready to drink it to the bottom, when he noticed out of the corner of his eye that something had changed in the courtyard. He looked outside and froze with his mouth open. An extremely weird-looking stranger stood in the middle of the courtyard and was frantically looking around while holding something that shone with bluish light. The stranger brought the object to his face and conjured something over it. He stretched his hand out, closed his eyes . . . and disappeared.

Zavalishin hiccupped loudly. His hand with the glass shook, spilling the moonshine over the table. But the young officer did not notice that.

Present Time. California. Hotel Room.

Dmitry opened his eyes. When he saw the familiar walls of his hotel room, he started jumping like a little kid with joy. *It worked! It worked!* Dmitry kept jumping around his room. *Wait! How much of the battery did that take?* He interrupted his joyful fit to check his iPhone. *A little more than half of the battery's left. Not bad!*

Exhausted from his excitement, Dmitry plumped happily down in his chair. Then he jumped again and ran toward the closet. Pulling the doors open, he grabbed the bag that contained his video equipment. He froze in the middle of the room, one outstretched hand holding the phone while the other held the bag and then he disappeared again.

1820. California. Fort Ross.

Zavalishin sat in the same pose with the same frozen stare. He looked straight ahead. With an effort, the lieutenant started to slowly bring the ill-fated glass of moonshine to his mouth. He was watching the courtyard, trying not to blink, but he still missed the moment when the stranger reappeared.

The man stood in the middle of the courtyard holding a big bag. Zavalishin had problems determining its purpose, though. After several seconds, the man again dissipated into thin air in front of Zavalishin's eyes like a mirage.

Zavalishin felt cold. He never knew one could sweat while feeling cold. The sweat was sticky and unpleasant.

Present Time. California. Hotel Room.

Dmitry was as happy as a child. *Jeff was right! I can bring anything through the portal!* He got a new idea. He rushed to the video bag and frantically searched for something. Finally, with satisfaction, he found what he was looking for—a solar battery charger. He slipped it in his pocket, grabbed the iPhone, and ran out of the room, forgetting to close the door.

A single lantern illuminated the packed parking lot. Cicadas screeched deafeningly. Shivering from the morning chill and crunching pebbles underfoot, Dmitry walked to their Toyota. He cast a quick glance toward the sleeping hotel, grabbed the van's door handle with one hand, and stretched his other arm in the already habitual gesture—in front of himself. He halted for a second, drawing a breath, and pressed the precious button on the smartphone's screen.

The van remained in its spot. But Dmitry was no longer standing next to it.

1820. California. Fort Ross.

Perfectly miserable Lieutenant Zavalishin was still seated at the table. His food and his moonshine had been forgotten. He was swaying from side to side, eyes closed. *This is what it means to be drunk as hell. I wonder why one person can drink all his life while another drinks just one glass and the devil himself comes to him.*

As if to confirm his words, the "devil" appeared again. This time he did not have his hellish traveling bag. He was empty handed but stood in a very strange pose: bent at the knees with a hand stretched as if he were holding something.

Look at how the poor thing is painfully distorted in God's daylight! Zavalishin thought. *Though this devil is not "as terrible as he is painted"* as one wise expression put it. Zavalishin was frozen in the barracks' window as the devil looked around and said in a human voice, "I see." He disappeared a third time.

Tears filled Zavalishin's eyes. "Of course I see! I see it clearly now!" Zavalishin rushed to the icons hanging on a wall in the corner. He fell to his knees and earnestly crossed himself. "Holy Mother of God, please forgive me! You have my word. I would never take a single drop of drink again!"

Zavalishin sealed his oath with a dull thud of his forehead on the floor. While kneeling and bowing before the icons, he shook noticeably.

CHAPTER 21

1825, December 13. St. Petersburg.
The Day before the Decembrists' Uprising.

Using the pause in the meeting, Sergey Uvarov rose from his seat. Despite his youth, the handsome, twenty-six-year-old prince was known in St. Petersburg as one of the most eligible bachelors. He was the inheritor of overwhelming financial means, chairman of the board of the Commercial Bank, and board member of the Russian-American Company. Unfortunately for court beauties, the prince was in no hurry to tie the knot. He was famous for his expression, "First, I need to serve the motherland while I am still strong; only then can I get married."

This saying drove the girls of courting age to hysterics, but among men of the state, it gained Sergey the fame of an extremely positive, talented young man. However, as always in Russia, "to serve the motherland" was understood differently by almost everyone.

"Gentlemen, allow me to add a few words," the prince said, enjoying the attention of the meeting's high-ranking attendees. "Judging by the return on our investments, what the Commercial Bank received from the Russian-American Company over the past few years, the state of its affairs is critical. If we fail to change the state's policy and put it back on the course set by Emperor Paul, the course favorable to our endeavors in America, all our efforts will have been in vain. What have we achieved so far besides receiving the highest approval for the naval officers to serve on the company's ships? Not much. That achievement is valuable, but it is not enough from the economic point of view especially if we remember that we, I mean the Russian-American Company, financed all the circumnavigations for the glory of the crown. Where is the state's support for our colonies as we see with other countries, if I may ask?"

The prince pointed to a huge world map, where dots and dashes contoured the lands owned either by the Russian-American Company or by the company's interests. "The policy of the Ministry of Foreign Affairs is frightening to say the least. It seems our empire has been more concerned recently with the interests of either England or France or Prussia but not its own! I assure you, gentlemen, that our great deeds will be forgotten if we lose Russian America!"

The prince paused dramatically. "Saying that, I have to admit, however, that when our enemies in the immediate vicinity of the emperor are carrying out international policies fatal to the interests of our company, to conduct our business as usual is simply irrational. Of course, I am a patriot, but first I'm a banker, and I have to show my investors a healthy return." Uvarov concluded his speech.

"I've read the proposition of Lieutenant Zavalishin about the seizure of northern California. It's rather interesting!" Mordvinov added out of the blue. "Annexing California may indeed help strengthen our possessions in Alaska, Kamchatka, and Sakhalin."

"If at the time the government had supported our actions in the Sandwich Islands," Kurakin threw in, "the island of Kauai and maybe the whole Hawaiian Kingdom, would be a part of Russian Empire now!"

"It's not too late to have a comeback with California," Severin, who had been silent all this time, added meaningfully.

"So from what has been said today, we can conclude," Ryleyev summarized with a sad smile, "that the interests of the present Russian government and our company have separated somehow. When exactly that happened is not of any importance now, but if that course continues, our financial interests in America are doomed. That again brought us to the conclusion we already knew and discussed many times before—without the emancipation of the serfs, without labor's freedom of movement and the abolition of slavery, we will not be able to keep America." Ryleyev looked at the faces around the table in a steady gaze. "By saying so, gentlemen, I have to agree that we have simply run out of options except for—"

"You're right, Ryleyev. Let the military act!" Speransky answered for everybody. "Only, we need to send a message to the governor of our American colonies about the decision we have made here today."

That proposition didn't meet any objections from the venerable assembly; everybody understood that the report of the day's meeting would take six months to reach Russian America in the best-case scenario; the events of the meeting that day would have been history. What kind of history remained to be seen.

"I've already conversed with his excellency in writing previously," added Ryleyev. "Since he had only recently accepted his post, he fully trusts in whatever decisions we'll make."

"Very well then." Mordvinov rose and took a look at his fancy pocket watch again. "Then, *mon cher*, your task will be to see that nobody even thinks the company had participated in the events that will take place tomorrow. Not in a week, not in a month, not in a hundred years! Is that clear?" Mordvinov slammed the lid of his watch as if to emphasize his words' importance.

"I'll do my best, Your Lordship!" Ryleyev answered with a bow. The count stared into Ryleyev's eyes and nodded, seemingly satisfied with the response.

Assuming the meeting was over, the guests started pushing back their chairs and rising. None suspected that for many of them, this meeting would be their last. These intelligent, powerful, noble people, the cream of the nation, were unaware of the role they were destined to play.

Soon, the new emperor, Tsar Nicholas I, who that day was only the grand duke and very uncertain of his own future, would emerge as the winner and as the crusher of the next day's revolt. He had a very cunning mind. He would appoint many of these men to be jurors in the trials of the hundreds of young officers who would dare to threaten the monarchy and thus enter Russia's history as "the Decembrists." Speransky, for example, would sign the death penalty verdicts, and Mordvinov—let's do him justice—would try to mitigate the punishments. His efforts would help convince the emperor to graciously reduce almost all the sentences to lifelong exile and hard labor. Even those punishments would later be reduced in length, and the convicts would enjoy relative freedom in settlements in Siberia. Only five officers would be hanged. Kondraty Ryleyev, the managing director of the Russian-American Company, would be among them.

Hand in hand, Mordvinov and Speransky were heading for the door when it opened. Orest Somov, the company's head clerk, who had left to answer the door bell earlier, came in. He was deathly pale and greatly excited, something even he couldn't hide. "Gentlemen, I would ask you to stay a bit longer," Somov managed to force himself to say.

"Goodness, my dear Somov, are you all right?" Mordvinov exclaimed with obvious worry. "You look like you've just been visited by a ghost." The count joked to lighten the atmosphere that had suddenly changed. Somov either did not understand the joke or did not acknowledge it. With widespread arms, he closed the huge, gilded doors as if he indeed expected guests from hell to break in. At least, that is what could be read on his frightened, bloodless face.

"Who knows, Your Excellency? You might be very close to the truth," Somov managed to say in a coarse voice. "Gentlemen, I would ask you to stay a bit longer. As for you, Mister Ryleyev, you are asked to step outside. S-s-someone is waiting for you there."

Everyone turned to Ryleyev. He gave Somov a puzzled look. Displaying calmness and self-control, Ryleyev put his papers on the table, and with a firm step, he headed for the door.

CHAPTER 22

Present Time. Northern California.
A Hotel near the Fort Ross State Historic Park.

Margo sat motionless in a lotus pose on a sunlit spot at the edge of the cliff above the roaring surf of the great ocean. High in the sky, an eagle soared, majestically surveying its vast domain: the coast with its rugged coves, the land with its bristling evergreens, the serpentine road along the sea, the mouth of the river flowing into the ocean, and the bridge connecting the river's banks.

The driveway turned off the highway and ran to the hotel, beautifully located on the tip of the rocky cliff. In a bird's eye, the hotel looked like a dollhouse, and the lonely figure of a girl sitting motionless on the edge of the nearby cliff looked like its forgotten Barbie.

Margo faced the morning sun's rays and seemed completely immersed in the surroundings. She wore a dark-navy silk kimono and a black belt around her thin waist. She slowly rose and stretched her arms. The wind immediately made the silk cling to her figure and started lovingly caressing her slim body. She began a set of exercises slowly, then she raised the tempo.

A series of smooth, flowing lunges alternated with brisk surges of her arms and legs that were deadly strikes against an invisible enemy. Her rhythm became faster and her movements more complicated. The routine she performed was called the dance of a fiery dragon in Wushu. Margo's execution of the war dance was perfect. Her arms and legs flew around rapidly, and then she would freeze for a moment, strike, and start her routine again with a turn, a forward somersault, a lunge, a jump, and a momentary pause. The fierce woman warrior froze in an incredible pose, swaying slightly on one leg, the other tucked under her. Her pose was that of a reptile ready to strike.

With a towel over his shoulder, Jeff approached the cliff along the path from the hotel. Like a mountain goat, he was playfully jumping from one rock to another with a happy smile. He was whistling an elaborate tune.

Suddenly, as if he had run into a tree, the young man froze! A scene of pagan beauty was before his eyes. Margo, bare to her waist was spinning in a whirlwind of an unknown dance at the edge of the cliff. She had dropped the upper part of her kimono so it wouldn't hinder her movements. The ends of her wide pants were rolled up and tucked under her belt; her slender legs were very visible. A serpent-like dragon tattoo on her sweaty skin wriggled and twisted to the rhythm of the girl's menacing movements.

Jeff froze like a deer in headlights. His jaw dropped. He stared at the girl, afraid to break her transcendent unity with nature. A blush spread over his cheeks. His eyes gleamed in genuine admiration.

After a few seconds, Jeff realized he had forgotten to breathe. Not being able to hold his breath any longer, he gasped loudly just as a treacherous pebble crunched under his sandal. Margo stopped. Everything, even the wind, stopped.

Margo turned and stared angrily at the unwelcome intruder. Something in her eyes made all the words stick in Jeff's throat. Slowly, as she came out of her trance, Margo's eyes became warmer. Jeff even thought he saw mischievous sparks in them. Not at all embarrassed by her nakedness, Margo slowly arched like a cat, pulled her kimono over her shoulders, adjusted her pants, and picked up her mat. She moved toward Jeff with an incisive smile; she swung her hips like a fashion model on a catwalk.

Jeff instantly and quite inappropriately started sweating. He licked his suddenly dry lips and stared at Margo with undisguised admiration.

Reveling in her complete hypnotic control over him, like a boa constrictor facing a rabbit, Margo came within a hair's breadth of Jeff's lips. He squeezed his eyes shut, thinking in disbelief she was going to kiss him. Jeff braced himself. He did not want to faint.

"Close your mouth, dude, or you'll catch a sore throat!" Margo whispered into his ear. Laughing merrily, she skirted Jeff, who was a statue, and ran up the trail to the hotel.

Jeff's face was burning red, but he couldn't give up. "Margo, wait!" he yelled to the departing girl.

Margo turned. "What else do you want?" She was laughing.

"Margo—" Jeff started, but he could not find enough words to make a complete sentence. He shook his head. "So, you, uh . . . you know, what's that called? Martial arts?" To emphasize his question, Jeff waved his hands in the air in imitation of karate movements.

"Go back to your room, martial arts boy, before you hurt yourself." Margo smiled sympathetically. "We gotta get going!"

Relaxed by her smile, Jeff shook off his initial shock. He assumed an indifferent pose, dropped the tone of his voice, and said, "I'll be right there. I'll take just a quick swim!"

"Hey you, victim of geographical idiocy, what have they taught you in school? It's not the Black Sea! Don't you know the water temp here is about forty-eight?"

Jeff could not pull back; that would show weakness. He nervously tossed the towel over his shoulders and continued bravely. "So what? When I was a little kid and lived in Odessa—"

Margo brushed him off as if he were a bothersome fly. She turned. "Make sure you don't freeze your nuts, Odessa boy!" she yelled and ran up the trail.

Downcast, Jeff descended to the ocean, but there he made a sharp turn and started walking back to the hotel. His desire to swim had completely vanished.

If Jeff had walked a bit faster, he would have been greatly surprised to see that someone else among the hotel guests was not asleep on this peaceful Saturday morning. The guy with the buzz cut they had met the previous night was sitting on his balcony dressed in jeans and a T-shirt. He sat in a plastic wicker chair and stared at the scene on the shore through binoculars. That morning, the "soldier" was not in the mood for any show-offs. When Margo appeared underneath his balcony on her way to the hotel, the guy took refuge in the depths of his balcony.

When the sound of Margo's footsteps subsided in a distance, the young man got up, went into his room, and locked his balcony door.

CHAPTER 23

Present Time. Northern California.
A Hotel near the Fort Ross State Historic Park.

It was late morning when Margo and Jeff, dressed as if they were going hiking in Yellowstone for a month and carrying huge backpacks on their backs, knocked on Dmitry's door. One look at Dmitry was enough to make them realize he had probably spent a sleepless night. His two-day stubble looked good, though, and his eyes shone with an intense inner light. He pushed the door open, checked his crew from head to toe, chuckled, and walked to his notebook without a word.

"I see!" Margo seemed to come to the conclusion first after she scanned the room. Without waiting for an invitation, she dropped her backpack by the door and dropped onto the bed.

"What do you 'see'?" Jeff asked, clueless, while carefully perching himself at the edge of the bed.

"Okay, I have some initial test results," announced Dmitry without taking his eyes from the screen.

"What test results?" Jeff still wasn't following.

"The test to move objects through the time portal." Dmitry didn't even try to hide his sarcasm.

"You mean you already tried it? Without us?" Margo asked menacingly.

"Oh, c'mon guys!" Dmitry waved them off wearily. "That was just the 'reconnaissance-in-force operation,' so to speak."

"Well, and how was it?" Margo was trying to hide her disappointment. "Judging by your look, it made you tired. Too bad you didn't ask for help."

Dmitry faced his crew. Margo and Jeff looked gloomy. "Okay, I've run some tests." Dmitry ignored his friends' moodiness. He didn't feel guilty at all. On the contrary, deep inside, he felt he was the only one who could control such an emerging situation. "So this is what I've been able to find out. During time travel, the weight of a transported object apparently shouldn't exceed the weight of the host or carrier—"

"Hey you, 'object'!" Margo turned to Jeff. "If you happen to be heavier than the boss, you're staying home! Got that?"

Jeff sighed miserably and said nothing.

"I don't know that for sure," Dmitry said. "I need to run more tests, but I was trying to take the van with me and it didn't slip through the portal."

"Whoa!" Jeff whistled. "You already managed to check even that?"

For some reason, this announcement made Margo excited. "Awesome! Too bad we can't take a car with us. It could've been so cool to roll into the Presidio San Francisco of the nineteenth century in a jeep!"

"Yeah!" Jeff said. "We could've taken Rezanov and Conchita for a ride in the hills!"

"I'm sure they would've loved that." Dmitry chuckled. "But for that, we would've had to travel a bit further into the past. When Nikolai

Rezanov was managing his love affairs in California, Fort Ross hadn't been built."

"So what? The fort can wait, but instead, we could've gotten to know Rezanov in person!" Margo started jumping on the bed like a little girl.

Dmitry thought for a second. "We might still do that, but later. I was checking something in the archives and found a very interesting year, when peculiar events were happening in Russian America. The people then probably weren't aware of it, but looking back at those events—" Dmitry suddenly became silent, lost in thought.

"Okay, 'looking back at those events—'" Margo interrupted his thinking process.

"Never mind. I just remembered something," Dmitry replied, chasing his thoughts away.

That made Margo jump around on the bed again. "C'mon, man! Jeff, tell him that for a woman, an unfinished process is like for a man . . . eh—" searching for the right words, Margo started snapping her fingers in front of Jeff's nose.

"To get his nuts clamped in a vice?" volunteered Jeff. For the first time, Margo hadn't immediately found what to say. For the first time, there was a glimpse of approval in her eyes.

"Yeah, man! Exactly!" She continued to play her righteous anger card.

Dmitry jumped off his chair and started pacing. "You think I'm hiding something from you? Believe me, not a thing. It's the other way around. Let's say I just don't understand many things myself yet! For example, why did all this happen to me? If there are no coincidences, why did I get this ability to travel back in time? Why me? Why not . . . someone else? What should I do with it?"

Dmitry stopped. Silence hung over the room. He turned to stare out the window. Jeff and Margo were motionless, keeping their eyes on him.

"I think there's a reason for this," Jeff uttered.

Margo snorted with contempt, but Dmitry, not noticing it, continued. "I told you I've been having strange dreams lately. About Old Russia, about Saint Petersburg, about Russian America. They were the weirdest dreams! Like about Russia's foreign policies associated with our colonies in America or about the Russian-American Company.

"God knows where I got this crap in my head! Why did the Russians leave this place? Why hadn't they stayed in America for good? 'We came, we checked, we left'? That concept doesn't click in place for me. It's just beyond my comprehension! I've tried to explain to myself that I've dug too deep into the materials while preparing to make that film, but then all that happened."

After another moment of silence, Dmitry added, "Maybe I was chosen for this somehow, but by whom?" Dmitry froze. He gasped, grabbed his head with both hands, and rubbed his eyes vigorously.

"A flash!" he cried out softly. "God, my eyes hurt so badly!"

Margo and Jeff jumped up.

For a moment, Dmitry thought he was going blind from unbearably bright sunlight. His heart was wildly pounding like hoofbeats in his brain! He heard a bloodcurdling scream from a woman. Everything ended as suddenly as it had begun. Still not believing it was over, Dmitry carefully pulled his hands away from his eyes. He was panting and nauseous.

Margo and Jeff were collectively a sorry sight. Their faces were frozen in fear.

"Jeez, you've scared shit out of us, boss! What was that?" Jeff had been the first to come to his senses.

"Whatever it was, it seemed to have passed." Dmitry tried to calm down.

"What's wrong, boss? Is it your heart?"

"No, I don't think so. My heart seems to be all right," Dmitry replied, hesitating for a second. He opened the balcony door. "Something happened to my head. I saw weird flashes. Okay, forget it! Let's go to the balcony for some fresh air."

They stepped onto the balcony. Jeff helpfully offered him a chair. Margo had lost her mask of independence; she had genuine concern in her eyes.

She's so sensitive, Dmitry thought. *And nice.*

"So what have we been talking about?" Dmitry asked. To smooth the situation, he tried his best to look cheerful, although the episode had scared him too. "Oh yeah. I remember. I was telling you about my dreams of Russian America. Can you imagine if that dream came true? It's not a joke! It happened! You have no idea what the Russian colony looked like. A paradise, El Dorado! They used to harvest three times a year! Fur processing and leather factories. Endless fields of grains! Shipbuilding facilities. The budget of the Russian-American Company was catching up with the budget of the whole Russian Empire!"

Margo still hadn't gotten over the incident and was unusually serious. She slowly took the chair opposite Dmitry. "Listen, boss," she uttered, "what if the Fates have given you the chance to sort things out? It's true that when someone wants something really badly, the whole universe rushes to meet his dreams!"

"It could be so," Dmitry said. "That's why I made a decision last night. I don't want to make a film anymore. I'm not interested in just shooting a film. I want to understand and maybe adjust history."

A moment of silence ensued. Jeff asked, "What do you mean 'adjust'? Even those who are not fans of science fiction know nothing can be touched in the past. Otherwise, you can damage the cause-effect relationship, break the invisible chain of events that leads to your birth!"

Dmitry nodded approvingly. "Good try, man! You've obviously done your homework, Jeff, but *causality* is just one theory and rather outdated at that. Physics has advanced a lot since the days of Aristotle, not to mention your own school years."

Margo pulled a cigarette out. Jeff stared at her with the eyes of a faithful puppy. With a sigh, she handed one to him. Taking a lighter from his pocket, Dmitry gallantly gave her a light.

"A modern theory states," Dmitry continued, "that at the moment of your influence on the continuum, whether it's accidental or intentional, the space-time continuum gets separated. One stream keeps flowing toward that important point in the world's history where a baby Jeff will be born. The other stream develops its own completely different way, considering that particular interference as a correction. In other words, one can interfere with time's events but cannot change the outcome because it would be different. It would already be a different reality. So each new intervention, so to speak, would alter the space-time continuum and divide its flow into a 'planned' one and an 'unplanned' or *altered* reality."

"Are you saying," Margo asked thoughtfully as if speaking to herself, "it's possible that in some realities dinosaurs may still exist?"

"Exactly!" Dmitry laughed excitedly. "I think it's very possible! The notorious meteorite that slammed into earth sixty million years ago was exactly such an external 'intervention.' It cracked the trajectory of our reality in two. Somewhere, the reality 'originally' conceived may still exist. It's very unlikely the universe denied itself the pleasure of continuing its fascinating experiment with dinosaurs!"

Jeff and Margo watched Dmitry talking excitedly, and their mood became visibly lighter too.

"I wouldn't want to be in that reality," Margo smiled. "Not for a second! Not even with you, boss."

There was a pause on the balcony. Dmitry looked at Margo as if he were seeing her for the first time. In a sense, that was exactly the case. Margo did not avert her gaze; she only slightly straightened up in her chair.

"Okay, let's assume for a moment you're right," Jeff said, reminding the others of his presence. "How would we be able to travel into the exact time and space we want to?"

"The correct word would be 'I'" Dmitry said, still looking at Margo.

"What 'I'?" Jeff frowned, feeling a catch.

"It would be 'the exact time and place *I* want to travel,'" Dmitry reiterated as he reluctantly turned to Jeff. "You, Jeff, aren't going anywhere yet!"

"All right." Jeff jabbed his cigarette out in the ashtray. "Let it be *you*! I just wanted to know who controls the process."

"The thought and the iPhone," Dmitry answered laconically.

Margo and Jeff jumped in with simultaneous questions. "What thought?" "Who's iPhone?"

"My thought," Dmitry replied in a calm voice. He was enjoying their elongated faces. Margo and Jeff exchanged glances and stared incredulously at Dmitry, not quite sure if he was joking. Dmitry seemed to be dead serious.

"Someone *up there*," he pointed to the sky, "God, universe, a higher mind, call it what you want, selected a courier to effect reality. The iPhone or its carrier are only the instruments by which that mind does what it wants to. It may sound crazy, but, as is widely known in modern physics, the most absurd explanation often turns out to be the correct one. I'm not sure if I fully understand it myself. I know only that I always turn up exactly where I wanted to be in terms of *space*, and the iPhone does the rest in terms of *time*. I just have to picture this place very clearly, though, and I have to choose the time on my app. That's it." Dmitry finished simply, as if he had just given them a cake recipe.

"Well, so what time did you choose?" Margo asked in a coarse voice.

Dmitry grinned and turned away from the girl, staring into the distance. The ocean was peaceful, matching its name. Crying gulls soared over the bay. There was not a trace of yesterday's rain. In the distance stood Fort Ross, undisturbed on its high cliff across the bay.

"Oh I choose a wonderful time!" Dmitry said with rather epic intonation in his voice. As if he had just changed his mind, he turned from the railing and stepped into the room. "Come in here," he called.

Jeff and Margo hurried after him, closing the balcony door behind.

After they disappeared into Dmitry's room, the door of the adjacent balcony also closed with a click.

CHAPTER 24

Present Time. Northern California.
A Hotel near the Fort Ross State Historic Park.

The adjacent room wasn't much different from Dmitry's. The young man with a buzz cut, the connoisseur of women's legs, stood by the table next to the room's TV. He was intently focused on twisting a device in his hands. He was dressed rather unusually, to say the least. His white linen shirt with wide sleeves looked rather outdated. His pants' cut resembled a bubble, and the legs were tucked into short boots made of rough-looking leather. A wide belt was bound a few times around his waist, and a hefty machete was stuck in his belt. A rolled piece of colorful woolen fabric—a blanket or a spacious poncho—was slung over his shoulder.

An actor who played the part of Sancho Panza would wear such a costume on stage. In truth, except for his costume, the young man did not resemble Don Quixote's plump squire at all. On the contrary, he was tall, sinewy, taut. His entire appearance spoke of his warrior bearing.

The TV was on, but instead of a regular broadcast, it showed everything happening in Dmitry's room. Even the voices came over the TV's speakers clearly. Continuing to fidget with the device, the young man turned his head toward the TV and adjusted its volume. "In the eighteen-twenties of the nineteenth century," Dmitry's voice came from the speakers, "one of the most interesting characters in Russian history came to Fort Ross with the expedition of Captain-Lieutenant Mikhail Lazarev, on the Russian Navy frigate *Kreicer.*"

At that point, the device in the hands of the young man flashed with a blue glow. Flashes of blue sparkles cast reflection on the walls. The light grew more intense before it dimmed. That was followed by loud cracking, clicking sounds similar to static electricity discharges. Something was clearly wrong with the device. The young man decided to use the first universal rule of any repair job. He put the device on the table and whacked it with a thick phone book. The crude method proved effective. The device lit up again with a steady light.

At that moment, the young man saw Dmitry on TV scream and collapse in his chair. He grabbed his head with both hands. He pressed his hands against his eyes as if trying to hide from blinding light. Dmitry convulsively slid off his chair. Margo screamed and rushed to him. Jeff dashed to the phone. His worried voice came from the TV speakers. "Let's call 911!"

The incident obviously affected the young man as well. He desperately whacked the device with the phone book again. The device's light died. On the television screen, Dmitry stopped rolling on the floor and quieted in Margo's arms.

CHAPTER 25

Present Time. Northern California.
A Hotel near the Fort Ross State Historic Park.

A flash! It hurts my eyes! Again, it seemed to Dmitry he was being blinded by an unbearably bright sun. The sound of his fast-beating heart echoed somewhere in his mind like the clatter of horses' hooves. A hellish cacophony of sounds exploded in his ears.

Wait! That's the sound of real horses' hooves! Something huge was rising in front of him, blocking the blinding light for a moment. He heard whistles, horses' neighing. An enormous black stallion was towering over him on its hind legs, furiously beating the air with its hooves. He could see a huge horseshoe move quickly in front of his face.

The next moment, something forceful pushed against his shoulder. As he fell, he managed to see it was Margo who had violently pushed him from under the horse's hooves. The girl's eyes were wide open. She was screaming at him. *How strange I'd never noticed how beautiful her green eyes are!*

The last thing he saw was Margo, who took his place in front of the stallion, disappear under the hooves of the agitated horse. Again, he heard a woman's bloodcurdling scream—a shrill, single note.

Slowly, Dmitry took his hands from his eyes. That desperate scream was still ringing in his ears. The first thing he saw was the bewildered faces of Jeff and Margo, who were bending over him. His ability to hear returned.

"Dim, what's wrong with you?" He could hear worry in Margo's voice. Jeff was kneeling in front of him with a glass of water in hand.

"We nearly called the ambulance!"

"Forget the ambulance!" Dmitry sat up and frowned, rubbing his neck. "I told you I'm okay! This is something different. I was hallucinating. God knows what it is, but it seems to me we don't have too much time left. I think the portal or whatever it is is closing. If we want to go, we have to do it now."

"Maybe we shouldn't, boss! Maybe all that's happened affected you in a weird way." Margo looked at Dmitry with concern. He shook his head.

"Where were we?" His eyes were burning with determination.

"You were telling us how one of the most interesting characters in the history of Russian America arrived at Fort Ross on the *Kreicer*," Margo said with a sigh.

"Oh yeah, sure!" Dmitry rubbed his forehead. "Zavalishin! That was the guy's name. Zavalishin." Dmitry rose, went to the table, and sat in front of his notebook. "Back then, Lieutenant Zavalishin was a handsome young man and looked more the rakish hussar than a naval officer. At that time, being a naval officer meant that the person was well educated and of noble upbringing. Zavalishin was also very clever. He had quite an encyclopedic knowledge and a wonderfully shrewd mind for someone in his twenties. His report to the Admiralty Board and to the emperor personally is still in the Russian Navy's archives. In his report, which he wrote upon his return from Russian America, he proved the necessity and possibility of the annexation of northern California to Russia! He based his report on his own experience when, while being here, he almost conquered California."

"What do you mean 'conquered'? How did he do that?" Jeff and Margo asked simultaneously.

"Just like that." Dmitry snapped his fingers and grinned at their amazement. His good mood gradually restored the atmosphere in the room. The images of his hallucinations dimmed in his memory.

"Well, maybe he didn't conquer California in the truest sense of the word, but as he later wrote to the emperor, he could've done so easily. So I thought, what if we meet him and prompt him with some additional ideas?"

Dmitry stopped smiling and gave his crew a stern look. "Are you guys going somewhere?" He nodded at their backpacks.

Margo and Jeff almost choked with indignation. They remained speechless for a while. Dmitry looked at their faces and broke out in laughter, clearly happy with his joke. "All right, all right. Just kidding!" Still laughing, he fished a small leather sack out of a bag by the bed and tossed it to Jeff and Margo. The sack jingled in Jeff's hands.

"What's this? Coins?" Jeff asked after taking a peek inside.

"These are Spanish doubloons of the eighteenth century, you fool!" Margo was happily pulling silver out of the bag.

"I thought, why travel empty handed? Right?" Dmitry beamed. "At least, we now have the means to buy horses at the market in Monterey!"

"Awesome!" Jeff relished the opportunity. "Where did you get them?"

"While you were asleep I visited a local antique dealer in Guerneville!" Dmitry was extremely happy with his resourcefulness. "Good thing there are more than enough Spanish galleons that sank off the U.S. coast. With the improvements in underwater search technologies, local 'entrepreneurs' have been looting them for more than a dozen years. So now we have a pretty good heap of doubloons!"

They heard the telephone ring in the next room. Nobody over there answered it.

"Why else did you go to an antique dealer?" Margo was happy his painful episodes had left without a trace.

"Why else?" Dmitry winked at her and reached inside his bag again. "Here's why! Try these on now!" Dmitry pulled out what looked like monks' garments and tossed them to Jeff and Margo.

"I borrowed these as if for the film. We wouldn't get too far wearing our regular duds." He nodded to Margo and chuckled, very pleased with himself. "Even with the horses!"

Margo as usual was in tight shorts and white tank top that didn't reach even the middle of her belly. Her minimal clothing exposed her body art. Besides the dragon, there were Chinese or Japanese characters covering her legs, arms, and neck.

The telephone in the neighbor's room kept ringing annoyingly.

"I have an idea," Margo exclaimed. She had fully recovered her playful mood. She jumped like a schoolgirl who had just aced a test. Her eyes sparkled. "I'll pretend to be an Indian princess, boss!"

That next-door telephone finally stopped ringing.

Jeff snorted, joining the fun. "Look at this Indian!" He pulled the monk's garment over his head. Margo stuck out her tongue at him, but she followed his example. She got her head through the opening in the garment and pushed the hood back. She froze in terror. She clasped her hand to her mouth to stop herself from screaming. Something had just gone wrong with Dmitry again. This time, he didn't roll on the floor in agony; he just stood motionless, his eyes closed. His eyeballs were frantically rotating under their lids. Tears appeared in the girl's eyes. She rushed to Dmitry, clasped his head in her hands, and pressed her body against his.

"Dim, what's wrong with you?" she whispered.

He did not answer.

Dmitry lifted his head. He was spread on the ground. Dust crunched in his teeth. He could see everything much more clearly. It was a bright, sunny day. He saw a white fortress wall, white dust, bright sun, and crowds of people dressed in white. They crowded around him. Hundreds of people! A stallion was beating its hooves about ten feet away. It was entangled in lasso ropes that six men, digging their feet in the ground, pulled on, but even they barely managed to hold the lathered animal. Dmitry could hear clearly the loud noises of a market, the neighing of horses, the whistles and hollers of the men, the women's shrill screams, the children's cries, and that heart-stopping scream of a woman he remembered so well that had given him an unbearable scare. Dmitry spat the dirt out of his mouth and looked around.

A heap of rags in a pool of blood lay on the other side of the bad-tempered stallion. Is that a body? Yes, probably. He could see a hand peeking out from under the rags, a white hand. With a tattoo. Next to the body stood Jeff in a dumb, brownish robe. He was deathly pale. A cry stuck in Dmitry's throat. Tears mixed with dust rolled down his cheeks. "Margo! Margo!" Dmitry thought his heart was going to tear apart.

"Here! I'm here! What's wrong with you, Dim?" Margo kept caressing his head. She didn't realize she had used his diminutive name.

Dmitry, emerging from oblivion, opened his eyes. She could see consciousness gradually returning to him. The look in his eyes became meaningful. He focused on Margo. Without a word, he grabbed her in his arms and started kissing her on the lips, on her face, eyes, and neck like a madman.

"Margo! Margo! Thank God you're alive! Margo, you're alive!" Dmitry kept repeating with tears in his eyes.

Margo, who only a moment earlier had passionately wanted nothing more than to be in such a position, froze. Jeff's jaw dropped as he watched the scene. He didn't know what to say; he just wanted to sink into the ground.

Dmitry came to his senses. He stopped squeezing the speechless Margo and carefully drew away from the girl. He blushed slightly. The dazed look in his eyes cleared. "Sorry, Marg, I don't know what happened to me . . . I got really scared. The thing is that I saw you, like . . . Well, never mind . . . It's just a stupid hallucination! Please forgive me. I wasn't myself."

Margo saw the sincere uneasiness in his eyes, but somehow, that was not what had surprised her. What surprised her was that she realized she didn't want to leave his arms.

"It's okay, boss. Everything's all right. You can hold me more if it helps."

Dmitry could barely restrain himself from grabbing the girl again. *My God, what a joy it is to see her alive!* Dmitry had no idea that seeing her, touching her, feeling her unharmed next to him would be of such cosmic significance to him! He looked at her with infinite love, as if she had come back from oblivion.

Jeff, completely befuddled, headed for the door. He heard Dmitry's stern voice.

"Where're you going, dude?"

"It doesn't matter," Jeff mumbled while trying not to look Dmitry in the eye. "I just want fresh air." It seemed a kind of black hole had suddenly formed in his chest, sucking all his insides out, and leaving him with absolute emptiness.

"Jeff, please don't go," Dmitry asked quietly with a slight smile. "What would we do without you? It was your idea from the beginning, and I won't do it without you. We need you! We have to go back in time together!"

Jeff turned slowly. Still not looking into his eyes, he gave a silent nod.

Everything was ready. Last-minute instructions had been given. Dmitry excitedly picked up his iPhone, carefully selected the already familiar date—June 14, 1820—pressed the "Go" button, and put the iPhone on the floor. The phone dutifully lit up with a blue glow that formed a flashing, expanding circle. The three friends joined hands. Margo's face shone with happiness and with an intensity that almost matched the iPhone's. Jeff looked at the iPhone intently. Dmitry was also focused. He nodded, and the three entered the glowing circle.

"To Monterey, the capital of Spanish California! To the marketplace!" Dmitry exhaled.

At that moment, the telephone in Dmitry's room started to ring, but no one was there to answer.

CHAPTER 26

1820. Spanish California. Monterey. The Marketplace.

A white, blinding sun, whistles, neighing of horses, noises, and cries! A stallion rises above Dmitry on its hind legs. Dmitry's nightmare repeats itself to the smallest detail, but this time, he is ready. He pushes a dumbfounded Jeff aside with one hand. He grabs a motionless Margo, dashes to pick up the iPhone, and like a professional football player, rolls with her away from the road, away from the menacing hooves of the stallion gone wild.

It all happened in a fraction of a second. Later, no one, including those who witnessed the incident, could understand or explain what had happened. Some asserted that the strangers appeared from under the ground and therefore were certainly servants of the devil himself. Other witnesses argued with foam at their mouths that the strangers fell from the sky and were therefore either saints or angels. In the end, the investigation into the appearance of the mysterious guests in the heart of New Spain came to a logical deadlock and was put aside until better times. However, that was all to come.

As for the new present, Dmitry, Jeff, and Margo rose from the ground, brushed dirt off, spat out dust, and silently looked around. The stallion that had been so frightened by the sudden appearance of the foreign-smelling strangers had calmed down. A crowd of onlookers who had gathered to view a free performance was reluctantly dissipating. The owner of the horse stood in front of Dmitry and bowed to him like a roly-poly toy, lifting the edge of his wide-brimmed straw hat.

"*Perdóname, Padre!*" the peasant kept saying, his look expressing genuine concern and regret.

"It's okay," Dmitry answered him, but in Russian, somehow forgetting to switch to English. Or better, Spanish. The incident about which he had been warned in such mysterious ways in his vividly realistic visions had affected him strongly. He started to feel dizzy from all that had transpired. However, Russian words did not confuse the peasant at all. He bowed even more politely, lifted his sombrero, and addressed Dmitry in Russian.

"*Pra-see-teetee, Gaspateen!*" said the peasant polyglot in understandable Russian. He tugged the stallion's bridle and hurried away.

He had spoken with a very strong accent, but it was clearly "I beg your pardon, sir!" in Russian. Dmitry looked at his fellow travelers to check whether he was dreaming due to acute stress. His friends stared at the departing peasant with the same stunned disbelief in their eyes.

Having decided to analyze all the miracles of the day at his leisure, Dmitry took Margo's and Jeff's hands and stepped into the dense crowd. A wave of pride and something else hard to describe was suddenly all over him. He felt upbeat and excited. Such happy deliverance from danger gave him confidence that the heavens were somehow favoring him. However, he hastened to get a grip on himself. The time had come to look around and get ready for whatever might come.

Monterey's marketplace lived up to its name and use. The hubbub of the multilingual crowd was very loud. As usual in the Hispanic world, the marketplace was in the city square, right behind the gate of the city wall. However, this settlement could be called a city only by a stretch; no other name for similar settlements was more precise. It was a small fortress, a presidio, with only a handful of stone buildings, including a church, some kind of governmental-looking building, and the fortress's walls.

If this is the capital, I wonder what the other cities of Spanish America look like? Dmitry thought. *This one is probably the governor's palace, or as they called that position back then, the viceroy's.*

Dmitry looked at the big white house built in the palace-castle style with a coat of arms on the façade. Small houses lined narrow streets. The nearby bay and ocean did not freshen the air, though. No wind dispelled the dense dust hanging in the air that had been raised by countless bleating, mooing, grunting, neighing, barking, and clucking creatures.

A church bell began to ring. Dmitry instinctively looked at his watch. Noon.

Jeff was the first to regain the ability to talk. "Whoa, boss! Your reaction was amazing! I thought that stallion would crush us!"

Margo didn't say anything. She just looked at Dmitry in such a way that words were not needed. Infinite devotion reflected in her eyes.

"C'mon, guys! It's okay. Don't mention it!" Dmitry seemed embarrassed. "Next time, we have to be smarter and choose a more desolate place to come out of the time portal." Dmitry decided not to tell his crew about his warning visions at that time; they had experienced enough miracles in the last twenty-four hours. "Let's skedaddle out of here! We've already created too much of a distortion here."

"What do you mean? Are you crazy? This place is awesome! It's filled with goods any museum would die to have! It's all antique!" Jeff was waxing positively eloquent.

"Forget it! We didn't come here for antique shopping!" Dmitry whispered in his ear angrily.

"Yeah, right! Then what are we here for?" Jeff did not want to give up, and he had not taken Dmitry's hint to talk in a low voice.

"We came here to buy horses and appropriate clothing and head to Fort Ross. Got that?"

Jeff sulked instead of replying. Dmitry turned; his whole demeanor indicated that conversation was over. He walked along the market stalls. Margo and Jeff followed him.

Margo also began to recover slowly from the natural shock. At least, she did not hesitate to turn to Jeff and hiss at him with a poisonous smirk, "Antiques collector, ha!"

The crowd Dmitry and his crew were trying to get through was a colorful sight. There were mostly Indians or Creoles dressed in white homespun shirts and pants. These Indians, as Dmitry identified them for himself, apparently had been already "civilized." They occasionally saw some "wild" Indians covered with colorful tattoos and with feathers in their hair. The rest of the crowd consisted of settlers, peasants of European origin. Dmitry even caught the eye of a well-dressed lady with a haughty look. Two soldiers walked in front of her, clearing the way. *She must be local nobility,* Dmitry mulled. The lady was dressed in black, according to the Spanish fashion of the time. Her eyes, two black olives, flashed at Dmitry from behind the fan with which she covered her face. Dmitry turned involuntarily and immediately ran into a young man striding toward him. The stranger was dressed in a loose linen shirt and velvet pants. The pants' cut resembled a bubble, and they were tucked into his short boots. A wide-brimmed black hat hid his eyes. He looked like an impoverished Spanish *grandee* who had just stepped out of a Velásquez painting. The stranger's hat fell off from the jolt of the impact and rolled into the dust.

Ooh, shoot! Like we didn't have enough already! A thought flashed in Dmitry's head. He instantly broke out in a nervous sweat. "*Disculpe, Señor!*" Dmitry rushed to pick up the hat, but the young man was quicker. To Dmitry's surprise, the man silently grabbed his hat and without a word slipped into the crowd. *Strange,* Dmitry thought, looking at his back.

In this case, Dmitry's thought *strange* referred not so much to the silent reaction of the young Spanish grandee as to how he looked. Contrary to Velásquez's images and other stereotypes entrenched in Dmitry's mind, the young man didn't have long hair. Instead, he had a buzz cut. Dmitry thought he had seen him before. However, due to the impossibility of that and the fact that his head was already spinning from all the experiences of the day, he decided not to think about the young man anymore. *Thank God he didn't take offense,* he thought.

CHAPTER 27

1820. Spanish California.
Monterey. The Marketplace.

"**S**o where's the local car dealership?" Dmitry asked, not specifically addressing anyone. The small crowd that had gathered around two merchants standing on a platform attracted his attention. Apparently, these guys' trade was going extremely well. Buyers jostled each other, and some hotheads even made attempts to cut through the line.

Dmitry's attention was drawn not to the crowd, however, but to those who towered over it. They looked exactly like Russian *muzhiks*, that untranslatable word that meant his country's peasants and villagers. No other word could properly describe these two guys! Dressed in a long shirts and sporting beards as wide as shovels, they had all the physiognomic characteristics by which muzhiks could easily be identified in any crowd or even in the jungles of New Guinea. Moreover, the goods they were selling were purely Russian handicrafts, wooden utensils, as if they had come right out of a Russian souvenir store. Only one thing puzzled Dmitry. The men talked with customers rather rapidly in Spanish.

Dmitry worked his elbows more energetically, trying to get to the merchants. Margo followed him like a shadow. Behind her, Jeff was huffing and puffing, carefully obeying the order to keep together. There was no way the crowd was going to yield, though. The people around the two merchants formed an unbreakable wall.

In desperation, Dmitry decided on a risky tactic. Clearing his throat, he drew a deep breath and shouted over the crowd in Russian, "*Privet, rebyata!*"

That simple Russian "Hello, guys" produced its expected effect. The merchants straightened up and looked around. The crowd, displeased by a slowdown in trade, decided to part to let the Russians pass through. The men noticed Dmitry. One of them gave the other a poke. "Look, Fyodor, isn't that guy Russian?" he surprisingly exclaimed as he slightly bowed to Dmitry. "Hello to you too, good man, if you are not joking!" He addressed Dmitry. "Where have you come from? You sure speak the language, but you look foreign to me."

"We *are* Russians!" Dmitry started gesticulating. "We are travelers. I was serving in the Russian Navy when I got an internship on a British galleon. The ship sunk near the coast of Mexico. I somehow got to California. I know there's a Russian fortress somewhere up north. That's where we're heading!"

Dmitry lied selflessly, using as many old Russian words and expressions as he could remember from college. Even Jeff joined Margo in sincere admiration of Dmitry's story-making abilities.

The look in the merchant's eyes became warmer. He squinted slyly and said cheerfully, "Then you're an aristocrat! I thought your hands were so white! Well, never mind. Our commandant, Kuskov, also comes from the navy like you, sir! So you'll probably get on well together. Our fort and village are not too far from here. I bet you can get there in three to four days. We just came from there. If you are in no hurry, wait for us, Your Lordship. With God's help, we'll sell all our goods quickly, and within a week, we'll head home together."

"A week!" Dmitry recoiled, hiding his hands in his robe's wide sleeves. "Oh no, thank you. Perhaps we'd better get there on our own."

"Who are they?" The man turned to Dmitry's companions not without interest. "Are they with you?"

"These ones?" Dmitry turned around and looked at his crew. "Yeah, they are with me. This one here is my servant, a valet—"

From the corner of his eye, Dmitry noticed Margo bury her face in the backpack she was holding in front her. Her shoulders were suspiciously shaking. Jeff turned red. Both of them were silent, though.

"The other is a . . . an Indian girl, we are . . . We've met." Dmitry mentally cursed himself for not preparing their "backstories" beforehand.

"Is that your tanya?" The man winked knowingly and grunted approvingly, pointing at Margo's tall and shapely figure that even her loose garment wasn't able to disguise.

"What's a tanya?" Dmitry didn't understand the man's question. "This here is an Indian girl—"

"That's how we call our Indian wives, Your Lordship. Good pick, by the way!" The man grinned, displaying a chipped tooth in his mouth. "I have one just like her at the fort waiting for me!"

It was Dmitry's turn to blush. He involuntarily looked at Margo. Two green eyes gleamed slyly at him from under her hood.

At that moment, a ripple of distortion went through the crowd. People stepped back in disarray. Those in front started pushing those behind them. Disgruntled cries could be heard. Dmitry turned and even stood on tiptoe to understand the cause of the confusion. He spotted it. A group of armed men, ten or twelve in number, had made a semicircle in front of two horse riders and unceremoniously raked the crowd aside with the butts of their rifles. The riders sat on their horses with arrogant looks, trying to run over some particularly obstinate people who failed to move aside.

One of the riders was tall, with an aquiline nose. He wore a black cocked hat over a red bandana wrapped around his head. His green jacket with wide sleeves was unbuttoned. A number of pistols were tucked in his silver-buckled belt.

He looks just like the captain of a pirate schooner! Dmitry thought, not without admiration. *If I were making a pirate movie, I would have definitely chosen this one to play the lead.*

The second rider was short and plump. He sat like a sack of flour on his stately stallion. The inconsistency between the rider and the horse was obvious.

That's probably his boatswain! Dmitry decided.

Despite his appearance, the second man did not lack arrogance at all. In addition, all the members of this motley crew were drunk and were obviously enjoying the commotion they were creating. The one Dmitry had dubbed the captain was solemnly silent as he glanced contemptuously at the crowd. The other was vehemently yelling at the crowd in English.

"Get back, you fools! Make way!"

The crowd pressed Dmitry to the counter. He noticed with concern that the stream of people had pushed Jeff and Margo away from him.

"Margo! Jeff!" Dmitry yelled. He was making a superhuman effort to force his way through the crowd to his friends. When he managed to get close to Margo, he reached for her outstretched hand when the lights went out in his head. He felt as though something had exploded in his brain. It took him several seconds to be able to think and see again. Surprisingly, he found himself lying on the ground for the second time that day. He again had the disgusting taste of dust in his mouth, but it was mixed with something else. *Blood,* he realized.

A grinning mug appeared in his field of vision and spat out in English, "Didn't I tell ya, Vicar, to get the *fock* out of the way?"

The mug said the familiar f-word but had emphasized an "o" sound. The bandit exhaled strong alcohol fumes into Dmitry's face. *They must be British,* Dmitry thought. He tried to get up, but something exploded in his head again, and he fell helplessly into a puddle of his blood. The crowd screamed and rushed in different directions, leaving space around Dmitry.

He saw what happened next through a veil and in slow motion. Margo suddenly leaped into the air. Her hood fell to her shoulders, revealing her face glowing with anger. He saw the colored tattoo on her neck and cheek. He saw eyes that radiated a cold gleam. Her hair done up in a warlike Mohawk blended well with the surroundings. One of her legs was pulled up while the heel of her other leg made a wide arc in the air, and with a savory, squishing sound, it nailed the man on his gap-toothed, grinning mouth. The pirate threw his hands up and crashed to the ground like a sack of beets. His musket, the butt of which he had just used to hit Dmitry, did a somersault in the air and fell directly into Jeff's hands. A startled Jeff quickly glanced at Margo and blushed slightly as she gave him an approving nod.

Unnatural silence hung over the marketplace. On one side were the pirates, taken aback but with guns at the ready. On the other side was Dmitry, who was slowly rising from the ground and wiping blood from his face, and Margo and Jeff, standing at Dmitry's sides. Jeff was holding the musket at the ready while Margo was standing in a menacing pose.

The pirate Margo had kicked lay motionless ten feet away. His head was unnaturally twisted to the side.

A roar broke the silence! The captain went berserk, as the girl had seemed a frivolous obstacle. He spurred his horse. It rose on its hind legs and darted toward the three friends. As he approached the trio, the captain deftly leaned from his saddle and not slowing his wild gallop snatched Margo by her waist and threw her across his saddle. Horse and riders thundered away at the same wild gallop.

Jeff and Dmitry, who had been thrust aside by the horse, jumped up and gave chase, but it was useless. Pirate, prey, and horse disappeared in a cloud of dust behind a bend in the road. "Stop him! Margo!" the men cried. A crazed Dmitry swayed from side to side.

Encouraged by the captain's brave act, the pirates revived their stupor and advanced on Dmitry and Jeff. One aimed a pistol at Dmitry. Occupied by their vain pursuit of the galloping horse, Dmitry and Jeff didn't notice when the young Spanish grandee in the black hat emerged from the crowd. Quick as a flash, he grabbed his machete and in one wide swing chopped off the pirate's hand.

A heartrending cry sounded above the marketplace noise. The crowd immediately turned to the new source of entertainment. The pirate doubled over with pain and was rolling in the dust. He shook his bloody stump in the air. His severed hand, still clutching the handgun, lay next to him in a pool of blood. The young man with the buzz cut pulled his black hat over his eyes and melted into the crowd.

The pause that followed these shocking events was interrupted by more intense commotion in the square. Frightened by what they had seen, people scattered in panic, trying to leave the dangerous place in a hurry. The air was filled with cries, neighing, bleating, swearing, and whining. City guards attracted by the commotion wielded halberds over the heads. Instantly sobered, the pirates faded into the crowd.

Dmitry and Jeff frantically thrashed about from one onlooker to another, who were recoiling in fright. "We need horses! We need horses!"

Dmitry kept yelling. He switched to Spanish, *"Caballos! Caballos!"* The tears of helpless despair rolling down his face left tracks on his dust-smeared cheeks. Exhausted, Dmitry fell to his knees.

"A horse! A horse! My kingdom for a horse!" he mumbled. His shoulders shook with sobs, but Jeff was unwilling to give up.

"Horses! Horses! We buy horses!" He kept grabbing the hands of the scattering peasants.

Suddenly, one of the muzhiks who were selling those wooden utensils emerged from the crowd. His face was focused and serious. He unceremoniously pushed Jeff aside and put his hand on Dmitry's shoulder. "Your Lordship! Follow me quick!"

Something in the man's voice made Dmitry immediately get up and follow him without a word.

PART THREE

War and Peace

The sun rises and the sun goes down, and hurries to the place where it rises.

—Ecclesiastes 1:5

Chapter 28

Present Time. Kremlin, Moscow.
Office of the First Deputy of the President.

In the office of the presidential deputy, a young man with tired eyes sat at a huge desk made of Karelian birch. Heavy drapes decorated with gold tissue shaded the luxurious office. The walls were adorned with mahogany panels, and in the corner opposite the desk stood an Empire-style tea table with inlay and gilding. Two chairs with burgundy velvet upholstery embroidered with gold double-headed eagles stood on both sides of the table.

The young man was completely occupied with composing a document on his notebook. The computer's modern look along with a multiline telephone panel on the corner of the desk contrasted with the imperial luxury of the office. A small lamp started blinking on the phone panel. The man was busy with his work and didn't pay any attention to it.

A few minutes later, a tall, double-folding door opened gently, and a secretary with an attractive haircut looked in.

"Sir, sorry for interrupting, but Sinitsyn on the line five!"

Without taking his eyes off the computer, the young man picked up the phone. "I am listening . . ."

"Sergey Petrovich," he heard, "you've asked me to inform you immediately if any *anomaly* occurs . . . Our sensors have just recorded one."

A few minutes later, a black Audi with flashing lights on the roof dashed out of one of the Kremlin tower gates. Two traffic police Fords with pulsing lights joined the black Audi in front and rear. The motorcade pushed honking Moscow traffic to the sides of the congested streets as it sped down the reserved middle lane of the snow-covered road.

Theirs was not a long trip. In just a little over a mile, the motorcade circled the wide Lubyanskaya Square dove into the open, massive, cast-iron gates of the Federal Security Service building. The gates immediately closed behind the vehicles.

Three stout, respectable men and an attractive young woman sat in front of the presidential deputy around the oval table in the small conference room. The men wore dark, impeccably made suits. The woman wore a gray extended skirt and white blouse. Despite their civilian clothes, the military bearing of the three men was unmistakable.

A plate with a name and rank was in front of everyone at the table. They all had notebooks bearing the logo that looked like an hourglass on the background of the Russian double-headed eagle. What was interesting is that the sand in this hourglass was falling in the opposite direction, that is, from the bottom up.

The inscription under the emblem read "FASTS, Federal Agency of Space-Time Security." A glowing electronic map of the world hung on the wall. A silver-haired man—his crew cut spoke of a military background—acted like an officer senior to the others. The plate in front of him read "Boris Sinitsyn, Colonel, FASTS." He was speaking in a quiet, confident voice.

"And the most important thing is that this violation of the space-time continuum was detected in the United States."

"Damn it! That's all we need right now!" the young presidential deputy got upset in a very boyish way.

"Well, it's good we learned about it in time, Sergey Petrovich," the second man uttered, hoping for praise.

Instead of answering him, the presidential deputy got up and walked to the map on the wall that also listed the different times. Those areas of the planet where the day has not started were cloaked in shadow.

"It's a pity, of course, that it happened on the other side of the planet and in that particular country! We could use this opportunity to collect more data," Sergey Petrovich said thoughtfully.

"The good thing though, is that it doesn't concern us directly," said the young man, turning to his obedient audience. He spoke with a note of optimism.

An awkward pause hung over the table. The men briefly exchanged glances and shifted in their seats, looking with hope at the woman. The plate in front of her read "Daria Shuranova, Lieutenant-Colonel, FASTS." She coughed into her diminutive fist and said in an unexpectedly ringing, almost girlish voice, "Unfortunately, Sergey Petrovich, this is not quite accurate . . . ahem, ahem."

The deputy stared at the pretty woman as a fox would at a rabbit. The young man asked in a rather dangerously soft voice, "What do you mean, ah, Lieutenant-Colonel? Please elaborate!"

"Ahem, ahem . . . This is not quite accurate . . . I mean, it does concerns us directly."

Everybody was silent. The young deputy slowly walked to the table. He pulled his chair out, deliberately turned it so it would face the woman, and sat. "Really? Interesting! And how might that be? Please continue, Lieutenant-Colonel, go on!"

"The thing is that the space-time disturbance occurred on Russian territory."

"Well, I am confused now. I thought you said—" the deputy started saying, but the young woman stubbornly frowned and found the strength to finish what she was trying to say.

"It occurred in California, ninety-five miles north of San Francisco, in the vicinity of the nineteenth-century Russian settlement named Fort Ross." She finished almost in a military style, stressing each word.

The presidential deputy got up and walked to the map. He looked thoughtfully at the American continent. "Well, in this case, this certainly changes everything," the young man said. Addressing the woman, he added, "You know what, Leit . . . ah, Daria, would you mind telling us in more detail about that . . . Fort Ross?"

CHAPTER 29

1820. Spanish California. North of Monterey Bay.

Three riders appeared on what was more a trail than a road that ran along the rocky shore above the ocean. The first rider was a large, bearded man in an untucked white linen shirt that inflated like a sail with each gust of wind. His two companions wore long habits made of rough pile wool of an indeterminate color. One led a downcast mule. The setting sun painted the clouds on the horizon in pink. The bearded man sharply pulled on his reins. His companions followed his example.

"There they are, Your Lordship!" the bearded man exclaimed with satisfaction and pointed toward the bay.

The man was one of the Russian merchants from the market. He had offered his timely help to Dmitry and Jeff and was trotting in front of them. The hoods of their habits were on their shoulders. Dmitry and Jeff rode closer to the man and stared in the direction he was pointing. Their faces, red from riding in the wind, were serious and concentrated.

A two-masted schooner without any insignia was anchored in the middle of the small bay, which was conveniently concealed on both sides. On the shore, six men sat around a campfire. Their rifles formed a pyramid close by. A huge wild boar was roasting. Jeff sniffed the air and swallowed.

"Those bastards are going to guzzle meat when we haven't had a bite since morning!"

Dmitry didn't answer. He turned to the muzhik and extended his hand. "I do not even know how to thank you, Fyodor!"

"Never mind, Your Lordship." The man shook Dmitry's hand firmly. "Please forgive me that I cannot be of more help to you. I gave my word to my commandant not to get my butt into any trouble. We should be as quiet as mice here."

"Yeah!" Jeff grumbled angrily, "Some have to be quiet as mice while others can do whatever they want!"

"Forget it, Fyodor! There's nothing to forgive! Don't even think about it!" Dmitry sincerely wanted to find the way to thank the kindhearted man. "Would you change your mind and take the money for the horses at least?"

"No, Your Lordship. You are heading to our settlement anyway." Fyodor shook his head. "You can just leave the horses there. You might still need your money. As for their all-permissiveness," Fyodor turned to Jeff, "you're right about that, Yefim!" Fyodor pronounced Jeff's name in a Russian manner. "Their secret is simple. They are bringing black slaves here, a free workforce for the Spaniards. It's beneficial for them. That's why they close their eyes on their rudeness and such arrogant behavior. There's no end to their insolence! According to the law, the British and the Americans as well as all others are not allowed to set foot on Spanish-American lands, but every law has its loophole. See? They don't even use a flag! They're like thieves, sitting there alone in the middle of the bay! Thieves they are indeed! Well, I've got to go, Your Lordship." He sighed.

"God bless you! Maybe we'll see each other again someday," Dmitry said.

Fyodor turned his horse, waved farewell, and started down the road they had taken.

Twilight was coming quickly. The setting sun was no brighter than the campfire. Dmitry and Jeff dismounted, tied their horses to a bush, and hid behind a big boulder. The whole bay lay before them as if in the palm of a hand.

"So what're we going to do now?" Jeff hissed after a short silence.

That question had been bugging Dmitry for some time already. During the ride here, he had cooled down a little. The idea of chasing armed pirates did not seem that bright to him any longer. Their hasty departure from Monterey had screwed up their plans to buy more-suitable clothing and, most important, weapons. Now they had to face a small army of bandits unarmed.

"I don't know yet," Dmitry replied in a quiet tone. He put his hand into his pocket to touch the comforting smoothness of the iPhone when a thought struck him. "Damn it! We forgot to charge it!" Dmitry pulled the device out from the pocket. The battery icon indicated the dangerous "less than 20 percent charged" level.

Suddenly, Dmitry felt that situation on the beach has changed. He carefully peered over the boulder. Below them, on the other side of the bay, a cart drawn by a pair of black bulls slowly rolled off the road onto a narrow strip of the rocky beach and headed to the pirates' party.

"Who is that?" Jeff whispered in surprise.

The cart was loaded with barrels piled in a tall pyramid and tied together. On top of the pyramid sat a man dressed in a white shirt with wide sleeves and velvet pants. A belt tightened his waist, and either a cleaver or a dagger protruded from under the belt. A black, wide-brimmed hat hid his face. It was difficult to say for sure, but judging by his constitution, Dmitry thought he was a fairly young man.

With a long pole in his hands, the stranger confidently controlled his bulls from the top of his pyramid by alternately poking the ribs of the animals.

The pirates, of course, noticed the stranger. They jumped from their seats and ran to their rifles. However, the cart's driver was apparently unimpressed with such greetings. Unfazed, he continued sitting on his barrels, swaying with the motion of the cart. The bulls calmly approached the camp of the night watch. Having almost reached the campfire, the cart stopped.

As far as Dmitry and Jeff could tell from their lofty vantage point, the pirates were acting belligerently. It was impossible to hear their words or the stranger's replies. The only thing they could do was to wait and see if the situation could offer a solution to their own problems.

Surprisingly, the conversation on the beach that had had such an aggressive start changed its tone. Dmitry and Jeff heard happy cries and even laughter. Negotiations apparently ended; satisfied with the results, the stranger jumped to the ground. Dmitry and Jeff could not hear what the stranger said to the pirates, but the calm silence of the bay at sunset was broken by an enthusiastic roar.

The loud sounds attracted attention from the schooner. The light on the ship started blinking, evidently sending a signal. In response, two pirates on the beach grabbed a blanket and started cover and uncover the light of their fire, thus blinking a response to the schooner.

Soon, a rowboat from the schooner has been lowered on the water and the creaking sound of oarlocks has followed. Cheering pirates ran along the shoreline between the cart and the water, yelling something excitedly to their friends in the approaching boat. They patted each other on the shoulders and gave friendly hugs to the stranger wearing a black hat.

"I'd be damned if they didn't get the booze," said Jeff licking his lips. "What do you think, boss?"

"There's nothing to think about! Those are the wine barrels," Dmitry replied. "The party is about to start. This might be very fortunate for us!"

Dmitry was not particularly surprised by the series of his lucky coincidences. Every time when something like that happened, he simply gave thanks to his fate for sending those chances his way. As if to confirm his thoughts, the pirates opened a keg and took turns taking abundant sips from the flow coming out of it. The bay shores resounded with excited shouts and roars of laughter.

CHAPTER 30

1820. Spanish California. Monterey Bay.

The schooner's crew had been in a depressed mood for two days already. They had not heard any news for a while from the Araucana Indians the pirates had brought with them from the north. The pirates had dropped them ashore a week earlier couple of miles north of the Russian fortress. According to the plan, from that point, the Indians had to travel to Fort Ross on foot and discreetly stay nearby while the schooner, passing San Francisco, traveled to Monterey to replenish its food and water supplies. Immediately after the raid on the Russian settlement, the captain intended to embark on the long journey to the Sandwich Islands and then Chinese Canton.

Developments in the Monterey market had made the pirates hide for a couple of days in their secret cove and wait until the dust settled. That of course delayed the execution of the plan that had relied on speed and surprise. The captain was depressed. He understood it would take the Indians some time to march to Fort Ross. The coastline's coves and bays did not facilitate rapid movement on land. Besides, they could maneuver only at night. Nevertheless, the Indians had to be in the position already, when they had to sit here, hiding from the Spanish coast guards doing nothing and waste precious time.

More important, the whole idea didn't seem as attractive as it had before. The Araucana warriors were supposed to attack Fort Ross, seize the warehouses filled with otters pelts, and deliver them to the captain. In the case of unforeseen complications for which the captain was always ready, everything what happened could be attributed to a feud between Russians and Indians. By the time the authorities investigated the incident, the captain and his valuable cargo would be long gone.

The money he could get in Canton and Macao for the pelts was worth the risk. He could make more gold with this one raid than with six loads of black slaves. He would then be able to think about getting a new vessel, or maybe two. He could think about settling in a more-civilized land where he could conduct less-dangerous business. The game was worth the candle; that was why the captain decided to try.

But the two days' hiding and waiting had not been planned. The captain sat at his desk in his spacious aft cabin. While he was drinking wine and nursing gloomy thoughts, he was leering at the gorgeous legs of his captive lying on his bed. She was tied up and seemed to be asleep, although he had had to punch her severely to calm her down. This wild beauty was so headstrong, almost like an untamed horse! Remembering how she'd broken the neck of that gap-toothed Sam with just one kick, the captain was in no hurry to untie his prey. The Indian girl wore a strange garment, but it added a certain spice to her situation. The robe had ridden up to her thighs, rather provocatively exposing her legs from which the captain had not taken his glance for the last half hour.

She was definitely something to look at, but it was not her beauty that held the captain's attention. The savage girl had very skillfully done tattoos the captain had not expected to see in these lands. He had seen tattoos like hers on Chinese monks from the high mountains when he had been in Canton three years earlier. To see the same tattoos on the local Indian girl was rather unexpected. He also had noticed that the girl's skin was much lighter than that of the local Indians, and she smelled of strange flowers or something else. In other words, his captive was full of surprises.

The captain hadn't succeeded to take a look at the girl in the nude, but he wasn't in a rush. He hoped to spend a marvelous time with her at night, and that thought improved his mood a little.

Screams and noises from the shore brought the captain out of his reverie. He picked up his guns and headed for the cabin door. There could be two reasons for the noise; either the Spanish coast guard had tracked down their hiding place, or the long-awaited messenger from the Indians had arrived. The last would be better, of course. The captain stepped on deck, but to his surprise, a strange sight appeared before his eyes.

"What the hell is going on there?" he asked the grinning boatswain.

"Sir, some crazy man brought a whole cart of wine!" The boatswain's eyes shone with genuine excitement. "He says he is British and came from the eastern American states. He has a trading post here, and he had not heard a real British accent in ages. He even cried! He said he was taking his wine to the market in Monterey, but he was ready to sell it to his countrymen at three barrels for the price of one!"

"You say for the price of one?" asked the captain thoughtfully. "Why not, let the crew have fun. And the wine we need anyway. Load that barrels onboard! We're having a party tonight!"

The last words of the captain were addressed to his crew, who had already rushed to carry out his orders with happy whoops.

The captain had another reason to be agreeable: he didn't want to share his captive with his crew that night, so he hoped that a couple dozen barrels of wine would help his companions forget about her.

When the cabin door closed behind the captain, Margo opened her eyes. She had been waiting the whole day for such a moment when she would be left to herself for a couple of minutes. Unfortunately, the captain had watched her very closely and had pawed her at every opportunity. She had kicked him in the groin, for which she had been beaten for a long time. After that, they tied her up again and left her alone. She kept feeling his hungry eyes on her all the time, but he had not approached her again.

The captain didn't have a clue that under her robe were her shorts and the belt with a knife hidden in the buckle. All she had to do was to be patient and wait for a moment when she could be by herself, at least for a couple of minutes, and then beware! That moment had arrived.

When the sound of captain's footsteps died behind the cabin door, Margo pulled her knees to her chin and slipped her hands, which were tied behind her back, under her thighs and tied legs. That was easy. She had already stretched the knot of the rope while she was pretending to sleep. Her escape plan had been thoroughly thought. Once her tied hands were in front of her, Margo jumped off the bed, lifted her robe up, and freed her hidden blade from the belt buckle. Another second and the ropes were on the floor.

Rubbing her numb wrists, she got out of the constricting robe. Holding her blade, she rushed to the window and opened the shutters. The current had turned the window toward the ocean, and she could not see anything on shore, but judging by the loud cries, whooping sounds, and flashes of torch light, something exiting was going on.

Margo leaned out the window. She hoped to see a boat tied to the side of the ship, but she could see nothing in the darkness. The girl imagined jumping into the freezing water and shuddered inwardly. She was not a sissy. In her youth, she had become fascinated with martial arts and had prepared herself for any trial, but she doubted she could make it to shore through such cold water.

How long would it take until hypothermia becomes apparent in forty-eight-degree water? Margo tried to remember various tables from her favorite books on survival in extreme conditions. *Is it something like five minutes? No, I wouldn't make it! I need to come up with another plan.* She frantically tried to think as she peered into the dark.

But her time was over. She heard the approaching footsteps. *Well then, let's bring it on!* Margo stood in the middle of the cabin in her combat posture. The key jingled and the lock clicked. The door opened and the captain appeared on the doorstep. The effect which she produced on him was exactly what Margo has counted on. The captain froze on the spot, his mouth open. In the shadows of the cabin, right in front of him stood a scantily clad beauty, a vision from a dream. It took him a couple of seconds to recognize that it was his captive. The Indian girl had lost her robe as well as the ropes he so painstakingly had tied her with. She stood in a strange pose, one leg tucked under her; a heron's pose. She had an evil, bloodthirsty smile on her face. However, what most impressed the captain at that remarkable moment, something he would search for a logical explanation for later on, were the words the Indian girl spoke in perfect English.

"Hi, sweetheart! Forgot something?"

Everything that happened next was no less astonishing, but the captain was never able to remember the details. The girl leaped into the air in an incomprehensible pirouette—she seemed to the startled captain to be levitating—and straightened her tucked leg at the level of his head. The last thing the captain saw on that memorable night was the girl's pink, astonishingly clean heel rapidly approach his mouth. His jaw crunched in his brain. That was the last thing he remembered. A bright flash of light extinguished his unbearable pain and took his consciousness with it.

CHAPTER 31

1820. Russian California. Fort Ross.

Ivan Kuskov walked in long strides on the side of the road that stretched from the fortress to the dockyard. The multicolored façades of various workshops, warehouses, freight houses, and even manufacturing workshops were visible on the recently added streets that branched out from both sides of the main road. The road was the life and soul of the colony. Judging from the busy traffic, things in the colony were going perfectly well. There was no bigger pleasure for Kuskov than to know that. He could hear the screeching sounds of ripsaws coming from the wood warehouses. Men stood in pairs on tall trestle scaffolds making boards out of the trunks of ancient pines. Through the open doors of blacksmith shops came the sounds of hissing iron and the clunking of heavy steam hammers. In front of the pelt warehouses, Indian women were processing fresh skins spread on special frames. A bit further, by the grain barns, sacks were being loaded on numerous carts that traveled loaded to the pier and came back toward the barns empty.

Two packet boats under the flags of the Russian-American Company and the Russian naval flag with the blue St. Andrew's cross had been loaded at the pier. Anchored in the middle of the harbor, three smaller, two-masted schooners were waiting for their turn to be loaded. Kuskov and Baranov used those ships for the internal needs of the colony, so they were navigating mostly between Alaska and California.

Alongside Kuskov, trying not to fall behind his long strides, an estate manager trotted along in short steps, hat in hand. Kuskov was giving the man orders as they walked. On the other side of the commandant, clinking his sword on his jackboots, Zavalishin walked in his unbuttoned uniform jacket.

"Sir!" Zavalishin was preoccupied with something. "I demand an answer! Right now!"

Kuskov let the estate manager go and turned to the lieutenant.

"I've already explained to you, Lieutenant, that I cannot leave the fort without appointing an active officer to stay in charge instead of me, especially when I have such an experienced officer like you! So your arrival turned out very lucky for all of us!"

"I don't think so, sir. I am, as you already mentioned, an active officer, and I am on a mission with this circumnavigation to collect important data for our motherland! I cannot miss the visit to San Francisco! Do you understand that? I am not going to stay behind and watch the farm!"

"I do understand, Lieutenant, but it seems you don't!" Kuskov exclaimed with a touch of bitterness in his voice. "Where have you learned all these foreign words? 'A farm'! This, my dear sir, is not a farm! This is an outpost of the Russian Empire and the commercial center of Russian California!" Kuskov made a sweeping gesture around him. "How much turnover have you seen lately in Mother Russia in recent years? Besides, all this, among other things, belongs to the company, which by the way has equipped your circumnavigation, sir, and which in its turn brings you well-deserved honor. I ask you not to forget that!"

For a moment, Kuskov stopped his speech as if wondering whether he had cited enough compelling reasons. "Also, I'm asking you to do it for just five to eight days!" Kuskov added in a more conciliatory tone. "I really cannot leave the place for this youngster Prokhor to keep an eye on!"

"Sir, please try to understand me." Zavalishin started begging. "If I sit here doing nothing even for one more day, I—" Zavalishin looked around in fear and crossed himself. "I might go crazy! I am already being haunted by visions!"

Kuskov looked at the young man with alarm. "Don't worry, son!" Kuskov patted him on the shoulder paternally. "We all have visions sometimes, and yours will pass I'm sure. Just don't get discouraged. God is merciful. Try to fast for the next few days, pray while you are alone, and everything will get back to normal." Kuskov tried to soothe the lieutenant as if he were a child.

Their conversation was interrupted. An Indian boy about ten years old flew toward Kuskov bareback on a dappled stallion. The boy sharply reined in his horse in front of the officers. He was bursting with self-importance and shouted breathlessly in Russian, "Sir Commandant, Spaniards arrived! From Presidio of San Francisco. Ten muskets and an officer!"

"Again?" Kuskov was very surprised. "Did they say what they wanted?"

"They said they needed to see you urgently!" The horse carrying the boy danced impatiently in one spot, raising clouds of dust.

"See!" Kuskov turned to Zavalishin. "They are probably worried we would forget about our visit!" He addressed the boy. "Ivan, go. Tell them I'll be right back!"

The boy saluted the officers and galloped toward the fortress.

"That's our blacksmith's son, Ivan," Kuskov explained. He noticed a surprised look in Zavalishin's eyes. "Our men take Indian women for wives. They make good wives, and this helps our cause. We didn't come here just to rob the land and be off. No, brother, we came here to settle down and be a good example of a thriving community for the others."

Kuskov said the last phrase thoughtfully and in a rather quiet tone. He did not look at the settlement, where he was expected by the Spanish, but instead gazed somewhere in the direction of the ocean. As if shaking off his stupor, he turned and quickly walked toward the fortress.

CHAPTER 32

1820. Spanish California. Monterey Bay.

Margo stuck her head carefully through the half-opened door. Something unbelievable was happening on deck. A huge barricade of barrels had grown in front of the hold's open hatch. Some empty barrels were rolling on the deck, and others stood opened.

Margo surveyed the bodies lying everywhere as if on a battlefield. She realized the reason for the noise and excitement she had heard in the cabin. *Seems like the boys decided to have a party but didn't calculate their capacity for wine. This was rather timely,* Margo thought while carefully stepping over sprawled bodies. A sharp stench of wine and feces permeated the still air. Margo gagged and covered her nose. While she was making her way past one of the open barrels, she caught an unfamiliar scent mixed with the smell of wine, but she had no time to deal with that. The way to freedom, certainly not without the participation of fate, happened to be open, and she had no intentions of passing it by.

The darkness was lit by torches everywhere. Looking around, Margo saw what she had been hoping to find—a rope ladder leading to a rowboat.

A moment later, Margo was in it. Her faithful blade flashed in the torchlight. The mooring rope plopped softly into the water. She pushed off from the schooner with an oar and disappeared into darkness.

Simultaneously, on the other side of the schooner, an Indian canoe approached the ship as quietly as a shadow. Sitting in the canoe was not an Indian, however, but the serious, focused wine trader. He didn't have his hat on, so it would not have been difficult to recognize the young man with a buzz cut.

He tied the canoe to the ship and noiselessly jumped onboard. He stopped for a moment and listened. The ship's crew was spread around in drunken delirium. An occasional grunt broke the silence from time to time. That did not surprise the man. Without skulking, as if he were meant to be there, the trader quickly walked to the captain's cabin. He silently crept to the door, pulled a pistol from his belt, and cocked the trigger. He froze for a moment. Then he kicked the door open with a swift blow and burst into the room.

In the middle of the cabin, among the debris of a broken table, lay the captain. Margo's robe and several pieces of cut rope were scattered on the floor next to the rumpled bed. The captain gave a low moan. The sound brought the trader out of his reverie. He bent over the pirate and put his pistol to the captain's forehead. The captain gave another slow moan, but it was evident he was still unconscious. After quick consideration, the young man took his pistol away from the poor fellow's head, straightened up, and left the cabin, quietly closing the door behind.

He tucked the pistol into his belt and retraced his way to the canoe. Giving a last look over the ship and her hapless crew, he jumped into the canoe. After a brisk moment, just as Margo had done, he disappeared into darkness like a ghost.

For a few hours, Dmitry and Jeff were watching in disbelief as the pirate party went wild. The results exceeded all their expectations. The thugs had drunk themselves to deranged states faster than the two had hoped for. Seeing that everything had quieted down, they descended to the campfire left burning on the shore. It was dark, and it was chilly. They still had no plans how to liberate Margo. The chances of staying dry during their rescue mission had disappeared with the last boatload of drunken pirates.

"Boss, do you know the water temperature?" asked Jeff shivering.

"Nope. It's probably chilly though," Dmitry answered without looking at Jeff.

"Yeah, it's only forty-eight degrees!"

"Well, we definitely can't make it to the schooner."

"Then what should we do?" Jeff asked in a whisper. "Once, when I lived in Odessa, one boy—"

Dmitry grabbed his hand. Both men grew silent. They listened intently. They thought they had heard a splash. A couple of minutes later, they could clearly hear the splashing of oars over the waves rolling onto the pebble beach.

"That's how we'll get onboard!" Dmitry's mood brightened instantly. "By boat! Crawl after me!"

They sprawled on the ground and crawled toward the approaching boat. After a time, their dark-brown robes fully blended with the ground.

CHAPTER 33

1820. Russian California. Fort Ross.

The Spaniards had made themselves comfortable in the reception room of the commandant's house. That was the name Kuskov had given the servants' room on the first floor of his house he used for meetings and negotiations.

The Spanish delegation, or visitors, as the Indian boy had called them, numbered eleven. The officer was seated at the head of the table and was ceremoniously drinking the hot tea an Indian woman dressed in a Russian jumper dress had poured him from the samovar. Two musketeers respectfully stood behind him while the others sat on benches around the room. The officer was a well-built, dark-eyed, handsome man in his forties. He was blowing on his tea and wiping the sweat on his forehead with a cambric handkerchief.

"Don Luis!" Kuskov greeted the officer in Spanish when he entered. "*Señor Comandante del Presidio de San Francisco*! It's a great honor for me that you found it possible to visit Fort Ross again. We are very happy to see you!"

The Spaniard rose to greet Kuskov with a friendly smile on his face.

"Your Excellency *Señor Comandante del Presidio de Ross!* I will not deny that despite the remoteness of our estates, the sincerity and cordiality of your reception each time compensate for all the hardships and troubles we may encounter on our way here!" the Spaniard announced with a flourish as if he were at a diplomatic reception. His eyes twinkled with mischief.

"The business which made me come back here so soon and distract you from your much-more important affairs is very urgent!" Don Luis added with a bow, noticing Kuskov's hint on his rather frequent visits.

"I have no doubts about it," Kuskov replied laconically. "Please sit down, *Señor.*"

Kuskov attempted to sit at the table, but the Spaniard kept standing.

"If Your Excellency does not object, I would like to suggest a short walk while my men and horses are taking their rest."

"It will be my honor, noble Don," Kuskov tried his best not to show his surprise.

Both commandants walked through the fortress gate. Once outside, away from prying eyes, they stopped and hugged each other like brothers.

"How were you doing? How's the family? How's Conchita?" Kuskov rattled off a series of questions.

"Oh, everything is normal, as it is always. My sister is doing fine, and she sends her greetings as usual!" Don Luis spoke Russian rather well though with a strong accent.

Kuskov had met the Arguello family when he was a young lieutenant under the command of the legendary Lieutenant-Captain Khvostov, when they arrived in San Francisco for the first time, in 1806, bringing His Excellency Nikolai Rezanov. At the time, Rezanov was co-owner of the Russian-American Company and had sailed to Alaska to inspect the company's affairs. They sailed to California on the *Juno*, which Rezanov had bought from the Bostonian captain who happened to appear at that time in Novo-Archangelsk, on the island of Sitka, the capital of Russian America. They sailed to establish friendly relations with Spanish California. Ten years later, Kuskov, already an assistant manager to Alexandr Baranov, traded for this land with the Indians, thus providing for a Russian colony.

Since that time, when Don Luis's father was the commander of the presidio, Kuskov's acquaintance with the commandant's family had grown into true friendship. After the father's, the son had succeeded him as commander.

How much time has passed since then? Kuskov sighed. *My God, better not count!*

Don Luis stayed tactfully silent, watching his friend get lost in memories. Interrupting the pause, Kuskov resumed their conversation. "How are things in Spanish America?"

"Lots of things going on, and the news that comes from both our capitals is not very good. It seems our rulers cannot agree on some things."

"It's sad," Kuskov sighed, "but as the saying goes, while they're far away, we have to manage to survive here."

"That's true, my friend, but unfortunately, we cannot do things as we please. We gave our oaths, and we wouldn't want to get in trouble by breaking them."

"Is this what makes you so sad?" Kuskov patted his friend on the shoulder. "Let's solve our problems as they arise. By the way, I discussed your offer with Baranov. We will buy an extra five thousand oxhides from you."

"Oh, *gracias, mi amigo*! *Mucho, mucho gracias*, my Russian friend!" Don Luis was noticeably elated. "That reminds me. Padre Antonio asks for a favor from you. Can you sell to the mission more of your vine shoots? The ones you sold to them earlier already seem to have taken roots well."

"Sell? No way! Never!" Kuskov paused. "It will be our gift!"

They become silent again. Kuskov decided to take the initiative.

"Tell me what happened. I don't think you came here for vine shoots."

"You are right, my friend." Don Luis grimly agreed. "That is not the primary purpose of my visit. I am faced with an unpleasant problem. I don't know where to start. Okay, some strangers were seen at the marketplace in Monterey," Don Luis hesitantly said.

"So?" Kuskov tried to encourage his guest.

"Well, in the court of the viceroy, they believe those people were Russians," Don Luis explained.

"Of course they are Russians! They even have your permission to travel to Monterey's market, my noble Don! Have you forgotten? Fyodor and his brother are our trading emissaries! Just as we agreed, once every four months—"

"No, brother," Don Luis interrupted Kuskov with a sigh, "I am not talking about those men. They are fine, and they are being watched. I am talking about the others. They were strangers!"

"My noble Don, we have known each other for many years, and we have always treated each other fairly and honestly, correct?" Kuskov stared into the eyes of the Spaniard. The latter nodded grimly.

"So take my word. If any of our settlers left without permission, you'd be the first one to know," Kuskov stated firmly. "There is simply no one besides those two merchants who left more than a week ago."

Don Luis continued shifting uncertainly from one foot to the other. Apparently unable to find more-compelling words in Russian, he switched to Spanish.

"Don Ivan, I'm not going to challenge your sincerity. I ask you only to understand how strict the Spanish laws are. You know that the whole territory from San Francisco to San Diego is closed to foreigners. I was given my post to ensure the strict execution of the imperial will. You know well that it is not easy for me to fend off the attacks of our enemies as it is. For a while now, my family and I have been accused of excessive sympathy toward the Russians."

"I know, my friend!" Kuskov shook his head. "I know, but I can assure you, I have every person accounted for. You know yourself we are shorthanded here. If even one of our people was missing, we would know. So no, that's impossible! Everyone except Fyodor and his brother are here in the settlement! But how did they decide those strangers were Russian? Do you think they could be deserters from another ship? You need to find out who came in lately."

"At first we thought so, but—" Don Luis interrupted Kuskov's speech quietly but firmly. He was obviously extremely embarrassed to question his friend's sincerity. "—the Indians at the market heard them speak Russian!"

Kuskov stopped walking. He stared at Don Luis, then he started walking again in silence. The confused Spaniard followed him.

"The devil must have had a hand in it!" muttered Kuskov, blowing off steam. "How many of them there were?"

Don Luis raised three fingers.

"Three?" Kuskov exclaimed. "That's impossible! I can understand one could have slipped away without noticing, but three? Impossible!"

"I am sorry, my friend, but that's the truth," Don Luis shook his head. "Two men and . . . an Indian girl."

"What?" Kuskov stopped, utterly surprised. "Why would an Indian girl go there? Your people in Monterey are definitely making up a story! Do you believe it yourself? Maybe our enemies are plotting something against us? Slanderers!"

"I don't know, Don Ivan," the Spaniard replied. "It could be so. I can't vouch for anything. The only reason we both do not face any direct charges yet is because they also spoke English, and that seems like a trick the Brits could play. It's not a secret for anyone that people here in our territories, including the Indians, do not speak English! But our sources assured us that all three strangers, even the Indian girl, also spoke English! This is nonsense indeed!"

The two friends started walking as they contemplated the matter, maintaining silence for a while. Kuskov turned to Don Luis. He looked very serious. "Okay, Don Luis. Let's solve this puzzle. You will give me permission to send a search party, and I promise you we will catch those strangers."

"Agreed!" the Spanish commandant replied.

When they returned to the fortress, Kuskov and Don Luis rushed to the commandant's house. "Call Zavalishin to me!" Kuskov ordered loudly while walking.

The Spanish were saddling their horses when Zavalishin rushed into the compound. He was running and buttoning his uniform on the go. He was accompanied by a warrant officer, Prokhor Zaborschikov.

"Well, Lieutenant," Kuskov said, "it seems to be your day! You are not going to be left in the fort. Instead, get your guard-de-marines ready. You are receiving a military assignment. Don Luis and I will give you all the details at the lineup of your detachment."

"Prokhor, dear." Kuskov addressed the warrant officer. "Please run to our winegrowers. Ask them to select some vine shoots to send to the Padre Antonio's mission. Be careful. Make sure they will not dry out on the way to San Rafael!"

CHAPTER 34

1825. December 13. St. Petersburg.
The Office of the Russian-American Company.
The Day before the Decembrists' Uprising.

Kondraty Ryleyev shut the door behind him and stepped onto the staircase. An unfamiliar man of indeterminable age was leisurely pacing the lobby below, waiting for him. Something about the way the man looked seemed strange to Ryleyev. *What is it?* Ryleyev couldn't tell. The man wore an expensive tuxedo. The collar of the starched white shirt was cutting into his muscled neck. *Aha, that's it! Isn't it too early for a tuxedo?* Nobody would wear a tuxedo until 7:00 p.m. One might be wearing a tux in the morning when returning home from a ball, but the stranger was emanating freshness and didn't look as though he had spent the whole night out; he looked as though he had just put that tuxedo on.

The strange gentleman held a black satin top hat. A black overcoat lined with fur was draped around his mighty shoulders. Melting snow sparkled on the wide beaver collar of his overcoat. Despite the man's civilian outfit, his well-built figure spoke of his military bearing. If only not for his expensive cloak, Ryleyev could've sworn the man was from the police! *It's doubtful the gendarmerie would wear such garments,* Ryleyev reassured himself.

Trying to look detached, Ryleyev ran down the stairs, welcoming the stranger on the move. "Oh, I didn't know the snow had started. I haven't even noticed!" he said in his most affable tone. He stopped in front of the visitor, greeting him with a slight nod. "So to what reason do I owe your visit, Mister—" Ryleyev paused and lifted his brow inquisitively. The stranger was in no rush to introduce himself, though. He looked at Ryleyev with apparent curiosity.

He is looking at me as if I were a specimen in the Museum of Anthropology. The stranger looked calm, respectful. *No, he can't be from the police.* Ryleyev was about to open his mouth to repeat his question when the stranger started speaking slowly, as if listening to his words' sound.

"Kondraty Ryleyev, I thought you would look much older," the stranger grinned all of a sudden.

He is definitely not from the police, Ryleyev thought. *He's just a lunatic!* As his worst suspicion faded, Ryleyev felt irritated. *He is so rude!*

"Pardon me?" he asked the man sharply. The stranger's reply exceeded all his expectations.

"My name is not important. You will never see me again. I have only the honor of giving you very important information that deserves your attention."

The stranger said it in such a tone that Ryleyev froze. If a moment ago he had been ready to point out the stranger's bad manners and maybe even show him the door, his inner sense told him the stranger had every right for exhibiting such behavior. Though Ryleyev was not going to give up just yet.

"It is very likely," he said coldly, "but I have to tell you that I do not meet people without a proper presentation. Kindly leave your business card indicating your concerns, and you will be notified when I can see you. Today, I'm very busy."

"Kondraty," the strange visitor addressed him very unofficially, almost in a friendly manner, "it concerns, hmm . . . How can I put it more precisely . . . It concerns tomorrow's *events*—"

Ryleyev became pale. He leaned on a small table in the lobby. The marble tabletop was cold, like the sweat on his palms. *My foreboding proved to be true*, he thought sadly. "Are you from the police?" he asked. His voice faltered treacherously. His assumption somehow amused his guest. The stranger, who all that time had remained serious and was even looking at Ryleyev with pity, broke into a smile and even chuckled.

"From the police? Ha ha ha! No, I'm not from the police! Although in some sense . . . Ha! No! I am, so to say, a private investigator. You can call me Colonel Sinitsyn. Then again, this does not mean anything. Ha ha ha!"

The stranger stopped laughing. For some reason, Ryleyev noticed how white and even his teeth were. Ryleyev had never seen such teeth before. "Please allow me, Colonel, to ah . . . You see, ah . . . What exactly do you mean by 'tomorrow's events'? It's not appropriate to call events that haven't happened yet 'the events,'" Ryleyev muttered deliriously as he was trying to buy time.

The stranger did not let him finish though. In a quiet, well-modulated voice, he recited as if chanting,

Ready the ropes for your masters' heads.
Ready the knives for your lords.
Hang the tyrants on the poles like lanterns,
Then your life will be bright and glorious!

To his horror, Ryleyev felt his forehead grow damp. He looked at the visitor, dumbfounded. Suddenly, he felt chilly. He even thought that an otherworldly cold emanated from the stranger. Ryleyev shivered. Not hiding his feelings any longer, he sank into a chair. "But how? Nobody has heard those lines yet! Nobody has even read them, since I wrote them this morning! Actually, I didn't even finish writing them! They're still here!" Ryleyev tapped his forehead.

At that point, he was not addressing anyone specifically. He seemed to be talking to himself, trying to find any explanation for all that the stranger was saying. *I'm probably losing my mind, but why so suddenly? It's crazy!* Ryleyev looked at the mysterious visitor again. "You are not a colonel! But who are you? Why have you come to me?"

The stranger shrugged his shoulders as if nothing unnatural had been going on. "Your secretary, Mister Somov, had the same face when I read his own poetry to him. Anyway, I hope, Mister Ryleyev, that now you believe I am—ah—more than well informed and have something really important to tell you."

The stranger looked at Ryleyev. Again, Ryleyev read only interest and respect in those eyes. *All this must have a logical explanation,* Ryleyev concluded. Having made the decision, he abruptly stood. He straightened his frock coat, and no longer looking at the stranger, said, "Follow me, please."

Ryleyev quickly walked into the inner chambers. The stranger followed in silence.

CHAPTER 35

1820. Spanish California. On the Road to Fort Ross.

In a small clearing in the shadow of an ancient sequoia, a campfire burned. The setting sun's beams streaming through the canopy of trees created an illusion of something majestic, out of a fairy tale. A waterfall could be heard in the distance.

Jeff held his video camera on Dmitry, who sat on a log. The sun's beams created a wonderful backlight while the fire's glow lit up Dmitry's face. He was holding a microphone and hugging Margo, who was wrapped in a wool blanket. She was cozily leaning toward him.

"So we conclude our first broadcast from the past. If everything goes according to our plans, which, thanks to someone, we haven't been able to implement yet—" Dmitry smiled and looked at Margo, who was eating a huge piece of cake. "—then tomorrow, we'll leave Spanish California and enter the lands of the Russian Empire near the River Slavyanka, destined to be called the Russian River two hundred years later!"

Dmitry paused in front of the camera to mark the finishing point. Jeff switched the camera off. "You should have added, boss," Jeff giggled, "—and if the cameraman will function normally!"

Everyone laughed. Margo said, "Well, you shouldn't try to attack an innocent girl! Especially one trying to get out of a boat in the dark on an unknown shore! You might end up without heirs!"

Jeff jumped up, doubled over in a buffoonish manner, and grabbed his groin. "Who knows? Maybe I've already lost my ability to have any heirs! Oh my balls! I've got to check them out right away!"

Another burst of laughter followed his statement.

"When we're back to our time, you'd better buy yourself a football player's cup and jockstrap. You'll need them, rescueboy!" Margo was wiping her tears from so much laughing.

"Better buy one with a heating function." Dmitry added fuel to the fire. "He constantly tries to dive into freezing water!"

Laughter, which was so much-needed to relieve all the stress of the last days, rang through the forest.

"Here's what you get for saving a girl from the pirates!" Jeff could not stop joking. "You either freeze your valuables off or get left with an omelet in your pants!"

Having laughed until their sides started hurt, the three friends finally calmed down. They were panting in exhaustion.

"On a serious note, though, thank you, guys!" Margo announced, suddenly serious. "I can stand up for myself, but it felt damn good to be saved! It was like being in an adventure novel!"

She looked at Dmitry, who was devouring her with adoring eyes. Only the snorting sounds of the horses grazing nearby broke the silence. Margo gently pressed her lips to Dmitry's mouth. Jeff rose from the ground with a groan.

"I'll go check that waterfall out there."

His friends hadn't heard him. Unable to restrain themselves, Dmitry and Margo joined in a passionate kiss.

The ancient forest stood in its pristine glory. Slanting rays of sunlight cut through dense foliage. The forest was overflowing with life. The restless movements and twittering of its inhabitants could be heard everywhere. A footpath that was almost covered with ferns ran to a creek glistening with sunbeams. Jeff took the path and went toward the sound of the falling water. Trout were moving their fins lazily in the numerous sloughs of the stream. The water was so clear that Jeff could see the fish in the stream from the path. Gradually, the current's speed quickened. This and the growing noise meant that very soon the stream would end its smooth flow in a downfall. It was so beautiful that Jeff regretted not bringing his video camera, but he didn't dare go back to the campfire.

After a time, the forest parted and an amazing panorama opened before Jeff's eyes. Forest on both sides of the river came directly to the precipice, ending abruptly and revealing a stunning view of the valley that stretched to the mountain ridge on the horizon. *This is the valley they would call someday Sonoma,* Jeff thought. *There would be no forest left, though. Damn, I should've gone back for the camera!*

Skipping from one stone to another, Jeff approached the edge of the precipice. He even sprawled on his stomach and crawled to the edge. What he saw made him freeze on the spot in awe. The waterfall was just a hundred feet in height. It plunged the river into the pond already formed by the water below. Huge boulders lined its border. The forest that had parted slightly to give space for the river's free fall surrounded the pond again. Mermaids splashing in the pond made the beautiful surroundings magical.

At least, that's what Jeff thought at first when he saw raven-black hair with bead strands, slanting eyes, high cheekbones, and tattoos on naked bodies. Six or seven—Jeff couldn't count them—Indian girls were having fun in a way their peers at any time and in any part of the world would have had. The girls climbed up the huge boulder that hung over the pond to jump into the water. Their wet, brown bodies sparkled in the rays of the setting sun that added a reddish hue to the surroundings.

One Indian dove into the water and swam to the other side of the pond in two strong strokes. She climbed on the rocks and stood under the waterfall. Jeff froze in awe. He was afraid to move and disturb the beauty of the moment. His face reddened, his mouth became dry, his fingers frantically dug into the stone. *It seems I won't have any problem with having heirs.* He chuckled inwardly as he fidgeted and adjusted his pants' zipper.

The Indian girl could not hear anything because of the noise of the falling water; likely, she had just *felt* his movement. Throwing back her wet hair from her face, she looked up and directly caught Jeff's admiring glance. The girl paused for a moment in surprise. Apparently, Jeff's eyes expressed no danger. Having come to such a conclusion, the girl smiled mischievously and slowly turned under the falling water and caressed her hips. When she looked up at the young man glued to the rock, she snickered. The man was a pity to look at.

Suddenly, the craving and imploring look in the young man's eyes changed in a flash. His eyes widened in horror, his mouth opened as if he wanted to shout something to her. He was staring somewhere behind her. The instinct of the daughter of nature worked faster than thought. Without second-guessing, without turning around, the girl slipped into the water in an instant.

That was what had barely saved her from being caught in the crudely made net that fell on the spot where she had been standing.

Jeff's erotic response to the scene vanished as if by magic. He jumped to his feet and yelled at the top of his voice, "Behind you!" But the girl had already disappeared into the water. A hefty man with a pierced ear and jackboots jumped out of the bushes. He swore, grabbed his empty net, and yelled something to the other side of the pond. Jeff did not hear what exactly the man had yelled, but he had no doubt he had spoken in English. The next events reminded Jeff of a nightmare.

Whooping and yelling, a gang of thugs that Jeff, to his horror, recognized as his "old friends" from the Monterey market, rushed out of the bushes surrounding the slough. They circled the naked girls and started throwing them roughly on the ground. The pirates treated the girls unceremoniously as they tied them up. The ones who were particularly headstrong got hit in the face, and they immediately went limp in the arms of the bandits. The pirates had also been excited by the erotic scene they had been observing.

One of the pirates grabbed one tied girl and bent her over the trunk of a fallen tree. He was readying to take her from behind but was kicked on his naked buttocks by the captain.

At first, Jeff did not recognize the captain at all. The pirate's former luster and splendor were gone. One of his eyes was completely swollen and bruised, his nose was broken, and he was missing front teeth; he was a boxer recovering from a very bad fight. He furiously ran along the pool, using a whip on thugs and captives without distinction. "Move, move, move!" he screamed desperately. "Whoever finds me that tattooed bitch will be a rich man!"

The pirates put all their catch in one spot. The girls who were conscious screamed and cried. To his enormous satisfaction, Jeff did not see "his girl" among the captives, but that was the last thing Jeff saw. A blow from a rifle butt made his mind go blank.

CHAPTER 36

1820. Spanish California. Mission San Rafael.

A guard was sitting by the wide-open gates of the Spanish mission surrounded by a high stone wall. He didn't know why he had been positioned there. *Why's this mission so important? Who am I guarding it from?* The local Indians were very peaceful; most of them had been converted to Christianity. Since the place was sparsely populated, there were not too many thieves there either. The people who lived on the scattered farms and plantations through the valley were all known and accounted for; everyone was in plain sight. The Russians, their new neighbors, were on the north side of the river, but again, they were very thrifty, hard-working people who were reliable in business and trade and had no reputation for committing any indecencies. Besides, they had enough of their own business to tend to since their territories were no smaller than those of the Spanish.

Although at times the guard heard angry speeches from some alarmists who stubbornly planted rumors that the Russians had grown in their ambitions and wanted to take land from the Spanish crown, not many believed those rumors. It was enough to look around and see there was plenty of empty land around to disprove that claim. Get your lot and work your land. *Why would anyone fight about it? Why was there any reason to quarrel? Man is such a creature that no matter how much he gets, it is never enough.*

When one gets old, one tends to get philosophical. The guard was old. Fifty years of age was no joke. He had seen a lot in his life. He didn't have a home in faraway Spain, so he had nowhere to return to. He had decided long since then that when his service was over, he would settle here. *Why not?* the soldier thought, smoking his pipe. *This country is no worse than any other. It's peaceful here, and that's the main thing.* This country reminded him of his native region, Extremadura. In his long twenty years of military service, there had been no action in California. All that time, he had served mainly as a guard. *What's not to like? I might even remain in the mission,* the old man speculated. *At least this place has God's presence, and there's nowhere to go anyway!*

The soldier crossed himself and yawned. He didn't mind being on duty. He would make up for his missed siesta the next day. Long ago, he had learned to nap while sitting or standing. If only his stomach, joints, and teeth didn't bother him. *Is it really possible to have nothing bothering a person? If nothing bothers you, you might as well be dead!*

His rinky-dink uniforms jacket was unbuttoned, and his head was bare. He squinted his eyes, letting the setting sun warm his wrinkled face. His ancient gun was wedged between his knees more for support than protection.

About ten other soldiers were resting in the shade by the one-story barracks inside the fortress yard and behind the wall of the mission. They were very similar to the guard. These old men were almost at the end of their service terms, and they bore this burden away from the tumultuous events of the era on the very edge of the empire.

In the depths of the mission fortress, across from a small square, a chapel stood in front of the gate, near the house of the abbot. Further on, along the walls, were household outbuildings and monastic cells.

Four Franciscan monks in brown habits belted with ropes were busy in the middle of the yard. The current abbot was a progressive man. He cared about God and their faith, he didn't let the monks get lazy, and he always came up with work assignments so the monks wouldn't get fat from being idle. At the moment, the abbot was serving as an example for the others. He was trying to put a new wheel on a cart the monks had bought from a passing trader at a great price.

The detachment of guard-de-marines under the command of Lieutenant Zavalishin and midshipman Nakhimov was cheerfully coming down the hill. Far ahead, they could see the Spanish mission, which was the goal of their day's travel. They sang as they walked along the road. *They've gotten so tired from being idle for so long!* Zavalishin thought. *I can definitely relate to that!* He was extremely happy with the turn of the events. "Thank you, Lord, for not leaving your servant!" Zavalishin kept repeating. A happy smile spread on his face. During his three months at Fort Ross, the lieutenant had visited Mission San Rafael several times and had become acquainted with the abbot in spite of the differences in their religious beliefs.

A couple of times, they had engaged in rather hot discussions they were able to conclude only with the help of three huge jars of wine. The monks had learned how to make great wine. The mission was in a valley with a specific microclimate. It was much warmer and drier than it was in the Russian coastal lands. Thus, the monks' wine came out sharp and rich in taste with a fine bouquet. The abbot added herbs to their wine that gave it a unique taste. Zavalishin advised the abbot to try selling their wine, and that had worked. The mission was earning its own money they used to finish constructing the church, to fix the wall, and to whitewash the monks' cells. Zavalishin even promised the abbot to buy a batch of their wine and take it with him on his long journey home so he could introduce it to Europe. Of course, Zavalishin was rightfully expecting a warm welcome at the mission.

The lieutenant sniffed the air. It smelled of smoke from human dwellings. Zavalishin turned to the midshipman and winked at him, saying, "What do you think, my friend Nakhimov? Should we check how ready the Spanish fortress is for an attack?" He was in a very good mood.

Nakhimov happily snickered back. "Are we going to storm the fortress? Do you think they would let us serve our sentences here as well?"

"Well, it's a great place to do hard labor." Zavalishin laughed heartily.

He turned to his detachment of fast walking guard-de-marines. "Hey, drummer, give us a roll! Detachment, line up! First singer, start a song!"

A loud drumroll and a ringing young voice broke the sleepy silence of the valley. The Russian naval flag with the blue St. Andrew's cross flew high.

CHAPTER 37

1820. Northern California.
Indian Settlement on the Border of Russian California.

Jeff struggled to open his eyes. The sun, shining like a huge, bright ball, made him see blood-red circles under his closed eyelids and did not allow him to open them. He recovered his hearing first. To be exact, it was not even hearing but a fury of noise in his ears. Jeff struggled to understand what the roaring noise reminded him of. It sounded like falling water crashing on rocks. Jeff thought the mighty streams of the waterfall were crashing down somewhere near his mouth, and he even opened it, trying to absorb as much of the life-giving water as he could. It was torture. Jeff could not take it any longer, and he moaned. Right at that moment, he felt drops of liquid on his caked lips. Something cold was put on his forehead. Wincing and trying to overcome the pain, Jeff forced his eyes open. What he saw did not immediately register in his fevered mind.

Next to him, actually leaning over him, was the Indian girl whose overwhelming beauty he had enjoyed during her nude swimming at the

187

waterfall. He recognized her immediately. The girl held a wooden dish. With a small wooden spoon, she took bitter liquid from the dish and poured it into Jeff's swollen mouth. Even those drops seemed like bliss to him. The girl's face was filled with tenderness. When Jeff opened his eyes, she smiled happily.

To his right, above his head, was the merciless sun. *Wait a minute! This is not the sun,* Jeff realized. *It's the light of the video camera!* That was why his eyelids had burned so painfully the last few minutes. The red indicator lamp also meant he was being filmed. Then, the "sun" was turned off, and instead of it, the happy face of another Indian woman looked at Jeff. The second girl's face spoke in Russian.

"Finally! Boss and I were considering buying a drugstore already. So how're you feeling, rescueboy? Do you remember anything that happened to you?"

"Margo!" Jeff exclaimed happily. It was still very difficult to speak. "What? Where? When?" he tried to put the words into a sentence but grew quiet when he realized his mouth wasn't working too well.

"Jeff, *What? Where? When?* is TV quiz show!" Margo giggled. She was extremely happy he had regained consciousness. "The year's 1820. We're in California. We're the guests of the Kashaya Indians. You, Oh Mighty Destroyer of Rifle Butts, risked your skull to save the daughter of the chief!"

Only then did Jeff understand why he had not recognized Margo right away. She was wearing an Indian dress made from fine buckskin and fringed along the seam. She had a wide belt made of braided straps. The dress, artfully decorated with beads, looked very good on Margo. Her arms as always were bare and revealed her tattoo that ran up her long neck and looked surprisingly fitting in the setting. Margo had white and black feathers woven into her braids hanging from her Mohawk.

"Wow, Margo! Look at you!" Jeff smiled. "I barely recognized you." He cast a glance at "his" girl again. She interpreted the look as a silent request and readily brought a spoonful of liquid to his lips. Jeff tried to give her a smile. More out of politeness than need, he swallowed a small amount of the potion.

Again, a great surprise waited for him. The Indian girl set the cup aside and leaned closer to him. She spoke in Russian a phrase accompanied by smooth gestures, as if Jeff was deaf and dumb. "Song of the Stream and Jeef are now friends!"

The girl smiled. She put her finger to her lips and then gently touched Jeff's cracked lips with it. Anyone in the world would understand that gesture. Lacking the strength to move, Jeff was all eyes, and he stared at the girl. He looked so confused that the Indian girl broke into laughter. Margo giggled as well as she recorded the touching scene on camera.

"Song of the Stream is the name of your new girlfriend, loverboy," Margo said, teasing him. Jeff tried to smile, but his lips were still struggling to move. It was evident that the potion the Indian girl was giving Jeff had not only healing characteristics but also an anesthetic effect. Jeff's mouth was numb, and with the numbness, the pain subsided. Barely managing to tear his gaze from the girl, Jeff turned to Margo.

"Where's Dmitry?"

"You won't believe this!" Margo put the camera down. "So much has happened! In short, you really have saved Song of the Stream! These paleface dogs—the pirates, I mean—hadn't had enough when I kicked some of their butts, so they organized a raid on the girls, but you stopped them! With your help, Song of the Stream managed to escape and run to her village for help. She picked us up, me and Dmitry, on her way back. We got there just in time! The captives were freed. You were found holding a rifle by the waterfall. Too bad the pirates got away. However, that's not all! A detachment of real Russian guard-de-marines are marching here this minute with Zavalishin as their officer in command! Do you remember Dmitry told us about him?

"So, the Kashaya are roasting a whole deer on the fire over there! There's going to be a huge celebration in our honor! They call it a powwow. You'd better get up!" Margo couldn't stop chatting in her happiness and excitement.

Jeff also felt delighted and at peace. He closed his eyes so the girls wouldn't see his happy tears.

CHAPTER 38

1820. Spanish California. Mission San Rafael.

The old guard, warmed by the sun and lulled by his philosophical thoughts, was napping. He was dreaming of the times when he was young and the enemy was about to attack. A drumroll had sounded. He dreamed of how it was both scary and fun and how he had badly wanted to take a dump.

Fly, which has flown into his open mouth, woke him up. For the first several seconds, the old man thought he was still dreaming. In the rays of the setting sun and under a high-flying flag, an infantry platoon was marching at him in attack formation. The air burst with a drumroll, and just like many years ago, he was again visited by an inappropriate desire to take a shit. Here and now.

The old man could not believe his eyes. His sleepiness disappeared as if by magic. His pipe fell out of his mouth. A Russian flag was flowing above the heads of the enemy's combat detachment that had formed a solid battle square.

As the guard tried to jump to his feet, he got entrapped in his rifle's sling and almost fell. His uncooperative stomach seemed to be waiting for just that moment. Taking advantage of the guard's momentary distraction, his belly issued a plangent, snorting sound and the contents of his bowels released into his pants.

Over many years of his service, the old soldier learned two things well: the first was that soldiers' pants were brown in color for a reason; the second was that it was better to run in the same direction the enemy was going, only much faster! That was exactly what the old man performed; he ran, lifting his legs high and wide to the sides.

To his credit, he tried to close the gate behind him, but either the doors were heavy or the hinges had not been properly lubricated. His efforts were to no avail. In the end, he left the gates as they were and resorted to the old, time-tested method of guarding. He filled his lungs with air and yelled.

The scream of the old soldier did not impress anyone in the mission's garrison. However, the veterans grabbed their old rifles, just to stretch their old bones, and gathered at the gates with curiosity.

"The Russians are coming! The Russians are coming!" the old soldier kept screaming and pointing to the attacking infantry detachment that had already started to re-form back into their marching lineup.

The heavy-built abbot gave up on the wheel and the cart he was attempting to fix. He pushed the soldiers apart and got to the front of the gates. Covering his eyes with his hand, the abbot looked in the direction of the approaching military group. "Well yes, the Russians are coming. So what? Why are you screaming like a madman, Hernando? Do you have sunstroke?" The abbot turned to look at the other soldiers around him. "Have you all gone mad? Go back to your barracks with your iron toys and stay there as quiet as mice! Lock the doors and do not peep outside. God forbid the Russians would decide that we were trying to defend ourselves from them! Begone! Sit there until I call for you."

It was evident that the abbot had a lot of authority in the mission. The soldiers rushed to carry out his orders readily, even happily.

The guard-de-marines looked dashing as they marched through the mission gates. The courtyard was deserted. Nakhimov lifted his arm, and the drumroll stopped. The young people started to look around suspiciously but with interest.

"Whoa," Zavalishin exclaimed. "Even my friend the abbot hasn't come out to greet us. So it seems we have experienced a complete victory, guard-de-marines! Well, have your snacks," he spoke to his detachment and turned to Nakhimov. "Midshipman, you and I are going to see if there's anyone alive around here."

While the detachment was settling down in the shadow of the mission wall, the church door suddenly opened. The burly abbot appeared on the threshold with a crucifix in hand. A procession of monks walked behind him. Singing something plaintive in Latin, the monks had tragic expressions on their faces and headed toward the Russians.

"Hey! Here's my friend!" Zavalishin winked at Nakhimov. He stepped forward and addressed the priest in Spanish.

"Abba Antonio, are you heading to the kingdom to come? Is that from the sound of our drums?" Mischief appeared in Zavalishin's eyes. "Are you heading straight to heaven or to purgatory first?"

The abbot recognized Zavalishin and cheered up noticeably but kept his guard. "Oh my son, is that you? God is great and gracious! Please, allow me to ask you, my young general, if you have come here with the whole army just to continue our theological dispute?"

"Heaven forbid, Padre! It is unwise and foolish of me to engage in a debate with the wisest prelate of the Roman Church!" Zavalishin parried in the same tone as the abbot.

"You are exaggerating, my young friend," the abbot said with feigned embarrassment, but he still cast a proud look at his multi-aged flock. Monks with downcast eyes stood silently behind him.

"No more than you are, Father. I am as far from the post of a general as my detachment of navy cadets is from an army. Although I am ready to accept your words as a compliment." Zavalishin bowed to the abbot with a smile. "Let me enquire as to the whereabouts of your own brave guardsmen, Father."

"They are . . . ahem . . . They are . . . participating in maneuvers," the abbot found the answer and started fussing. "Why are we all standing on the doorstep? Come to our rectory! Share our daily bread!"

Just as Zavalishin predicted, the process of "sharing daily bread" turned into a whole feast. The table was crammed with fruits and vegetables, and the monks had already rolled out their second barrel of fine wine. Zavalishin had been counting on that. He really wanted to please his fellow soldiers with homemade food and delicious wine after a day's march. The monks, by the way, diluted the wine with water, and Zavalishin's young guard-de-marines liked it very much.

When all became mellow and flushed from the feast, Zavalishin leaned to the priest and asked him the question that had prompted their visit to the mission. "Abba Antonio, we are looking for three runaways: two men and a woman. Most probably they escaped from a ship. Have you heard anything about them?"

The abbot was slightly tipsy since he was the only one who drank wine undiluted. He raised a cup that looked like a small bucket. "What's wrong, *Señor*? Has our wine lost the qualities you had always praised?" the abbot asked with real offense in his voice. He had noticed that Zavalishin hadn't touched his wine.

"I do not drink alcohol anymore, Abba Antonio. Congratulate me on my benevolent intentions," Zavalishin replied sadly.

"How is it possible? You Russians yourselves presented us with this vine." Father Antonio looked into the crater of his cup. "So taste your own gift!"

In reply, Zavalishin pushed his glass even farther away. "I can't, Abba! I gave my word."

"How can it be? Has my young friend given his word not to drink my wine?" the abbot cried with drunken surprise. "What is the reason?"

It was evident that the abbot was very upset. In truth, Zavalishin was also feeling bad. He had become very fond of wine during his travels. He enjoyed its taste but never cared for its intoxicating effect. The worst thing was that all his cadets were looking at him with perplexity at the moment. So Zavalishin was barely holding to his word.

"After all, wine was blessed by Christ!" Father Antonio exclaimed in frustration, not aware of any other argument to which he could resort.

Zavalishin took his glass, lowered his head a bit, and smelled the aroma of the wine. "Well, if you say that He Himself blessed it." Zavalishin hesitated. "Should I drink it one last time? The day was so hot. What do you say, Nakhimov?"

In response, Nakhimov took a sip of wine and winked at his superior slyly. "As far as I know, Lieutenant, you swore off only vodka."

"Well done, midshipman! You're a wiz!" Zavalishin exclaimed. He was happily relieved. "For I, my friend, thought I would leave these lands without trying this noble drink ever again. You really saved me!"

Zavalishin switched to Spanish and looked at the abbot. "Oh Lord, save and protect me!" He shook his head and drank the wine in one gulp. There was no one happier than the abbot at that moment. He broke into a blissful smile. While Zavalishin ate goat cheese and peaches, the priest patted him on the shoulder.

"Now I recognize my Russian friend!" he announced. His eyes became moist from his overwhelming feelings.

"They passed our mission not long ago," Father Antonio suddenly continued without any connection. He took a bite from a whole onion with a crunch.

It took Zavalishin a couple of seconds to understand that the monk had just answered his earlier question about the runaways. Trying to contain his excitement, Zavalishin waited for the abbot to refill their glasses with wine. He carefully asked, "How long ago did they pass the mission, Padre?"

"Just yesterday," responded the abbot readily. "We wondered where they might come from. They did not look like Russians. As for the woman . . . the woman was an Indian, and a gorgeous one!" For a moment, it seemed that the priest had forgotten his vows, for his eyes had lit up. He smacked his lips, hiccupped, and reached for another pheasant wing.

No wonder the Romans used to say "In vino veritas," Zavalishin thought. *The situation seems to be resolving itself so easily.* He said, "We are looking for them to prove to our neighbors they are not Russians! Where can we find them?"

"I think you should look for them among the Indians," the abbot noted reasonably.

Zavalishin and Nakhimov rose, having been satiated by the meal. Concern was reflected in the abbot's eyes. "Are you leaving already, my sons? What about our theological dispute? Don't you know that wine provides great inspiration for debates?"

"Thank you, Padre! We will definitely continue our discussion at a more appropriate time. Right now is not a good time for dispute."

The abbot rose and silently poured wine into the glasses. This time, all three drank and enjoyed it silently.

"What about the traditions of hospitality? What about God's gift?" the priest muttered drunkenly as he continued his efforts to persuade his guests to stay. "We haven't finished the wine! We haven't eaten the entire roast!"

Zavalishin only shook his head. He stumbled slightly, stretched with satisfaction, and left the table. All his people had long been waiting in the monastery's courtyard. Only he and Nakhimov remained with the abbot. *It's time to go,* Zavalishin thought. *If we march fast enough, we can probably get to the Indian settlement before sunset!*

"My orders demand attention, Padre! We'll debate next time." He smiled at the abbot kindheartedly. The abbot suddenly frowned rather sternly, although mischief gleamed in his eyes.

"What if I wouldn't let you heretics go? The door is locked. You can't touch me, for I am *persona sacrosancta*! If you do, you'll go directly to the eighth circle of hell. I will not let you go until you recognize the Vatican doctrine of purgatory, my sheep!" With these words, the abbot moved to the door with an unexpected agility considering his size and slammed and locked it. With a triumphant expression, he put the key in a bottomless pocket of his robe.

Zavalishin sighed and smiled at Nakhimov, who cast a look at a weighty bench by the door. Without saying a word, while the abbot tried to figure out what they were doing, the young men grabbed the bench, laughed, and began battering the massive wooden door. They accompanied each blow with a valiant chant.

The burly abbot froze in surprise, but then he grinned drunkenly and joined the officers. The work went quickly with his help. In a minute, the trio fell through the broken door, laughing uproariously, into the mission courtyard.

CHAPTER 39

Present Time. Moscow. Lubyanka Square.
Federal Agency of Space-Time Security.

A young man with a buzz cut sat at the table in a conference room on the second floor of a massive gray building in one of Moscow's central squares. At one time, his life had been as ordinary as those of millions of other inhabitants of earth. He used to have a name. He of course, remembered it, but he didn't like using it even when referring to himself; his name was a link to his past. The young man didn't want that connection even in his thoughts. He liked his current status, and besides, he couldn't go back to his past anyway.

He currently had a number, 14, instead of a name. It wasn't among the first ten, but it wasn't among the last either. Moreover, his number said a lot to insiders. The first two tens of the agents in the special operation force CHRONOS of the Federal Agency of Space-Time Security, Monitoring and Correction, officially called the FASTS, had exceptional privileges. As often happens, these privileges were accompanied by huge responsibilities, but could it be any different? As a former officer of the Russian Air Force, Fourteen had learned to take responsibility for his actions long ago. He had also learned to bring all his abilities to bear on the cause and the idea. He did it well, and somewhere deep in his soul, he suspected that if it had been otherwise, he would never have reached the important position he was in at that time. Because of his dedication, he had been given special trust.

In critical situations, which his new operation never failed to provide in abundance, his rank, his number, allowed him to make his own decisions. To draw an analogy with conventional military structure, he was on the level of a senior officer, though CHRONOS didn't have conventional army ranks. His rank, by which his fellow citizens usually distinguished people like him, was not needed because his communication with fellow citizens didn't exist anymore.

The organizational structure of CHRONOS was not quite usual, or to be more precise, it wasn't usual at all. His rank equated to . . . well, to a deity quite literally. In their service slang, the officers whose numbers were below twenty were called *gods*. Those with numbers above twenty were called *angels* in their code language. The rookies, whose numbers came last, were simply called *ghosts*.

More precisely, there were only ten gods: himself and nine others whose numbers ranged from eleven to twenty. No one has ever seen the first ten. There was a rumor that circulated especially among the cadets that the first ten didn't exist, that they were just a myth with roots that stretched back to the first days of the agency's foundation, but those were just rumors. He knew the first ten existed and he was sure that one day he will join their ranks.

However, he had never seen agents with single digit, but unlike the cadets, he knew he would never see them. It was forbidden; it was considered bad manners to even mention them at agency meetings.

Why, he couldn't say, but during the years of his unique service, he had learned not to ask too many questions and keep his guesses to himself.

The most important thing that made him feel proud and satisfied with his service was that all the agents in his group were highly respected and trusted; that was more than enough for him. That was what he was willing to give his life for.

Fourteen kept his hands in front of him. He was sitting straight out of habit, ready to get up at any second. He listened attentively to Lieutenant-Colonel Daria Shuranova, who was walking in front of the electronic map of the world in her gray skirt. Her official suit didn't make her any less attractive. Everybody in the organization agreed on this. However, the position the young woman held in the bureau cooled even the hottest heads.

The difference in their ranks did not allow Fourteen to look Daria in the eye, but that was okay with him. Instead, the young man looked at the lieutenant-colonel's legs, and that sight suited him better than any illuminated map. However, for the sake of decency, he appeared to look at the map from time to time.

"Such anomalies, as we recently learned, have happened in the course of history before." The young woman was continuing her report. "Some managed to travel back and forth on the time line. Some disappeared forever without any chance of return. As a rule, and depending on the epoch or their personal ambitions, such people were later called 'prophets,' 'geniuses', 'visionaries', and so on. Only now, after the brilliant breakthrough of our physicists, and with the appearance of the first STPG, 'space-time portal generator,' we can conduct a systematic study of the anomaly."

Daria paused. Two members of the staff in white gowns quietly opened the door and entered the conference room. *From the lab,* Fourteen noted. The lab assistants pushed a wheeled cart that held a semitransparent plastic box labeled with numbers and a bar code. One lab assistant opened the box and retrieved some accurately folded clothes. He carefully laid everything on the table: white shirt, brown velvet pants, boots of rough cowhide, belt, and an item that looked like a long knife or a short sword in a sheath. The second assistant walked to Daria with a folder. He took out a form that she quickly studied. She signed it with a sprawling signature. Both assistants left as noiselessly as they had entered. The procedure hadn't taken more than a minute.

Daria walked to the table and picked up the shirt. "You do remember, Fourteen, that these things are only imitation, don't you? None of these items can be left behind. Do you understand?"

Fourteen remembered that of course. He jumped to his feet and reported by the book, "Affirmative, Lieutenant-Colonel!"

"At ease, Fourteen." Daria held a hand up. "Where were we? Oh, yes, the study of the anomaly. Basically, this study is our main duty. I wouldn't overemphasize it if I say it's a national security question. It has direct relevance to us all! We are here to protect our state and it's secrets by all means.

"Our second goal is to try to utilize our possible advantage for the maximum benefit of our country. We still call it a 'possible advantage' because we don't know for sure whether other nations have similar devices for space and time travel. All this is so new that even the strategy and the tactics of using an STPG, its potential, as well as the ideological, sociological, and moral aspects of its use are still being developed by our agency with the direct participation of the president." Daria had stressed the word *developed*. "So try to avoid your independent decision making and actions! Strict compliance with the task in the shortest possible time is what's needed now! Is that clear, Fourteen?"

"Affirmative, Lieutenant-Colonel!"

"So our primary goal will be to discover answers to three standard questions we ask any anomaly: Who are the travelers? What are their goals? What are the consequences for national security?"

Daria turned to face the map. "Now to the most interesting part. Come here, Fourteen."

CHAPTER 40

1820. Northern California.
The Kashaya Indian Settlement.

For the umpteenth time that day, a small group of Kashaya Indians had become very excited. The heroes of the occasion appeared on the path that ran from the hill to the village. A detachment of the guard-de-marines was approaching in a marching formation. They were carrying the Russian naval flag with the St. Andrew's cross and the flag of the Russian-American Company.

Dmitry and Margo, with their arms around each other, stood next to the tribe's elders, who had come out to meet the Russians. They were staring at and enjoying an impressive spectacle. The wind blew the banners; the setting sun glinted on the officers' epaulettes.

Zavalishin held a sword with a gilt hilt. He marched at the head of the detachment, hair flying in the wind. Midshipman Nakhimov walked to his left and a step behind. Seeing the village down the hill, Zavalishin eloquently waved with his glove, and the breathless silence of the village was broken with a rhythmic drumroll. The detachment closed ranks. Indian tom-toms echoed the guard-de-marines' drums. Margo reached into her belt bag, a gift from Song of the Stream, and pulled out her palmcorder.

"Damn! Nobody's going to believe us! They'll say we staged the crowd scene," she whispered excitedly without taking her eye off the camera.

Dmitry expressed his own doubts. "I suspect we've been shooting all this activity for private use only."

The whole population of the Indian village had come out to meet the guests. These naïve children of nature lined up along the path and didn't try to hide their excitement. Raising clouds of dust, the kids jumped in excitement around the squad. Village mutts of every size and color joined the kids' excitement. The dogs' barks filled the area.

Zavalishin waved his sword. The squad came to a halt. The drumroll ceased, and like an interrupted echo, the Indian tom-toms stopped. Zavalishin sheathed his sword and took several steps toward the elders. He made a slow, deep bow. As if by command, the elders took several steps toward the detachment. One stately and rather young elder whose jet-black hair fell in loose waves over his shoulders took a few steps forward and stopped in front of Zavalishin. The Indian slowly raised his right hand with the palm facing the squad.

Zavalishin straightened from his bow and glanced at Nakhimov. A slight movement rippled through the Russian squad. An orderly hustled to Zavalishin and handed him a box. Zavalishin opened it and went to the chief.

"Great Chief of the Kashaya people, please allow me on behalf of your brother, the chief of the Russians who are your neighbors, to present you with this modest gift as a sign of our endless devotion and love!"

Zavalishin handed the box to the chief. Inside it were two pistols elaborately decorated with silver inlay lying on blue velvet. Sincere delight showed in chief's eyes. He bowed in gratitude. He ceremoniously accepted the box and solemnly handed it to the warrior who had emerged at his side as if from beneath the ground. The chief turned to his people and gave a sign. A girl stepped from the crowd of the welcome party. Margo and Dmitry, who were stealthily recording everything, recognized the girl.

Song of the Stream was wearing a long, homespun cotton dress tied with embroidered belts three times, under her bust, on her waist, and just above her knees. Her hair arrangement looked like an *ikebana* made of feathers, flowers, and strands of beads. The girl's bare arms as well as her face were covered with a colorful tattoo. She looked very impressive. In her outstretched arms, she held an elaborately beaded item—a belt or a ribbon. The chief nodded in approval to Song of the Stream, took the ribbon from her, and handed it to Zavalishin.

Dmitry leaned to Margo and asked her in a whisper, "Do you know what the chief is presenting to Zavalishin?"

"A ribbon is the most valuable thing the tribe has. It's like a banner," Margo whispered. "If such a banner is presented to the chief of another tribe, it means the inextricable connection and union of two tribes."

As he handed the ribbon to Zavalishin, the chief spoke in Russian, slowly and carefully searching for the right words.

"Oh Great Warrior Who Came on Big Canoe! I know you are a guest and a friend of my brother, the great chief of the Russians. Please accept our gift that was made by my daughter, Song of the Stream, in accordance with the sacred traditions of our ancestors. Our gift might not be as opulent as yours, but it means that from now and until the moon ceases to exist, the land of the Kashaya tribe is your land too and the Kashaya people are your family!"

The chief solemnly put the ribbon on the outstretched hands of Zavalishin. The latter again bowed deeply. It was evident that he was excited. Zavalishin turned and carefully handed the ribbon to his orderly. The guard-a-marines masterfully shouted "hooray" three times, and the lieutenant and the chief embraced and kissed each other three times, according to Russian tradition.

As if on cue, everything started in motion, and the fields resounded with shouts of joy. The Russians and Indians became a fun crowd that moved slowly to the middle of the field to the fire with the roasting deer.

"I believe the official part is over?" Margo turned to Dmitry.

Dmitry breathlessly watched Zavalishin and the chief approach. They were smiling while discussing something. Behind them, Nakhimov and Song of the Stream walked, and they were also talking vividly. Margo and Dmitry stood still, too excited to move.

Dmitry exhaled. "I can't believe we're about to talk to Lieutenant Zavalishin!"

Song of the Stream left the company of Nakhimov and trotted in a dignified manner to Zavalishin. She told him something rather quickly, addressing her gestures to the couple standing with the elders. Zavalishin nodded and walked briskly toward Dmitry and Margo. As they walked, the Russian officers bowed respectfully to the elders of the tribe and presented pipes, tobacco pouches, pocketknives, mirrors, and other gifts.

Dmitry was excited. He took a deep breath, grabbed Margo's hand, and stepped forward. Song of the Stream happily smiled as she turned to Zavalishin.

"These are the people, who with their friend Jeef, helped save us! Brave Jeef was even wounded! He—What's wrong with you, White Brother?" the girl asked.

Zavalishin stopped and stared at Dmitry so abruptly that Nakhimov and the orderly bumped into him from behind. They almost dropped the tray with the presents they were carrying. Zavalishin became very pale. Perspiration beaded his forehead. Without taking his eyes off of

Dmitry, he started to dry his wet forehead with his glove but suddenly crossed himself meaningfully. His hand was shaking.

Dmitry, who almost started his well-thought-out greeting, remained standing, taken aback by Zavalishin's reaction. He turned quickly to make sure the lieutenant was not looking at something going on behind him. There was nothing behind Dmitry except excited, active villagers preparing for the feast.

"It's *him* again!" Zavalishin muttered in a doomed and tragic voice. "I told you, Dmitry, not to drink. It will make things only worse, but you refused to listen."

Dmitry's jaw dropped. "I haven't been drinking anything," he said, shocked.

His response and his puzzled look seemed to surprise Zavalishin even more. If before he had looked at Dmitry from under half-closed eyelids as if expecting him to disappear at any moment, his eyes were at that point wide open. "What are you? Tell me this instant! Are you human?" Zavalishin hissed.

All the others stood crestfallen. Margo gave a surprised look to Dmitry, to Zavalishin, and back to Dmitry. The Indians too shared surprised glances. Song of the Stream kept looking from her father to her new friends and back. A frowning Nakhimov put his hand on the hilt of his sword. The orderly stood at attention, drawing his head into his shoulders.

"Well, I was just going to introduce myself," said Dmitry slowly while trying to understand what was going on. "But how did you know my name?"

"What?" Zavalishin was shocked.

"Dmitry. You said it yourself!"

"Dmitry is *my* name, demon!" Zavalishin was outraged. "You can take my life, but you cannot take my name!" Zavalishin cried as he leaned forward.

The chief stopped smiling. Nakhimov made two steps forward and stood by Zavalishin. His hand held his sword's hilt. Song of the Stream was observing the scene in horror. Margo frowned. Her hand shifted unnoticeably to her belt buckle.

"Why are you calling me a demon?" Dmitry felt the slight sting of offense. "My name is also Dmitry. What's wrong with it? What's wrong with you, Dmitry Zavalishin?" Desperation sounded in his voice.

It was hard to say what had affected Zavalishin more, the fact that he had been addressed by his full name, the stranger' sincere tone, or that the stranger had a human name, but it seemed that Zavalishin had awakened. The look in his eyes become more conscious. He shook his head and ran his hand over his forehead. He stared at Dmitry with new interest, as if he were really seeing him only then.

"Please forgive me." Zavalishin coughed with embarrassment. "I am not myself today . . . Forgive me my question, but who are you?"

"I am a traveler, Lieutenant Zavalishin. I travel God's world with my friends. I have taken ships under different flags, and I have traveled alongside traders and merchants. During my travels, I have missed my homeland, Russia. We arrived at Monterey on a Spanish vessel, and we were heading to Fort Ross to see the Russians, but we've gotten ourselves into a fine mess."

Dmitry was giving his prepared speech in short sentences. From the corner of his eye, he noticed the tension among his listeners had slowly receded. Although Nakhimov still had his hand on his sword, he was listening with interest. The powerful figure of the chief, who had acted as if he were about to attack earlier, had visibly relaxed.

Margo stood beside Song of the Stream and whispered something into her ear. The Indian girl stepped forward. She waited for a pause in Dmitry's story before she addressed Zavalishin.

"White Brother! The same paleface dogs who attacked us kidnapped my sister at the marketplace in Monterey! Only the courage and valor of The One Who Bears Your Name saved my sister from certain death and shame!" The Indian girl gracefully pointed at Dmitry. "He made his way to their large canoe, and with the help of his faithful friend Jeef, he beat them all and saved her! Then they saved me!"

The Indians looked at Dmitry with respect. He in turn blushed slightly from this new interpretation of his exploits. He had no doubt who had made up such a story. He cast a quick glance at Margo. She winked conspiratorially.

"Tonight, we are having a big powwow to honor your brave tribesmen and also to honor you, oh White Brother, and your warriors!"

The Indian girl finished her pantomimic story and stopped to take a breath. Her cheeks were flushed. The chief looked at his daughter with admiration. Nakhimov couldn't take his eyes off her, but Zavalishin was looking at Margo with apparent interest.

"At first, I thought you were an Indian," he said to Margo. "I can see now I was mistaken. Who are you, Miss, and how did you get here?"

Margo looked in Zavalishin's eyes calmly. "It's difficult to explain, Lieutenant Zavalishin. I can tell you only that I am an American and due to circumstances, I am traveling with my . . . my fiancé!" Margo cast a quick glance at Dmitry, who turned even redder.

"We could tell you many things," Margo continued, drawing everyone's attention. "I hope we will have time for that, but now I need to tell you something very important, the reason we were in such a hurry to get to Fort Ross. When I was a prisoner on the pirate's schooner, I overheard their conversation and learned they were preparing an attack on the Russian fortress."

Everybody stared at Margo in shock; it was clear that this information was a surprise to them. Zavalishin looked at Margo with undisguised interest. He addressed her in English. "You said you are an American, so why do you care about the Russian settlement?"

"Because they will attack the Russian settlement and then the Indian village. I don't like it! They're cowardly thugs who must be stopped and punished!"

Zavalishin turned to the midshipman. "Nakhimov, signal the gathering! We are leaving! We cannot wait a single minute!"

He addressed Margo again. "If the information you gave us is true, my lady, and I have no ground to doubt your words, we all will be in great debt to you!"

The chief suddenly joined the conversation. He was still carefully selecting Russian words. "I know that the great warrior is as fast as a young deer! Although, please, consider that the big canoes of the palefaces can go only in the direction of the wind. Today, the wind blows in the opposite direction. Also, the sun has finished its walk through the day. Take a rest, and let your people rest. Be our guests. Tomorrow, my best warriors and I will travel with you and your people! We shall arrive at Fort Ross way earlier than those cowardly dogs who travel in a big canoe. The great warrior will not miss his victory!"

Zavalishin lifted his face to the sky in which small clouds floated peacefully. The trees were rustling and swaying in the wind. Having done a mental tally of something, the lieutenant turned to Nakhimov but changed his mind. He turned to the chief.

"Oh Great Chief, my brother, you are as smart as you are brave!" Zavalishin bowed to the chief. "It would be an honor to be the guests of your people."

He turned to Nakhimov and ordered, "Dismiss the gathering! We are staying."

CHAPTER 41

1820. Northern California.
The Kashaya Indian Settlement.

The tribe gathered by the campfire. The bodies of oiled, half-naked Indian warriors shone in the glow of the fire. The enthusiastic audience clapped their hands to the rhythm of the tom-toms. In the center, next to the fire, Margo writhed in the fast and beautiful dance of the fiery dragon.

For a long time afterward, the elders told stories of the great powwow that had happened that fateful day. Great warriors had gathered for that meeting, and the Great She-Warrior Mar-Go bestowed the audience with her presence. The beauty and strength of her fearsome but artful performance of the deadly dance won over the hearts of the Kashaya people. The mother snake herself had entered the body of the beautiful Mar-Go. Everyone saw it! For one cannot perform such movements no matter how hard one tries unless one knows how to let the spirit of the great totem—the mother snake—influence them. The tribe of white brothers from Fort Ross had luck on their side; the very incarnation of the great serpent would guard them day and night. Then there was a great battle and a great victory!

Both Dmitrys sat on a log a little farther from the fire, watching, as were the rest of the villagers, Margo's skillful, sharp movements. Dmitry took his eyes from the camera with which he had filmed the dance.

Zavalishin sighed with a sad smile. "The only thing I regret," Zavalishin said quietly, "is that I won't be able to share everything you have told me with anyone. They would think I had lost my mind! I'd better be quiet about it. To tell you the truth, I would not believe it if I hadn't witnessed myself your, as you call it, 'time jump'! It's unbelievable what science will be able to do in the future!"

"You're right. It's better be quiet about all this," Dmitry said. "Just remember well everything we talked about. You know what? Write about it in your report to the tsar. Maybe in the new flow of time, your report will be taken into account and something would be done about it unlike in our history time line!" Dmitry had stressed the word *our*.

"What do you mean?" Zavalishin was puzzled.

"Well, it is known that in *our* history, you would have written such a report, or from your point of view, it's better to say that you *will* write it, but it won't be of any help. That's why I am saying that maybe in the new flow of time, something will be different and changed for the better."

"*Our* history, *your* history—it's still hard for me to comprehend all that." Zavalishin sighed. "For me, there's only one history. My life and my hopes are in it."

"That's true, of course. However, because of this unique phenomenon I have told you about that, believe me, is hard for me to understand as well, there appears to be an opportunity to look at the whole course of historical developments in Russia in the next centuries as if from a different point of view! Traitors are pushing the country down the path where, thanks to its geopolitical position, Russia will always be at a disadvantage. It will spend untold resources trying to overcome this disadvantage while trying to consolidate its position in the European arena. As a result, it will miss the opportunity to gain a foothold in the East, and the time will come when an entirely different continent will rule the world!"

"To tell you the truth, it is hard to believe this." Zavalishin shook his head thoughtfully.

"Yes, it's difficult to believe it now, when everything is so new here in America, so . . . wild, but that's a fact! Yes, during the last century, we have conquered the access to the Baltic and Black Seas, but look at the map! One look is enough to realize that these seas are nothing but two closed water pots from the geopolitical point of view. Any small squadron of navy can cover two narrow isthmuses—the Danish Straits in Baltic and the Bosporus and Dardanelles in the Black Sea—and the entire Russian fleet in both seas would be paralyzed!"

"Dmitry, do not forget that you are talking to a man who is teaching navigation and geography at the Imperial Marine Cadet Corps!" Zavalishin smiled sadly.

"Of course I remember! That's why I'm telling you this. No one else will understand me better than you! Whereas, here in the Russian far east, there is this great ocean that would allow our country to become a leading maritime power and thus a world leader! You know perfectly well that the country that rules the seas rules the world! It has always been like that, and it will always be that way! Right now, Russia has two coasts along this ocean from Kamchatka to China and from Alaska to California! Get settled here! Do not flirt with the Spanish! The Spanish crown will lose this land within two years anyway! There's really no one to conquer here. The land is empty!" Dmitry gestured in agitation.

"True, there's nothing to conquer here," Zavalishin agreed with a sigh. "You come to any presidio with a squad of soldiers and they drop their rifles and roll the wine barrels out. 'Just don't hurt us!' they say."

"See, I told you! You should write about this, and this time, you should describe all the riches hidden in the land here. Maybe this time it will work!"

The more Dmitry talked, the more it seemed to him that he couldn't express something that was important. That *something* was on the tip of his tongue, but he couldn't find the right words. Zavalishin seemed to notice it too.

"Calm down a bit, Dmitry. I believe I understand what you're saying. The only thing I don't understand is why you think it will work this time when it didn't work last time? Also, the riches in the depths of this land are good, but who on earth will work the land? Our Kashaya brothers? They still live in a primitive communal system!"

"Emancipate the peasants!" Dmitry suggested passionately.

"Whoa! Listen to what you are saying! You, my friend, are contradicting yourself!" Zavalishin cried in shock. "If we free the peasants, who will do the work then? Who will remain to work the land in Russia? They will all walk away!"

"Nobody is going to walk away if everyone has a house and a job. If there's none in Russia, bring the peasants here! The Russian-American Company will not be able to develop this continent all by itself!"

"I've heard something similar already. They said in our corps that some hotheaded officers in St. Petersburg and Moscow are writing a new economic program; they want to reform Russia. They even want to install a parliament!"

Dmitry froze in his seat. It seemed he had managed to grasp the thought that had long been running from him in his head. "Wait a minute! December 14! The Decembrists' revolt of the year 1825! This will happen in five years! That's when they had to emancipate the peasants! Who the heck needs parliament?"

"What are you rambling about, Dmitry? What 1825? As God is my witness, we are still in 1820!"

But Dmitry was not ashamed of the agitation that consumed him. He rushed to Zavalishin and grabbed his shoulders, shaking the young man. "Zavalishin, my friend! Please promise me that you will think my words over and that you will write a letter to the tsar. I think I understand! That's where the catch is! Russia needs not only a parliament but also the peasants, its workforce, to be set free! With this workforce and the blessings of the tsar, we can develop the whole world just as the English did when they formed a constitutional monarchy!"

"If you are so good at geography, Dmitry," Zavalishin spoke as he carefully freed himself from Dmitry's grasp, "then do not forget that England is no bigger than the Russian province of Pskov. When they took the land from their peasants there, those countrymen crawled around the globe like cockroaches. In Russia, only Siberia could absorb all your workforce without a trace and not choke!"

"Oh yeah? What about Ivan Dezhnev, who sail through the Bering Strait eighty years before Bering did? What about Shelikhov? They didn't get lost in Siberia! What about Baranov? If it didn't happen to them, it wouldn't happen to the others!" Dmitry was very excited. "Give them freedom and good direction! Show them the way! Bring them here for everyone's good and for the glory of Russia!"

Zavalishin was watching Dmitry intently. Slowly, the excitement of the other man caught up with Zavalishin.

"Maybe what you're saying makes sense, Dmitry. I promise you one thing—cross my heart—I will think it over carefully! You have the word of a gentleman!"

Early in the morning, before sunrise, before the embers of the campfire had burned out, the combined detachment of Indians and guard-de-marines was headed to Fort Ross. They traveled in complete silence, some on horseback and others on foot. They stretched like a small army along the narrow road that ran along the shore for almost a mile. The chief and Zavalishin were serious and focused as they rode in front of the group. Behind them, also on horseback, rode Margo and Dmitry. Leading the consolidated unit behind them were the horses carrying Nakhimov, Jeff, and Song of the Stream.

The army was an impressive sight in the predawn haze.

CHAPTER 42

1820. Russian California. Fort Ross. Early Morning.

Fort Ross was ready for battle. The whole population of the Russian and Indian villagers had gathered in the fortress the night before. When the savages attacked, the fortress came to life. The bell in the chapel's tower that also served as a watchtower started to boom loudly. Gun crews began to bang the lids of ammunition boxes. Realizing they had nothing to lose and had nowhere to retreat, the savages rushed to the walls of the fort in a hurry to meet their doom. The young corporal Prokhor Zaborschikov was flushed with excitement. His sword was drawn. He deftly climbed the ladder to the observation deck.

"Squadron, prepare for the battle!" Prokhor yelled in a clear voice as he calculated the distance to the approaching wall of the Araukana Indians.

Kuskov walked to the fortifications in a rapid step. Dmitry did not lag far behind him.

"Sir, I want to ask you, when Nikolai Rezanov came to these shores with you for the first time—"

Kuskov stopped for a moment. He turned to Dmitry perplexed. "What are you talking about, good man? Which Rezanov are you asking about? Our minister of commerce? His excellency has never been to this shores! He had never visited California!"

"What do you mean 'minister of commerce'?" Dmitry halted as if he had run into a wall. "He was . . . What about Rezanov arriving on the ship *Juno*? What about Conchita? What about their love? The famous Californian poet Bret Harte would also write about it!" Dmitry incoherently muttered as he tried to cry over the noise. He was completely stunned.

It seemed that Kuskov was surprised even more than Dmitry. "What are you talking about? What does Donna Maria have to do with this? Who is Bret Harte?"

"Wait, sir!" Dmitry could not give up. "Hadn't Rezanov arrived here on the ship *Juno*? Hadn't he offered his hand and heart to Conchita? Hadn't he died in Krasnoyarsk on his way back to St. Petersburg?"

"Goodness gracious!" Kuskov brushed Dmitry off. "Are you insane, brother? I don't know where you've picked up all this stuff, but someone played a bad joke on you. Believe me! Fifteen years ago, His Excellency Nikolai Rezanov arrived in Kodiak and then in Sitka, straight from Petropavlovsk in Kamchatka. He arrived with the circumnavigation expedition of Captain-Lieutenant von Krusenstern. That year was bad, and the whole Russian colony in Alaska was dying from hunger. For sure they would have had scurvy by winter. So His Excellency Chamberlain Rezanov and Alexander Baranov, the ruler of our Russian-American lands, decided to send Lieutenant-Captain Khvostov to California. They were given the order to bring as much bread as they could buy from the Spanish.

"The Spanish turned out to be very stubborn, and they didn't want to sell the bread. Khvostov was not a fool, and he seduced and kidnapped Conchita, the daughter of the commandant of the Presidio of San Francisco! The Spanish had no other way but to sell the bread and host an official wedding. Then, His Excellency Nikolai Rezanov, who at the time was the chairman of the board of directors of the Russian-American Company, made the order to come to terms with the local Indians and to buy their land from the Spanish border and north, toward our Alaska. His order was to turn those lands into our breadbasket. He left for St. Petersburg, where he still lives. God grant him a long life! I swear this to you! I was here in person with the Khvostov expedition! We carried out his orders to the letter, and you can see it for yourself! We built the fort as a stronghold on our southern border, and we are developing the lands. Why are you looking at me like that? I am still alive and sane, aren't I?"

Dmitry was a sorry sight in Kuskov's eyes. He could not believe his ears. Kuskov had not made up a single line of his story; he had told it as it had really happened. As he was talking, Kuskov had an expression of astonishment and curiosity as if he expected Dmitry to break into a smile and say he already knew all this, and yes, that's the way it was, is, and will be.

Dmitry couldn't breathe. He looked in Kuskov's eyes, stunned. He was about to open his mouth to ask Kuskov something again, but he never had the time. At that moment, the sky suddenly lit up with a myriad of lights. Just like all the defenders of the fort, Dmitry looked up. The hood slipped off his head to his shoulders. A gust of wind that appeared out of nowhere disheveled his long hair.

With all his effort, Dmitry was running toward his friends. No more than twenty feet separated him from the clearing. "This way! Faster, Margo! Help him!" Dmitry tried to yell above the noise of the battle while gasping for air. "Jeff, drop the friggin' backpack!"

Snatching his knapsack from his shoulder, Dmitry took out his iPhone and hurriedly pushed some buttons. He had already programmed their return date. One press of the button separated him from his familiar reality. *We'll make it,* Dmitry thought as he sized up the noticeably reducing distance between his friends and him. *We have to make it!*

He pressed the button and threw the phone on the grass in the direction of Margo and Jeff. Upon reaching the ground, the iPhone lit up with blue, pulsating light. Dmitry was the first one to jump into the circle lit with neon flashes. Seconds later, Margo threw herself into his arms. Jeff literally stumbled into the glowing portal with all his bags.

At that moment, a hissing sound sliced the air. A tomahawk flew like a lightning bolt through the smoke. Running savages emerged through the smoke as well. With a dull thud, the tomahawk embedded itself in the backpack hanging on one strap across Jeff's back. The long-suffering backpack, as if it couldn't withstand such abuse any longer, fell at Dmitry's and Margo's feet along with the tomahawk. However, the force of the impact threw Jeff out of the glowing circle and he sprawled on the ground about ten feet from the portal.

That second, Dmitry and Margo disappeared. Only a faint bluish light outlined the border of the portal.

Suddenly, a canister shell exploded directly behind the backs of the savages who had run into the clearing. Jeff lost his hearing for a second. The earth shuddered deep down and seemed to rise up. Everything was shrouded in black, acrid smoke. For a moment, everything that used to be on the ground was up in the air, and everything that went up came down, including chunks of soil with the remains of the uncut rye and torn body parts of the attackers.

Jeff was saved only by the fact that he hadn't had time to get up after his fall. He pressed his body to the ground, covered his head with his hands, and held his breath. He waited for the rain of dirt and human remains to stop. When the ground returned to horizontal, Jeff spat dust as he tried to get up slowly. He was still a little stunned, and he couldn't think straight about what had happened. He tried not to look at his feet. He knew the ground was littered with human remains. He was already nauseated as it was.

The surviving Indians who had earlier surrounded him were shocked at the fate of their comrades. They backed away in horror, then turned and ran.

Still shell-shocked, Jeff did not hear the sound of stamping hooves and hundreds of running feet. He saw Kashaya warriors skirting him on both sides in their chase of the savages. He also saw a dappled mustang galloping toward him at full speed. Song of the Stream was on its back.

At that moment, he allowed himself to lose consciousness.

CHAPTER 43

Present Time. Northern California.
At the Entrance to the Museum
of the Fort Ross State Historic Park.

The doors of their rented minivan slammed simultaneously. With a hand trembling from all the shock and excitement they had experienced, Dmitry stuck the key in the ignition. The engine roared to life. The radio, which had been left on at full volume, came on with a blast. Dmitry backed up sharply, honking furiously. He was angry at himself, angry at the tourists who were around, and angry at the whole world. Dmitry pulled up to the exit of the ill-fated parking lot of the Fort Ross museum. Some fat moron was insanely clicking his photo camera.

"Margo, can you turn that damn radio down a bit?" Dmitry winced. Only then did he notice the girl's shaking shoulders. She lifted her tear-stained face from the backpack and turned the radio down. She sniffled like a child.

"What are we going to do now, Dim?"

"What?" Dmitry shrugged his shoulders, trying to look calm and speak with confidence. "We'll recharge the iPhone, and I'll go back to get Jeff! Don't worry! Besides, I saw for sure that he fell on the ground *before* the explosion."

"I'm not worrying." Margo tried to pull herself together. "I think we can always get there like five minutes earlier, can't we? Tell me!"

"Theoretically, yes, it's possible," Dmitry sighed. He suddenly hit the steering wheel with his hand. "Shit! We left so many tracks there! That's what drives me nuts! I knew we should have left before the battle started!"

"Well, we tried, Dmitry," Margo said placatingly.

"We didn't try hard enough!" Dmitry failed to calm down. The thought he was releasing his anger and irritation on the innocent girl didn't help. Margo turned and stared out the window.

"It's all my fault! I wanted to ask Kuskov more about the company's connection at the court and about Rezanov, but he blurted out such things that—" Dmitry stopped and glanced at Margo, who was staring out the window thoughtfully.

"Why couldn't we just stay casual observers? Why do we always get in a fix?"

"What about me?" Margo asked suddenly without facing him. Dmitry didn't get what she meant.

"What do you mean you?"

Margo faced him. "What am I going to do while you . . . while you're back there?" Her green eyes looked questioningly at Dmitry.

"You? Well, you can wait for me at the hotel," Dmitry said hesitantly. "Have a drink, have a good meal. I'll be quick!" Dmitry glanced at his watch. "We spent days out there, but here, only a few hours have passed! I mean local time—"

Margo turned again to the window. They reached the hotel and sharply turned into the parking lot. Without a word, Dmitry and a completely upset Margo got out of the car and headed to the hotel entrance.

PART FOUR

The Relative Concept

What has been is what will be,
and what has been done is what will be done;
there is nothing new under the sun.

—Ecclesiastes 1:9

CHAPTER 44

1820. Russian California. Fort Ross. Early Morning.

Through the acrid black smoke, the outcome of the battle under the walls of Fort Ross had not yet been decided. Kuskov had given the order to fire not only with canister shells but also with incendiary rounds. The smoke and stench were beyond description. Kuskov secretly hoped the wild Indians would become scared at the very beginning of the battle and run away. Yet naked savages smeared with black paint moved like ants from a disturbed anthill. They ran like an avalanche to their imminent death.

This is the massacre of the innocents, Kuskov thought sadly as he was watching the battle from the wall of the Fort. *Although that depends. If we had not received such a timely warning, things could have turned out completely different. These savages are beyond counting!*

The artillery squadron under the command of Corporal Prokhor Zaborschikov alternated canister shells with incendiary rounds and skillfully delivered their fire across the front lines of the advancing enemy. Black smoke stung the eyes of the savages. Despite this, the first group of particularly nimble men began to climb the walls of the fortress with ropes and hooks. Unfortunately for the defenders, the wind began to blow the thick black smoke toward the fortress. The attackers noticed that too. The black paint covering their bodies made them impossible to distinguish through the thick smoke. They appeared from a curtain of smoke and disappeared into it again like ghosts. In this situation, the bows and arrows of the Kashaya and the Aleut defenders as well as the rifles used by the small garrison became useless. The defenders started to prepare for hand-to-hand combat.

The outcome of the battle was inevitable nonetheless. After the artillery shelling, the scattered and disoriented savages didn't pose a serious threat.

Kuskov turned. Inside the fortress and in front of the closed gates, a horse detachment of Kashaya warriors stood still, awaiting the command. Kuskov could feel the pleading, impatient eyes of his corporal boring into the back of his head. Kuskov turned to face Zaborschikov.

"Well, Prokhor, you may release your hussars!" Kuskov chuckled. "It's time!"

Kuskov had barely finished his phrase before Prokhor raced to the gate with a drawn sword. He shouted orders on the go. The heavy fortress gates swung open, and an equestrian avalanche of Kashaya Indians darted off toward the foot-borne attackers with a terrifying battle cry.

This battle is over, Kuskov thought sadly. *I only wish we could have saved the bread plants.* He slowly descended the stairs to get off the wall.

Zavalishin's detachment of guard-de-marines who had gone to intercept the pirates at Rumyantsev Bay had started the final stage of their military operation. With their clothes off, their hands and feet tied, and their mouths gagged, the pirates were left to lie like sacks of potatoes on the pebble beach by the water. Disguised by the clothes lifted off the pirates, Russian guard-de-marines were approaching the schooner in three rowboats. The boatswain, in one of the boats, sat at its nose and stared morosely at the approaching hulk of his schooner. His hands were untied, but Zavalishin's marine dirk pressed into the boatswain's side was causing him great inconvenience. Nakhimov sat on the boatswain's other side.

"Remember," Zavalishin leaned over and spoke quietly into the boatswain's ear, "if something goes wrong, you'll be feeding sharks with your own guts in no time! Get up!"

Despite the years spent at sea, the boatswain could swim only as well as a stone. He of course was not going to inform the Russian about that. He groaned as he got to his feet, and he waved to the watch keeper. "All hands on deck! The damned Russians beat the shit out of the red asses! They're after us now!"

The sound of running feet could instantly be heard on the schooner's deck. The captain appeared on deck. In his customary manner, he opened his mouth to spit curses, but he suddenly remembered he had an articulation problem due to his missing teeth. With an animal roar, he yanked the guns from his belt and aimed them at the unfortunate boatswain. That was when he noticed Zavalishin.

"Who the hell is with you?"

"That's one of the Russians! A captive! We took him for ransom!"

A rope ladder was thrown down from the schooner. There was the sound of the anchor chain lifting. The rowboats turned sideways and gently touched against the schooner's hull. Zavalishin, pretending his hands were tied, went to the ladder first. He was followed by the boatswain and Nakhimov, who was the one at that point pressing the dirk against the boatswain's back.

The captain bent to get Zavalishin onboard as he kept yelling orders with his body half-turned.

"Hoist the sails! All of them!"

"Too late!" Zavalishin said as he jumped on deck.

The captain turned sharply to him. "What?"

The lieutenant inched toward the captain and barked into his face as if the pirate were deaf. "I said, too late!"

With these words, the brave lieutenant struck the captain violently on the captain's already aching jaw. Nakhimov knocked the boatswain off the rope ladder, and he fell into the ocean, shrieking wildly. Russian guard-de-marines started to climb the schooner, guns and blades in hand.

The fight didn't last long. In fact, there was no fight. In less than a minute, the remaining pirates along with their captain were face-down on deck and hands tied behind their backs. A moment later, the coastal waters of Russian America resounded with a unanimous trifecta of "hurray!"

Dmitry appeared in front of the wide-open gates of the empty fort. He had heard the cannon shots. The yelling of people indicated that the fight had turned into hand-to-hand combat a distance from the fortress.

Dmitry crouched as he ran to the spot from which they had teleported not long before. He wore his familiar monk's habit and held the iPhone. *Look at all this smoke,* Dmitry thought while trying to use his sleeve as a smokescreen. *You wouldn't recognize friend from foe in this!*

The wind that had stubbornly carried clouds of smoke toward the fort changed direction briefly as if it had heard Dmitry's complaint. As a photo emerges on a piece of paper in a bath of developing chemicals, the battlefield slowly took shape before his eyes.

Far ahead, Dmitry saw Prokhor Zaborschikov with his sword raised high, yelling something as he ran. A motley crew of fortress defenders, some with rifles and others with spears, followed him. Dmitry saw Kashaya warriors gallop across the field in different directions.

It seems they've already started to clean up, Dmitry thought not without satisfaction. Still bent to the ground, he tried to be inconspicuous. In short dashes, he kept getting closer to the right spot. The clearing to which he was headed appeared not far ahead, but Jeff was nowhere to be seen. Dmitry froze. His heart beat in his throat like a booming warning bell. He could see nothing but the smoke that had started to dissipate and the endless ocean ahead.

Breathing heavily, Dmitry looked around. *Just don't panic,* he said to himself several times. He stood straight and shielded his eyes with his hand to get a better look. Dmitry looked carefully, then he chuckled happily. Through the dissipating smoke, he saw Jeff, alive and safe, being led like a battle hero toward the fortress. His legs wobbled a bit; that was why he was supported by Prokhor Zaborschikov on one side and by a very pleased Song of the Stream on the other. Jeff had an absolutely blissful smile on his face. He didn't waste any time and held the Indian girl around her waist while whispering something in her ear. Armed Indian warriors walked by their sides and behind them.

See, Jeff? All good things come in good time! Dmitry thought and smiled. A heavy weight had been lifted from his shoulders. This was one of the rare minutes some call pure happiness. Dmitry felt the urge to run to them. He even started to move, but on impulse, he changed his mind. While still on the run, he stretched out his arm with the iPhone and pressed that treasured button.

CHAPTER 45

Present Time. Northern California.
A Hotel near the Fort Ross State Historic Park.

Margo stood in the shower, letting water caress her face. Until then, she didn't know a person could miss such a simple convenience so much. She leaned her head back and almost physically felt the thin and prickly water sprays carry away her accumulated fatigue and troubles of the past several days. *Has it really been days? We were there for days and here, only a few hours have passed. It's so weird!*

She had been so caught up in the rapid pace of the recent breathtaking events that she hadn't had time to reflect on and address everything that had happened to her. A belated assessment of the events started. She felt her life had changed direction and had acquired a new dimension.

Direction! My life just got a new meaning, a new value! Just the other day, she had had it all planned out, but everything had changed so dramatically. Because of her passion for martial arts, Margo was fond of Eastern philosophies. She *knew* life existed only in the current moment, this particular second. Yet before that day, this knowledge was somehow dormant in her. Now she had absorbed this wisdom with all her heart. Something that had seemed to her an abstract idea before had become an indisputable truth in the last few days or hours.

Margo remembered a phrase from a book on esoteric practices that had argued the possibility of predicting the future. She could not remember the exact phrase, but its meaning was something like the following: one who possesses a gift or special skills can only see the past. The present appears to a person the way he or she imagines it to be. The future—this is true only for the enlightened ones—appears as a pulsating mist the outlines of which are uncertain, vague, mystical, and ambiguous. Margo finally understood the meaning of these words. *Of course! How could it be otherwise when the future changes continuously and we are the main cause of it! The future is woven of countless knots or intersections of a person's own choices. Every second, consciously or not, a person chooses and ties the threads of fate into new knots, thus weaving the fabric of his or her universe.*

Interesting, Margo thought suddenly. *No wonder the Moirai, the three Fates of Greek mythology, have always been pictured with a spindle. They controlled the metaphorical thread of life of every mortal from birth to death. I will definitely have to discuss this with Dmitry.*

The thought about Dmitry brought her back to reality from the depths of philosophical reflections. She turned off the water and opened her eyes. She had trained herself not to pay attention to bruises and scratches, but those she had reminded her of their existence. Her broken lip was swollen. It didn't make her look bad; rather, the opposite. The swelling gave her lips sex appeal, Margo decided. *Yet it's still not good. This scratch on my cheek will most definitely turn into a good bruise.* Yet in general, she had managed to get off with nothing more than a fright. *It could've been worse,* Margo logically concluded. She touched her hips. *Dmitry—*

Somehow, she could not quite comprehend to the full extent that part of her extraordinary adventure. She always considered him interesting, and somewhere deep inside her heart, she knew he liked her. She just didn't know what to do with this knowledge. To be exact, when she participated in innocent flirting as if it were a game, she allowed the events to unfold freely without trying to control them or pushing the situation. There had never been a need for that! They saw each other practically every day. All this time, she was in a state of anxious waiting, and at the same time, she felt a joyful thrill of romantic uncertainty.

Sometimes at night, especially when they were on field trips, she had trouble falling asleep when he was in the next hotel room. Yet she enjoyed the beauty of anticipation. Then things started to happen fast!

Margo giggled as she looked at her reflection in the mirror. The unnerved expression on her face seemed funny even to her. Nevertheless, she liked the way she looked. In the mirror, she saw a beauty, maybe not in the classic sense of the word, but she considered herself quite a gorgeous girl by modern standards. She had long legs and was well built, like a model on the cover of *Sports Illustrated*'s swimsuit issue. Tiny drops of water glistened on her flat stomach. A golden California tan looked really good on her.

Through the opened bathroom door she could see the white sheets on the untouched hotel bed. Her robe, shorts, and tank top lay in a heap on the bed. Margo wrapped herself in a towel, and crooning "Hotel California," she stepped into the room.

Dmitry burst into the hotel room from the time portal still on the move. He almost knocked Margo off her feet. She screamed. Though, it had all happened so fast, in just a fraction of a second, that she didn't have time to get really frightened. Dmitry happily beamed at her.

"Jeff is all right!" He breathed out prepared phrase, although this was not necessary, judging by his happy face.

Then he saw Margo in only a towel, and froze. His confused expression instantly changed into one of admiration. His eyes got that very special expression like the one they had had the other day on the balcony, when Margo realized for the first time he was not only interested in her but also seemed to desire her. And very much.

Margo didn't say a word. Instead in one smooth motion she undid the knot and dropped the towel on the floor.

Margo stretched as she got comfortable on Dmitry's shoulder and pressed her body to his. "Dim, what really happened there? What happened to Jeff? Why did you come back alone? Nothing bad happened to him, right?"

Dmitry blissfully stretched out on his back. With one arm, he pressed Margo tenderly to him, and his other arm was under his head.

"Of course it hasn't. Everything's fine. You know, I think he's better than fine! I believe that he's found his happiness and that going back to reality is the last thing he'd want right now." Dmitry contemplated his answer. He turned so he could see Margo's eyes. Their lips almost touched.

"This is all so strange," Dmitry whispered. "Just recently, it seems I didn't even know you, and now . . . I can't imagine my life without you. It happened so unexpectedly!"

"Why do you say *unexpectedly*?" Margo smiled. "It took us a hundred and ninety-four years to get to know each other!"

Dmitry laughed happily. They locked their lips in a passionate kiss.

After they had enjoyed each other again, Margo sat on the bed in a lotus pose, wrapped in the sheet. She turned to Dmitry. "So now what?" She asked the question that hung in the air. "To tell you the truth, it's strange for me to think about my past. You know, don't call me pathetic, but I somehow feel responsible for all our people there."

Dmitry looked at her with a smile. "You know, I think about it all the time too! I can't think about anything else."

Without a word, both looked at the iPhone on the bedside table. The green indicator light of the completely charged battery seemed to beckon them. Margo and Dmitry's eyes met. The burst into happy laughter and fell on the pillows.

"So what did you talk about with Zavalishin?" Margo inquired curiously as she got comfortable on his shoulder. "I was spying on you. You were so excited!"

Without an answer, Dmitry carefully freed his arm from under her head. He gave her a tender kiss on the nose, got up, and wrapped a towel around his hips. He walked to the balcony door, lit a cigarette, and took a drag on it with evident satisfaction. "You know, the conversation with him gave me a new idea! Check it out. We're in the twentieth year of the nineteenth century . . . I meant to, in *that* time—" Dmitry seemed to be confused for a second.

"Just go on!" Margo smiled to him. "I myself don't understand what time I belong to anymore." She got more comfortable in bed, just like a little girl getting ready to listen to an interesting fairy tale. Her eyes twinkled with happiness.

"Well, that's what I've been saying," Dmitry continued, returning Margo's smile, "the year 1820. In the following years, Spain will lose vast expanses in Central and South Americas, and numerous small countries will be formed in its place. The pressure on the Russian border in California will weaken since the Spanish will have their hands full with their own problems. So I thought it might be a perfect moment for Fort Ross and Russian America in general to firm up! Yet as we know, that didn't happen in our time continuum for some reason. Thus, when

I talked with Zavalishin, I recalled Kuskov's complaints about the lack of working hands, and suddenly it dawned on me! The Decembrists' revolt would happen five years later! Only, unlike in our reality, it has to be successful!"

"What does the Decembrists' revolt have to do with Russian America?" Margo stared at Dmitry with surprise.

"Don't you see it?" Every time when the Decembrists were the subject of conversation, Dmitry got very anxious. "If the revolt will be successful, serfdom will fall and millions of working hands will be freed up!"

"So?" Margo still didn't understand him or pretended she didn't.

"So the Russian-American Company will finally have a workforce for its foreign dominion!"

Margo paused to ponder. Thanks to her questions, Dmitry also withdrew into his thoughts. He sat in a chair and lit another cigarette as he stared blankly, trying to grasp a thought that ran through his head. He didn't manage to come up with anything, so he slapped his knees and got up.

"Well, in short, based on what I've just said, I decided to visit St. Petersburg on the eve of the revolt and find out why it has failed." Dmitry paused and gazed at Margo. He still could not make up his mind whether to tell her about what Kuskov had told him about Rezanov during the attack. He didn't have any reason to keep it from Margo; he simply had a feeling he was on the verge of an important discovery that was close but still elusive.

"Though I believe I'll have to postpone the implementation of my idea." Dmitry had made up his mind. He gave Margo a meaningful look.

"Postpone?" the girl echoed without thinking.

She got out of bed, put her shorts and tank top on, and sat by Dmitry, ready to listen. Dmitry was deep in thought. He watched cigarette smoke floating in a bluish wisp out the balcony door.

"I have no idea how to tell you this." He started very cautiously. "The thing is that Kuskov told me that Nikolai Rezanov, the chamberlain and the winner of the heart of beautiful Conchita, had never been to California."

"What do you mean, Dim?" Margo stared at him in surprise.

"I mean what I just said." Dmitry nervously chuckled. He stood in a pose of a tragic actor and recited, "Nikolai Rezanov, the minister of commerce, is perfectly alive and well, and he lives in the capital city of St. Petersburg. As for Donna Maria de Arguello, or 'Conchita,' the heroine of Bret Harte's and Andrey Voznesensky's poems, who became, by the way, Khvostov's wife, lived with him, as befits a good wife, in Petropavlovsk in Kamchatka. Khvostov, former captain-lieutenant of the ship *Juno*, is a very successful governor of the aforesaid city."

"Now, on a serious note," Dmitry switched to his usual tone of voice, "what I am saying is this. In the reality we just visited, Rezanov has *never* been to California. However, what's interesting is that *that* reality had an undeniable analogy to ours. The story of extraction of bread from Spaniards and the seduction of the commandant's daughter repeated exactly as we know it but . . . with different actors!"

CHAPTER 46

Present Time. Northern California.
A Hotel near the Fort Ross State Historic Park.
Half an Hour Ago.

When Margo and Dmitry, upset and shocked by the events at the fort, left their van in the parking lot and disappeared through the hotel doorway, a dark blue Ford with tinted windows rolled smoothly into the parking lot. The wheels softly crunched pebbles. The Ford parked next to the minivan. The invisible driver turned the engine off. It took a good half hour before the driver's door opened.

The same young man with a buzz cut, the hotel guest in the room next to Dmitry's who later became such an avid but secret helper of the three friends, stepped out of the car. This time, Fourteen was dressed in usual jeans and a T-shirt. He purposely slammed the door loudly and headed to the entrance. Then, looking like he changed his mind he stopped and remained outside. He took the car key fob out of his pocket and pressed a button on it. The Ford blinked its front lights and obediently locked itself up. The young man waited for a while and pressed the button again. Then again. No one noticed his strange manipulations; the parking lot was empty. The day was in full swing; there were countless sights to see, and if any guests remained in their rooms, they were rushing to get out as quickly as they could to enjoy the Californian sun and explore the surroundings. In any case, nobody paid any attention to the young man or his tricks.

Fourteen waited a while. When he was sure nobody had noticed him, he put the key in his pocket and briskly walked back to the car. Not his car though. He approached the rented Toyota and took a penknife out of his pocket. He played for a second or two with the lock, opened it, and entered the van. The Toyota's alarm wailed indignantly.

At that point, even if there had been the proverbial bystander nearby, he or she would most likely have felt sorry for the guy and his efforts to calm his rebellious machine. Fourteen somehow managed to silence the alarm. The parking lot was once again quiet.

It was also unclear which car the guy had gotten into, since no one exited the van, not in a minute, not even in an hour or two. No bystander would have had the patience to wait that long. Too bad, for any bystander would have discovered something strange: the van was empty. The man had gone away without opening a door.

CHAPTER 47

Present Time. Northern California.
A Hotel near the Fort Ross State Historic Park.

Margo lit a cigarette. "So what does it all mean?" she asked.

"Well, to tell you the truth, I didn't get it myself!" Dmitry combed his hair with his hand as if trying to keep his thoughts from running away. "To be honest with you, my head is spinning! It could be that the anomaly gives us the chance to see not quite the development of famous historical events but deviations from them. What do you think?"

"What if the anomaly picked us to *correct* this 'deviation'?" Margo frowned.

"You just don't get it, Margo! Imagine for a moment how our history would have developed if we accept the fact Rezanov hadn't died but, as Kuskov said, had become the minister of commerce in Russia! Can you imagine that? This means that the expansion of Russia to the East, as well as annexation of California, could become a reality!"

"What about love?" Margo inquired hesitantly and in a low voice.

"To hell with love! As the French say, 'Behind every misfortune there is a woman!'"

Before he even finished his phrase, Dmitry realized he had made a mistake. Margo got up wordlessly and stepped onto the balcony. Dmitry didn't know how to fix the situation, so he followed her. They stood on the balcony for a while, each thinking private thoughts.

Margo turned to Dmitry. "Okay, let's assume it could be so," she said calmly. "Then what if the anomaly sent us into that very time so we could make corrections and give the events the direction similar to *our* reality? What do you think? So that we could change events in such a way that Rezanov would be able to come to California and meet Conchita! Then what? Have you thought about that?" Her green eyes stared at Dmitry. "By the way, boss, have you by any chance ever heard the phrase, 'Love will save the world'? Even though it wouldn't be sophisticated enough for you because it wasn't said in French, it was said much earlier than your phrase was. Maybe it even appeared at the time humankind was born, though I'm afraid *man*kind never got the true meaning of it!"

Margo defiantly ground out her cigarette in the ashtray, signaling their conversation was over. She walked to the bathroom. Dmitry was taken aback. He had to admit the girl's words had logic. That meant he had to make a choice. *If you ride to the left, you will lose your horse,* Dmitry sneered inwardly. *If you ride to the right, you will lose your life.'* The situation started to remind him of a puzzle or a chess problem in which real nations rather than pawns and knights were pushed around the board.

It's hard to be a God. He remembered the title of his favorite Russian sci-fi novella by Strugatskys brothers and got lost in his thoughts. *Okay, let's start from the beginning. Rezanov joined Krusenstern on the first Russian circumnavigation. Why? This one's easy. Because his*

Russian-American Company sponsored the expedition, and Rezanov himself would have easily been its secret initiator. The company needed a sea lane between St. Petersburg and America. What's next? By then, Rezanov was the royal chamberlain. Not bad for a provincial nobleman. Besides, all the company's activity and all its prosperity rested on him, or more precisely, on his connections at the court. At the same time, the emperor entrusted him with a secret diplomatic mission to Japan, a country that was then closed to the rest of the world.

If that mission would succeed, Rezanov's career would skyrocket; in case of failure, he probably would have needed an alternative.

Now, as it is known, Rezanov's mission to Japan failed, so he immediately hurried to Alaska, to his lands, so to speak. Of course he would later need California, but he, being a statesman, most probably wouldn't have gone there in person! It's unlikely he would make such a move without the emperor's mandate, for such actions could complicate the already-difficult Russian-Spanish relations.

However, in our history, he did visit California! So there must have been a reason for him to go there. I wonder what made him do it?

Dmitry rubbed his forehead. The riddle turned out to be not as easy as it had initially appeared. The main thing, which was scary, was that there were numerous variants of consequences that were impossible to calculate or foretell.

Okay, Dmitry sighed. *Take a pause for the cause or your safeguards will burn out!*

Still, a certain thought was close to the surface of his mind, but he just couldn't catch it. Suddenly it dawned on him! The solution he had been looking for had been right in front of his nose! *It's not important how it happened! The important thing is to not interfere with the flow of events no matter what!* Dmitry started to sweat when he imagined for a moment what could've happen if he hadn't found the solution.

"Of course! Let the history of Russia in that time flow develop with Rezanov alive! Russia needed him alive more. Here was a great chance to turn the tables on the history! An awesome chance to turn the tables! Dmitry even giggled, he was so happy with his word play. "It turns out that to help history, it's better to just step aside and watch things happen. Okay, I will step aside. Just to think what great possibilities would open for Russia! It also means that my conversation with Zavalishin and his report about the state of affairs in California could actually bring results in this time flow! Whoa!" Dmitry became breathless with excitement.

He had been so immersed in his thoughts that he hadn't noticed he had been talking out loud. But that way, it was easier for him to stick to the thread of logic that kept trying to evade him. Besides, there was no one to interrupt or bother him. Margo was in the bathroom, drying her hair. Behind the wall, however, either a TV was on or someone was talking loudly.

"I will not be able to explain all this to Margo right now, and I should definitely distract her attention!" Dmitry reasoned on the go. The recollection of Zavalishin had reminded him of their conversation around the campfire and also about the Decembrists.

"Moreover, we also have something to do! We need to check the other time line of our history. This one, for sure has to do something with our time flow or, more precisely, we have something to do with it!"

Since the solution to the problem had been found, Dmitry's mood improved greatly. He walked into the room from the balcony. The door to the bathroom was open. "Margo," Dmitry called. He walked to her and gently hugged her from behind. "Let's go to my room. I need to check something on the computer."

Even though she was still very upset, Margo packed her beauty bag and silently followed Dmitry.

As he opened the door to his room, Dmitry immediately walked to his notebook. He turned it on and became completely immersed in work. Margo lingered by the wardrobe in the hall, carefully studying her reflection in the mirror.

Suddenly, a car alarm wailed in the parking lot, but it quickly went silent.

On impulse, Dmitry whistled softly, keeping his eyes on the computer. "Margo, do you know how many books, essays, and other literary garbage have been published on the history of the Decembrists' uprising starting from the end of the nineteenth century?"

"How many?" Margo asked. She leaned toward the mirror to put lipstick on her swollen lips.

"More than seven hundred!" Dmitry exclaimed with much excitement, as if he has just discovered the universal law of gravity.

"So?" Margo puckered her lips to check her work.

"So I think," Dmitry continued, unfazed by the fact that his audience's attention was elsewhere, "if the historians repeatedly came back to this event, something about it must've nagged them. That means that not all the answers to their questions have been found!"

Margo finished beautifying her lips. She took tweezers out of her bag and started plucking her eyebrows. That car alarm wailed outside again.

"So what do you think, huh?" Dmitry continued his research. "What kind of a dork is playing with the car alarm out there?" Dmitry leaned back in his chair and turned to Margo, who was focused on applying eyeliner. Dmitry was carried away with the sight. He felt a rush of tenderness toward her. *She's wonderful!* He knew rather well the cause of her expectant and somewhat sulky silence.

"Margo, I need to figure it all out. It's a crime not to use the opportunity we have!"

The clinking of various bottles, tubes, and other makeup in Margo's beauty bag got louder.

"I have to go to the Senate Square on December fourteen, 1825! Do you understand? I have to figure out what happened there and maybe adjust something if I can! Also," Dmitry had trouble finding the right words, "we can't risk it anymore. I'll travel alone. I'll be quick! I'll go there and be back in no time, I promise!"

Without a word, Margo finished her makeup session and stepped into the closet. "Do you know where our long-suffering backpack is?" Margo suddenly asked as if nothing had happened. Her voice was muffled by the huge interior of the closet. "The one with the tomahawk in it. Have you seen it, boss?"

The word *boss* unpleasantly grated on his ears. *She's still upset!* Dmitry felt sad. "It should be in the closet," he said as he walked to her. "Look for it thoroughly."

"That's exactly what I'm doing! It's not here." Margo looked around the closet while deep in thought. Dmitry hugged her from behind. He didn't want to think about the stupid backpack. The only thing he wanted at the moment was for this woman, who had become so close to him and who filled his heart completely, to stop sulking and not be upset anymore.

Margo tensed but didn't rush to get out of his arms.

"Forget it, Margo!" Dmitry said as he tried to make peace. "Maybe we left it in the van."

Margo turned and buried her face in his chest. "Yes, you're right. I left it there. All the SD cards and camera are in it! Everything we shot *there.*"

"So what? They're not going anywhere." Dmitry tried to calm her down. "Why do you need them now?"

"I just wanted to download all the material to the computer, while . . . while you're away."

Dmitry took her face in his hands and carefully lifted it. Her green eyes looked at him in a serious, focused manner. Not being able to restrain himself, Dmitry smiled happily and gave her a tender kiss on the lips.

"Don't you worry about me. I'll be careful! What's the most important thing in our business?" Dmitry tried to cheer her up. "Correct! To keep the iPhone charged!"

Margo managed a smile. "I bet the backpack stayed in the van!"

Encouraged by her tacit consent, Dmitry was pleased, and he cooed while holding her in his arms, "I left the keys on the bedside table for you. But first," Dmitry gave a conspirators wink to a guarded Margo, "we will go someplace together! Not too far. Just some hundred and eighty years into the past."

Margo could hardly keep from jumping with happiness.

CHAPTER 48

Present Time. Moscow. Lubyanka Square.
Federal Agency of Space-Time Security.

Comfortably ensconced in plush chairs in the small viewing room, Lieutenant-Colonel Daria Shuranova stared absentmindedly at the screen while listening to Fourteen's report. On screen, Margo was performing her dizzying dragon dance before the awestruck Indians.

"It is evident," Fourteen continued, "that the client has a device that helps him generate a time vortex. It has nothing to do with our own Space-Time Portal Generator. The anomalistic abilities of this device have been discovered by mere chance. The client is clearly experimenting, and he is completely unaware of the possible consequences of such experiments."

"Did you get a chance to witness the actual 'jump'?" Daria interrupted him without taking her eyes off the screen.

"I was not able to see the actual jump." Fourteen blushed slightly. "However, I had learned that the device generates a force field strong enough to give a 'jump' to at least three people and their luggage. According to the client, the total weight of all the material items cannot be more than the weight of the organic carrier. In other words, only the things the client and his fellow travelers can carry are able to go through the portal."

"Got it. The video camera is a clear example, but what if they decide to take something else? Say, modern guns? Can you, Fourteen, even for a second imagine the consequences of such actions?"

"Yes, Lieutenant-Colonel! There's definitely a risk, but—" Fourteen paused.

"But what? Continue, Fourteen!"

"You see," the agent continued with hesitation, "the client and his fellow travelers surprisingly feel a great responsibility for what happened to them. I would even say they see this time travel as a mission."

Daria took her eyes off the screen when Dmitry smiled into the camera as Fourteen finalized his report. She turned to look at the agent. "Fourteen, there's only one step between a mission and a messiah!" She adjusted her glasses. "Besides, as one of your acquaintances from the century our department works on said, 'In history, we hear a host of examples.'"

Daria pressed the button on the remote to turn the video player off. She rose. The light came on automatically in the small but comfortably furnished room. The agent was on his feet a bit ahead of her.

"Quite right, Lieutenant-Colonel, but our greatest fabulist, Ivan Krylov, also says, I mean said, in this fable, 'But we don't write history!' We, on the other hand, if you allow me to note it, are doing just the opposite!"

Daria poured Perrier into her glass, put the bottle on the silver tray, and turned to the agent. "I was not aware of your literary abilities, Fourteen," she said with a little sneer. She checked the agent with an interest as if she had just met him. His eyes gleamed. His cheeks blushed. It was unclear to Daria why he had blushed, though. *It's probably too stuffy in here.* "Well, continue!" she encouraged the young man.

"By a surprising coincidence," Fourteen continued readily, "the activity those travelers perform are almost identical to our department's strategy at that time span. Most probably it's explained by the fact the client is well read in this historical period."

"Fourteen, what did you mean by 'almost identical'?"

The young man chuckled slightly as he searched for the right words. "You see, Lieutenant-Colonel, according to what I have heard from Dmitry, that's the name of the leader of those travelers and the owner of the Space-Time Portal Generator, they might react unpredictably to our temporary correction of Rezanov's case."

"What do you mean by 'unpredictably', Fourteen?" Daria's voice rang with inner tension.

"The thing is, they are under the romantic influence of the legend about the love of Count Rezanov and beautiful Conchita."

"Why do you say 'count'? He never was a count." The young woman had asked that purely out of reflex; it was clear she was thinking about something else.

Regardless, Fourteen considered it his duty to explain it to her. "According to a poetic legend—"

"Oh yes, I know. The poets made him a count." The lieutenant-colonel nodded. "So what is your plan of further action?"

"I have an idea, Lieutenant-Colonel! I think that Article 4 of our organization charter is quite applicable to the client."

Daria turned to the table with the Perrier, poured some into a fresh glass, and walked to Fourteen with it. The young man took the glass and nodded in gratitude in a military style.

"Drink, drink," Daria said. She took a small sip from her glass as well. "It seems too hot in here."

The young man drank his water in one gulp with great thirst. He evidently felt rather warm.

Daria ended the interlude. "Well, your code number allows you to recruit. Just make sure to get an approval from Colonel Sinitsyn. Until then, before the decision is made, the client is your personal responsibility. Do you understand me, Fourteen?"

"Yes, Lieutenant-Colonel!" the young man responded cheerfully. "May I be dismissed?"

"Yes you may," Daria answered as she turned. The agent clicked his bootheels sharply and nodded to her back. He spun and marched to the door. It was evident he was bursting with joy. When the door closed, Daria allowed herself to relax. She plopped down on the plush couch, kicked her shoes off, and put her feet on the chair in front of her.

"Kindergarten!" the young woman said out loud. She pressed the button on the remote, dimmed the lights, and closed her eyes.

CHAPTER 49

1825, December 13. St. Petersburg.
The Office of the Russian-American Company.
The Day before the Decembrists' Uprising.

When Ryleyev saw his guest off by walking him to the door, the members of the board of directors of the Russian-American Company were long gone. Sinitsyn's and Ryleyev's footsteps echoed in the empty halls of the company's building. Their good-byes also felt completely different from the greetings earlier. At that point, Ryleyev was absolutely calm, despite his pale face and sad eyes. His guest, on the other hand, looked very emotional. He took his expensive coat with fur lining and his gloves, and he turned to face Ryleyev again.

"In a sense I envy you, Mister Ryleyev! Not everybody gets to end his life the way you would. You would be forever written in the history of Russia as its true son and a real hero! It doesn't matter that in a different perspective . . . Never mind. Trust me, if the military branch of your organization will come to power—" Sinitsyn made a meaningful pause as he looked Ryleyev in the eyes. The other man only sighed deeply in reply.

"I understand. I always hoped we would be able to hold them!"

"You might have," Sinitsyn suddenly agreed. "I actually *believe* that you and your company would've been able to!" Sinitsyn specifically stressed the word *believe*.

"Yet the risk is too high, Mister Ryleyev. When we leave a chance to turn things in an unplanned way, history never misses an opportunity to take advantage of that. The next hundred years will be full of great ideas with bad implementation and, respectively, with catastrophic consequences! Just trust my word on that! Though, as you see, we try to do something about it. As for your specific case tomorrow, I have already told you everything about it. If *Messieurs* Trubetskoy, Pestel, and the others will succeed with their crazy scheme, then Russia, as we know it will cease to exist in ten years. You can be absolutely sure of that, for we've checked it out.

"By the way, something similar will happen at the beginning of the next, twentieth, century. The aftermath will be similarly catastrophic. So, Mister Ryleyev, tomorrow is the one of the crossroads of history, and you are the one to lead its course! The final decision is still yours, but . . . I hope—"

"Of course," Ryleyev looked as if he had just come out of hibernation, "rest assured that tomorrow's revolt . . . won't happen!"

A visibly satisfied Sinitsyn put his hat and gloves on and suddenly stood at attention, saluting Ryleyev in a military manner. "Sir, to the end of my days, I will cherish these several hours I was so lucky to have spent in your presence!" *That sounded rather melodramatic, but it was sincere,* Sinitsyn reflected sadly.

Ryleyev's big, gray eyes looked at him questioningly and even with surprise. Without another word, Sinitsyn turned and stepped into the street.

Ryleyev was not in a rush to close the door behind his visitor. Frosty air pleasantly cooled his hot forehead. Cannon shots sounded from the Peter and Paul fortress. *It's 3 p.m.,* Ryleyev thought instinctively. *This is one never-ending day!*

The snowing had stopped. The wind that picked up from the Nevsky Bay was sweeping the pavement diligently. For a long while, Ryleyev stared after his strange guest who had pulled his hat over his eyes and had wrapped his coat tightly around him. He walked across the Blue Bridge toward Senate Square.

CHAPTER 50

1820. Russian California.
On the Road near Fort Ross.

A very colorful group of riders appeared on the road that stretched from Fort Ross to the south, toward the border of Spanish California. Dmitry and Margo led their horses by their bridles while Jeff rode a chestnut mustang. The horse was stocky, and he rode bareback in Indian manner; his long legs almost reached the ground.

The friends evidently made fun of something. Judging by Jeff's shy smile, he was the butt of their jokes as always. Jeff was dressed in Indian attire from head to toe. He wore a light yellow pair of pants made of fine deerskin decorated with fringe. The breastplate armor was artfully composed of bones and stones of different colors. His head was adorned with a whole structure of feathers, which fell onto his back in two ribboned tails also decorated with feathers. Due to the galloping change of recent events, Jeff had noticeably lost weight. His paunch had disappeared without a trace. His lightly tanned skin and Jewish facial features made him practically indistinguishable from the native sons of the American land.

A group of Indian riders in full warpaint led by Song of the Stream followed the three friends from a distance. Far away, Fort Ross was still visible on its cliff.

"You wouldn't change your mind now, would you?" Dmitry asked Jeff with a smile, evidently continuing their conversation. "What if after a couple of years you want to get back to civilization. Then what?"

"No, Dim, I wouldn't want to go back," Jeff answered quite seriously. "I am here . . . how should I put it . . . I want to live and die here!"

"No way, Jeff. They won't let you die so easily!" Margo turned the seriousness of the moment into another of her jokes. "It wouldn't be easy with such a guard!"

All three involuntary turned to look at the Indians and Song of the Stream, who kept their escort at a polite distance to allow the friends to say their goodbyes in private. Admittedly, she looked spectacular—a real Indian warrior princess. When she noticed the friends turned to look at her, she waved.

"Seems like you might die only of sexual exhaustion!" Margo could not help joking. All three friends laughed.

"C'mon, Margo!" Jeff dismissed her with a gesture. "I'm serious. Only now have I understood the real meaning of the proverb 'a time for everything'! I have found *my* time!"

Everyone becomes quiet. The three friends walked in silence, deep in thought. Vineyards occupied one side of the winding road, and peach orchards the other. As usual, the cicadas screeched loudly. On Sundays the road was practically deserted. Most of the population of Russian America had gathered at the fort's chapel and for a traditional market day.

"What about you two? What's next?" Jeff ended the silent pause in their conversation.

"I have couple of ideas," Dmitry replied after he and Margo gave each other quick glances. "You know, all my life I was fond of history, and all my life I thought if only I could get to some particular moments of it. Now when it's possible, how can I simply refuse such a chance to travel in time?"

"Dim, are you back to your idea about Great Russia with Russian America?" Margo said. "Can someone explain to me why Russia needs so much land? Why do you keep dreaming about conquering America? Isn't it better to make something out of what you already have?"

"Well, maybe you're right! But . . . I don't know." Dmitry nodded to her with a smile. "The America we experienced here had never happened in our reality. What caused it? I don't know, maybe it's us who already altered the flow of history, but don't you agree it's a good alteration? Don't you agree it's gorgeous here? America the beautiful indeed! I'm dying to see the variant flourish to its full potential! By the way, I want you to note, guys, that we didn't change anything! We just created an alternative reality!"

"Listen. What if you can make corrections in American history too?" All of a sudden Jeff got excited. "So that we whites wouldn't be such assholes toward Native Americans!"

"Look at him! He's already thinking like a great chief! Hey, Crazy Horse, try to stay safe!" Margo laughed, but her laugh didn't sound relaxed. Everybody understood that the future of Jeff's new family was not certain, though it seemed joyful to say the least.

"C'mon, guys," Dmitry replied with a conciliatory smile. "To be fair, we need to admit that atrocities were committed not only by whites, or Europeans. I think, such behavior is in human blood. We are all Cain's descendants!" Dmitry stopped walking and patted Jeff on his knee in a friendly manner. "But you're right, and I'm sure you'll become the Great Chief Jeef!"

They all laughed again. Jeff turned to his escort.

"Maybe you'd still change your mind?" Dmitry said uncertainly to end their prolonged farewell. Jeff faced his friend with a smile.

"For what? Go to work tomorrow?" Jeff's voice was laced with sarcasm. "No way. I'd prefer to fight here. You never know. Maybe we've changed some things for the better in Indian history as well. If not, I'll try to change it in a natural way!"

He turned to look at his "princess" with adoration. Song of the Stream, taking that look as an invitation to join them, separated from the other riders and galloped toward the three.

"I understand you!" Dmitry stretched his hand to Jeff. "Well then, good-bye my friend!"

But Jeff grabbed Dmitry's hand as if he had remembered something. He turned to Margo to include her in the conversation.

"Look, guys, would you leave me the Polaroid?" Jeff burst out while he turned his head from one friend to another, "I'll be very careful, I promise!"

"Well, watch out," Margo chuckled as she took the camera out of her bag. "If something happens, you know about the consequences! Make sure no archeological expedition can ever find it!"

"Don't doubt it!" Jeff exclaimed excitedly as he grabbed the camera and played with it happily.

"Jeff," Dmitry interrupted, "let's agree where you will hide the camera for us to find later."

"Sure!" Jeff beamed. "Listen here—"

Despite all Dmitry's efforts, it took the friends a while to say their good-byes. Song of the Stream added fuel to the fire, and both girls duly cried.

Jeff waved his last good-bye, and rode with his princess to their people. He has not looked back again, probably to not show his feelings. A moment later, he and the rest of the riders disappeared in the distance.

Margo sobbed as she clung to Dmitry. They stood on the empty road and held each other for a long while until Dmitry pressed the button on his iPhone.

CHAPTER 51

1825, December 15. St. Petersburg.
The Day following the Decembrists' Uprising.
3:00 in the Afternoon.

A low winter sun hovered grimly over the frost-bound Neva River. A single ray of sunshine escaped the darkness. It sparkled for a fleeting moment against the needle-shaped spire of the Admiralty Building before disappearing behind the heavy cloud again.

The square in front of the Winter Palace was a picture of absolute chaos. The ranks of military personnel formed a solid square in one spot, while in another, the ranks broke. The sounds were overwhelming: the clopping of the aides-de-camp's horses' hooves on the stone-block pavement, braying, gendarmes' whistles, people running and crying, and swearing when being bumped into or pushed. Civilian carriages were forced to stop at the quickly erected barricades. Unimaginable confusion! The city looked like it was under siege.

Standing still, as if at the parade, a platoon of drummers of the Preobrazhensky Regiment dressed in characteristic green uniforms with red cuffs enthusiastically cut through the dry, frosty air with a series of drumrolls. It seemed they were there by the order of an excessively zealous officer but had apparently been forgotten.

A man walked along the embankment of the Moyka River. He didn't pay any attention to the surrounding chaos. His feet, shod in jackboots, involuntarily adjusted in step to the drumbeat. The man wore a military uniform of a second lieutenant of a sapper regiment, and a military-style trench coat was over his shoulders.

As he approached a big four-story building in a Russian classicism architectural style with white Corinthian columns supporting a gable, the man stopped. He raised his head and looked at the impressive sign of gilded letters: "The Russian-American Company." He stood for a few minutes before crossing the road toward the building. He hesitated at the entrance and then knocked loudly. No one answered. The man waited for a while before pushing on the door. It happened to be unlocked. The man entered the building.

Dmitry closed the door behind him and stood still for a moment. His heart hammered in his chest so hard that he thought its loud beats would carry throughout the empty building.

A wide marble staircase soared upward. Getting hold of his emotions, Dmitry slowly ascended the stairs. When he reached the second floor, he paused in front of the door with a plate that read, "Reception of His Excellency Mister Kondraty Ryleyev, the Manager of the Russian-American Company."

Dmitry knocked on the door carefully, but the door opened by itself. A man sat in the depths of the spacious office with his back to the door. He was facing the fireplace. He acted startled, aware he was no longer alone. But he didn't rush to turn to his guest. He leaned toward the fireplace and stirred a burning pile of papers in it with a poker. The crackling fire attacked the thick folder with new strength.

Dmitry was silent. He tried to swallow the lump in his throat. The man stood, slowly put the poker in a holder and turned to the newcomer. A young man of medium height with big gray eyes looked at Dmitry with interest.

He does resemble the pictures of him in history books. The men looked at each other in silence. Ryleyev was pale but calm. He said slowly, "I was warned of your visit . . . Dmitry."

Dmitry remained silent. He didn't quite realize what had just happened. It was so unexpected; it didn't fit the framework of any logic. His brain refused to accept it as reality. When his mind registered Ryleyev's words, Dmitry thought he was going to faint. If his consciousness, of course, had not left him already. Amazed, he remained silent.

Ryleyev grinned with just the corners of his mouth. He stepped to the table. "Your . . . colleague has already told me everything." Ryleyev picked up an envelope from his table and offered it to Dmitry.

"What? Why? What 'colleague'?" Dmitry managed to whisper.

Instead of answering, Ryleyev continued to hold the envelope in front of Dmitry. "He asked me to give you this . . . He said you would understand everything."

The envelope was sealed, as expected, with a wax seal. Despising himself for the fact that he could not get his treacherous hand to stop from shaking, Dmitry took the envelope. It was not an envelope but just a triple-folded piece of paper sealed in the middle in the manner of an envelope. With trembling fingers, Dmitry broke the seal.

The inner side of the paper had a business card attached to it with a piece of common scotch tape from a modern stationery store. On the card was a gold embossed Russian double-headed eagle. In its claws, the eagle had an inverted hourglass. The business card had an inscription: "Boris Sinitsyn, Colonel, Federal Agency of Space-Time Security. Russian Federation."

On the piece of paper, right under the attached business card, the handwritten note read, "Dear Dmitry, When you come back to *our* reality, please call this number . . ." At the bottom of the note was a seven-digit phone number with Moscow's area code.

Dmitry slowly raised his eyes to Ryleyev.

Epilogue

All streams run to the sea, but the sea is not full;
to the places where the streams flow from,
there they return.

—Ecclesiastes 1:7

Present Time. Northern California.
A Hotel near the Fort Ross State Historic Park.
Six Years Later.

The sun was setting when another group of tourists appeared on the path that led from the hotel to the ocean. They seemed to hurry in the direction of the vista point at the very edge of the cliff above the ocean. Two little boys, ages three and five, skipped along the narrow path as they held hands. Their parents did their best to keep up. From time to time, they called to their excessively rambunctious children.

Except for his hair, Dmitry had not changed much in these years. His nice, short, modern haircut made him look at least ten years younger. Margo looked practically unrecognizable. Youth's defiance had given way to confident beauty. She had gotten rid of her famous piercings. She still had her tattoo, but it was covered with jeans and a long-sleeve top. She was still far from being a grand dame, but she had definitely acquired the status of a beautiful woman with a calm and confident smile. It seemed she had traded hairstyles with Dmitry. These days, she wore her black hair long, and the ocean's breeze ruffled it enthusiastically.

Just like several years ago, Margo and Dmitry carried a wicker basket by the handles from which protruded a French baguette, a bottle of wine, and a bag of food. The only new detail of the picnic basket assortment was a huge bottle of juice, which was probably for the youngsters.

Not much had changed on the California coast in six years. Just as before, the great Pacific's waves rolled onto shore. Just as before, the hotel near the state historic park was full with guests. Just as before, Fort Ross stood on the top of the cliff on the opposite side of a horseshoe-shaped bay. A tall, wooden totem of an Indian god stood majestically in the center of the vista point.

"Mom! Dad! Let's stop here, by the monster!" Overexcited by all the unusual experiences of the day, the kids jumped up and down around the totem.

"We were just heading there," Dmitry replied as he approached the pole, "although, this is not a monster but a very kind man!"

"No, he's not kind! Check out his teeth!" The brothers rushed to prove they were right.

"So what? He has teeth," Dmitry said with a chuckle. "That's because he's smiling at you!"

The kids got quiet for a moment, assessing the new information. The elder boy looked conspicuously at his father. "Why does he smile at us? Does he know us or what?"

Margo, who was busy spreading a cloth on the ground, laughed. "Sure, he knows you!"

Dmitry exchanged glances with Margo, and he also chuckled.

"Mom, I'm scared!" the younger boy suddenly squeaked. He stepped away from the totem just to be on the safe side. The elder boy, seeing his parents' reaction, looked at both of them skeptically.

"Yes, it's true," Dmitry didn't give up. "He even prepared a present for us!"

The word present worked like a charm. The younger boy stopped hiding behind his mother, and a hopeful smile lit the elder boy's face.

"Did you say present?" he exclaimed while smiling hesitantly. He apparently decided that whatever strange game the adults played, if it ended with presents, it could be worth it.

"Go and check for yourselves!" Dmitry continued. "Here's a spoon for each of you. Imagine you're pirates in search of hidden treasure. Dig under the totem and you'll surely find a present!"

A smiling Margo watched her men's games. After a while, as they blissfully stretched out on the blanket with glasses of wine in hand, Dmitry turned to Margo. "Everything is just like it was then, isn't it?"

The parents had already pulled out fruit and cheese. The children were busy digging at the foot of the idol.

"Listen, Dim, even if there's nothing there, we'd have to make something up," Margo said as she chuckled, watching her little ones working so enthusiastically.

"They're stubborn!" Dmitry added not without pride. "Hey you, treasure hunters! Come and eat, and we'll look for the treasure later."

Just as he said it, the brothers gave a victorious yell as they bumped their foreheads into each other. They were reaching into a hole they had made.

"The present!" the youngest screeched happily. The elder boy was surprised at how quickly and excitedly the adults joined their game.

In a ceramic pot wrapped in a piece of cloth soaked in wax was a Polaroid and a pack of slightly darkened pictures. The pictures were of a smiling Jeff, or Song of the Stream, or the two surrounded by a bunch of kids. Silent tears ran down Margo's face. Dmitry patted his wife on the shoulder while he smiled happily.

"Mom, Dad! Who are these people? Are they real Indians?" their elder son asked. The younger boy was a little upset that the gift was not Lightning McQueen, nor even Thomas The Train.

"Very real!" Dmitry answered his elder son. He held the photos with one hand and hugged Margo's shoulders with the other. Margo started blowing her nose in her handkerchief.

Adults are so strange, the elder brother thought, noticing his parents' emotions. *Only a second ago they were in a good mood, and now they're ready to cry! But that happens to me sometimes too.*

Margo and Dmitry stood and held each other at the edge of the cliff as they watched the red sun sink into the ocean. Their peace was interrupted by a cell phone. Dmitry pressed the answer button with a sigh.

"Hello? Yes, Colonel . . . We're fine, and the vacation is good! . . . No, why? . . . Well, I think we can manage it. Okay. Yes, sir! Talk to you later."

Dmitry watched his wife while he talked on the phone. His eyes were full of love. As for Margo, she kept staring at the horizon. Her thoughts were far away.

Dmitry didn't have to tell her about the phone call word for word or comment on it. Everything was clear as it was.

"When?" was the only question Margo asked him.

"Tomorrow," Dmitry replied laconically.

"So we still have lots of time!" Margo laughed as she turned to face her husband and placed her hands on his shoulders.

"Yes, Lieutenant!" Dmitry gave her a boyish wide smile. "Besides, you and I both know that time is such a relative concept."